Kelly Romo's *When Sorrow Takes Wing* takes the reader on a riveting journey through one woman's experiences during the Cristero War in mid-1920s Mexico. Romo brings this tragic episode into sharp relief and gives us an unforgettable portrait of ordinary people struggling to survive, to practice their faith, to keep family at the center of their lives. The story is by turns tender, honest, shocking, and empowering, and the characters seem as vivid as if they were alive today. I can't stop thinking about this book. I can't recommend it enough.

MIKE MAGNUSON, AUTHOR OF *THE RIGHT MAN FOR THE JOB*

Kelly Romo has crafted an excellent novel. The book chronicles a working class family, the Castillos, who are deported on false charges. Back in Mexico, the federal government has closed the churches and priests are shot or hanged. Mariana, the vivid heroine, joins other women aiding the revolutionaries at great peril. I marveled at the womens' bold actions despite the dangers. These strong, brave women are unforgettable-- as real as your fist. And this marvelous book is too. I'm recommending this splendid work to everyone I know.

CRAIG LESLEY, AUTHOR OF *THE SKY FISHERMAN*

WHEN SORROW
TAKES WING

KELLY ROMO

For JoAnne —

Never underestimate the power of people standing up for what they believe in.

Kelly Romo

July 20 23

PAPERMOON
PRESS

For my children: Brittany, Brennan, and Ryan
My greatest joy

"Man is born free, but is everywhere in chains"

—JEAN-JACQUES ROUSSEAU

CHAPTER ONE

August 1927
Stratton Ranch
Santiago, California

MARIANA AND JENNY sat on the porch swing waiting for
Jenny's father to come rolling up the drive in his fancy convert-
ible motorcar with the top down, goggles on his eyes, and his
arm hanging over the door. He drove everywhere, always dragging a whirl of dust behind him.

Autry, the youngest peacock of the ranch, came strutting
toward Jenny's big house in his full splendor—in iridescent
gold, emerald green, sapphire, and amethyst. The crest on his
head swayed as he moved, like the headdress of Huitzilopochtli,
god of the sun, war, and human sacrifice.

With a couple of hops, Autry fluttered into the fig tree,
posturing himself on one of the boughs. His lacy train dangled
beneath him and the wisps of his feathers rustled in the breeze.

He pulled his head back, aimed his beak up to the heavens, and let out a high-pitched, *may-AWW, may-AWW, may-AWW*.

"Señora Hernández used to tell me that the devil never noticed the garden until the peacock flashed his tail," Jenny said.

"Do you think he will bring the devil?" Mariana did not need another thing giving her nightmares.

"It's just an old wives' tale."

"Then you should listen," Mariana said. "Old women are the wisest of all."

Autry let out another horrible cry.

The single crack of a shotgun burst from the house, and Autry dropped from the tree. The girls leapt from the swing, scampered down the steps, and turned to look up at the second story. The white face of Jenny's mother peered out the window, just above the black barrel of a shotgun.

Mariana's heart pounded, and Jenny's hunting dogs, Cody and Belle, came racing around from the back of the house.

"Leave it," Jenny yelled. "Down."

The dogs stopped inches from the bird and dropped to their bellies.

"*Ay Dios*," Señora Hernández cried and barreled out the front door, with wide eyes and clutching a wad of her skirt in one fist. She bounded down the porch steps, her feet moving faster than Mariana ever thought possible for such a round woman. The face of Jenny's mother disappeared, and the curtains swung shut.

The poor peacock lay in the dust beneath the tree as dead as a feather duster. One moment, proud and preening, and the next, a limp glassy-eyed heap of feathers. Mariana's stomach turned.

"*Ay Dios*," Señora Hernández said again. "What did you do?"

"It wasn't me." Jenny pointed up to the window. "It was Mother."

Señora looked about to go into one of her warnings about

the fate of liars, so Mariana gave witness for Jenny. "It is true. Her mother shot it out the window."

Just then, Jenny's mother emerged from the front door in an emerald gown and corset, standing as rigid as a statuette, like she always did whenever she came to the barrio to give Americanization classes to the women. She taught them how to speak English, as well as how to properly clean their houses and care for their children, even though she did neither of those at her own house.

Without stepping off the porch, her mother asked, "Is it completely dead?"

"*Sí*," Señora said. She looked so guilty you would have thought she shot it.

Jenny's mother gave Señora an icy scowl. She did not abide anyone speaking in Spanish at the big house. Mariana knew that. Everyone knew that. And everyone also knew that Jenny spoke Spanish as well as most of the people in the barrio.

"Yes," Señora said. "It is now in heaven."

"Animals do not go to heaven," Jenny's mother said. "Take it to the Mexicans. They will be glad for the meat."

"Oh, no, the people will not want anything to do with one of Señor Stratton's peacocks."

"Well, I don't care what you do with it. Just take it away, and don't let Warren see it." Jenny's mother waved her arm in the air, turned, and went back into her big house. She was one of the most beautiful Anglo women Mariana had ever seen. She looked like a porcelain doll, but just like porcelain, you had to be careful with her or she was liable to crack.

"Get me a rake and a gunny sack." Señora fluttered her hand at Jenny. "*Rápido*, before your father gets home."

Mariana waited with Señora, who cursed in Spanish the entire time Jenny was gone. She flipped the bird over, inspecting it. Maybe she had changed her mind about taking it to the barrio. Hopefully she would not give it to Mariana's family. After watching the murder of the poor thing, she could not stomach eating it.

Jenny finally came running back, holding the sack on the end of the rake and as far from her body as possible. Jenny had caramelcolor hair, cut short like all the other Anglo girls in town. She was a pretty girl with freckles across her nose and a vivacious, independent spirit, nothing like her mother.

"Hold the sack open for me," Señora said and grabbed the bird by the neck.

Jenny shook the bag from the end of the rake. "I'm not touching that thing. There could be black widows on it."

"*Ay Dios!* Do you see any black widows on it? Open it up."

Jenny looked to Mariana, but she shook her head. They both knew that Jenny was the brave one, so she pinched the sides of the sack and peeled them apart.

Autry's regal headdress drooped over the side of Señora's fat hand as she lowered him into the sack.

"Rake the gravel flat, like nothing happened." Señora twisted the top of the sack and clutched it in one hand. "*Rápido.* Your father will be home soon."

Both dogs sniffed at the ground where Autry had fallen. They refused to move out of the way while Jenny raked the gravel smooth.

"Virginia," Jenny's mother screamed from her window. "Come up here."

"Finish for me." Jenny extended the rake to Mariana. "I'll be back."

Mariana took the rake and crossed herself, hoping the omen of death would not bring her bad luck. When she finished raking, she sat on the porch steps to wait. Jenny's ranch had 175 acres of Valencia orange groves, apricot, walnut, and pomegranate trees, horse stables, and a driveway lined with palm trees that circled around a fig tree that looked like it came straight from the Garden of Eden. Her house was the color of a yellow canary with red pointy roofs, just like in the fairy books. Mariana imagined all sorts of magic happening inside it, but she would never know because she was not allowed through the door.

Finally, Jenny came around the back side of the house with the sack.

"Come on," she called to Mariana. "We need to get rid of this."

"My family doesn't want it."

Jenny laughed. "It's just the feathers and appendages. Señora is making a soup out of the meat."

"For who?"

"My parents, I guess. I'm not eating it." She lifted the bag and made a nasty face. "Let's dump them into the river and let them wash downstream and into the ocean, just like Father does with the bad oranges."

The screen door banged shut, and the dogs came scampering around the corner to follow Jenny and nose at the sack.

"This is not for you," she said, and she looped around to the east side of the grove, away from where the pickers worked that day.

As Mariana and Jenny moved deeper, the trees closed in behind them and wrapped them in a blanket of leaves and light and shadow. Already picked of their ripe oranges, the branches held nothing but glossy leaves and the hard green lumps of next year's harvest.

"Heard a shot," a deep voice burst from behind a tree.

Mariana gasped and both she and Jenny turned to stone. Cody and Belle moved forward with ears flattened and hair raised.

Walt, the ranch's *trouble man*, stepped into the row with a shovel slung over his shoulder.

"Oh...it's only you." Jenny slipped the bag behind her. "You shouldn't sneak up on people."

5

"I heard a shot." Walt stood there with his shirtsleeves rolled-up and strings of greasy hair hanging below his hat brim.

"Just shooting at tin cans," Jenny said.

Walt let out a short laugh. "Only heard one shot. Too much of a kick for you?"

"Yes, something like that."

"What do you have in the sack?" Walt took a step forward, and Cody growled, baring his teeth.

"It's all right, boy." Jenny put her hand on Cody's back. "It's only Walt."

"Hopefully he hasn't got rabies from one of the coyotes," Walt said and turned back toward the grove. "We'd have to put a bullet in him."

Cody's muscles did not relax until Walt faded into the trees. The children called him *Señor Comadreja,* Mr. Weasel—not only because he looked like one with his small head and beady eyes but because he always hunted rodents and would pop his head up to watch the children whenever they passed by.

One time, Mariana saw him piping exhaust fumes from the ranch truck into the hole of a rabbit den. After that, she had many nightmares of him coming to their house in the dark and placing a hose in one of the windows.

When they made it to the river, the bank was littered with empty tin cans, a twisted strand of barbed wire, strips of dusty tree bark, and thousands of eucalyptus pods that hurt like the devil when you stepped on them with bare feet.

Jenny up-ended the gunny sack and shook the remains of poor Autry into the water. The quills floated down—a flotilla of iridescent boats in emerald and amethyst with eyes of turquoise and amber flashing in the current. Cody and Belle paced back and forth along the bank, stopping and pointing and pacing again.

"When Father finds out, my mother will have hell to pay,"

Jenny said. She poked at the head with a stick as she tried to help it catch the current.

"I'm surprised she shot it. She does not seem like a woman who would handle a gun," Mariana said. Señora Stratton never had a hair out of place or a single chipped fingernail the entire nine years she had known her.

"Not that I approve of her murdering the peacock," Jenny said and flipped the head into deeper water. "But I rather like this gun-wielding version of Mother."

The fleet of feathers would have been beautiful if not for the morbid event that preceded their journey. The head still lay beneath the surface staring straight up. Mariana crossed herself and said a Hail Mary for him. Regardless of what Señora Stratton said, she pictured him in heaven and standing before Saint Peter at the pearly gates. Why wouldn't God want all his beautiful creatures there?

"Let's go home that way," Jenny said and pointed toward the sound of the pickers.

"So you can see Emilio?"

Jenny did not answer. She just turned and, swinging the empty sack beside her, strolled off toward the picking crew. The late afternoon sun sifted through the leaves, cooled the grove, and cast shadows across the rows and trenches. Up ahead, two crows picked at the carcass of a poor dead rabbit, while above it in the branches, a dozen others called their raspy *krah, krah, krahs*.

Mamá always said that crows were a bad omen, and she never let them near their house. If she spotted any in the yard, she would go after them with a broom. Her youngest sister, Catalina, would scream and cover her eyes—afraid the birds would peck them out.

Jenny and her dogs bounded forward, sending the crows into a mad and squawking flutter. Their wings beat against the air and leaves until they all broke free, into a black swarm in the sky.

Jenny giggled, ran off with her dogs, and signaled for Mariana to follow. Mariana did not run. If she twisted her ankle in one of the irrigation trenches, she would not be able to start her new job the next day. She finally got a position at the packing house and she did not want to do anything to jeopardize it.

Jenny stopped just before the picking crew and twisted a bright orange off one of the trees. The oranges were supposed to be clipped off, not twisted—but if you are the daughter of El Patrón, you could do it however you wanted.

The men, perched on ladders almost perpendicular to the trees, clipped and dropped the fruit into their bags. They spoke and playfully teased or called down instructions to their little boys. The boys, with their scrawny arms and shocks of dark hair, picked oranges from the lower branches and added them to their fathers' field boxes.

Jenny stood there and stared at Emilio. Each time he reached for an orange, his wrist peeked out between his cuff and his glove. He clipped the fruit free, cradled it in his palm, and let it roll into his new picker bag before reaching for another.

Jenny and Emilio thought that they were sneaky by hiding their feelings for one another, but Mariana knew her brother and she recognized the intense gaze that came onto his face whenever he looked at Jenny lately.

"I'm afraid for Emilio," Mariana said.

"Whatever for?" Jenny asked.

"I see the way you look at one another."

Jenny did not answer her.

Mariana slipped her hand into Jenny's. "Your father will never approve."

"Would yours?"

"No. That is two good reasons why you should stay away from him."

Papá, the foreman of this picking crew, put two fingers into his mouth and whistled one long and shrill note. The men, dressed in faded blue shirts with no collars and patched denim trousers, descended from their ladders. They all headed to their field boxes and unbuckled the bottoms of their bags. The oranges rolled out and topped off many of the boxes.

Tomorrow, she would be at the packing house wrapping each of those very oranges in tissue paper and placing them in boxes for shipment to all parts of the world. Mariana scraped her fingernails across the rind of one of the low-hanging oranges—a thing she had done since she was a child so that the scent would linger on her fingers all day long. At night, when she lay in bed afraid of the dark, all she had to do was bring her fingers to her nose and breathe in some sunshine.

When Emilio turned toward them, Jenny smiled and waved. He looked over at her with his thick-lashed eyes and a hint of a smile, but he suppressed it as he unbuckled the bottom of his bag.

Noticing who had distracted Emilio, Lázaro shot Jenny a nasty glare. Since Emilio and Lázaro were the same age, some people thought that they were twins—with all the blessings of good looks passed out to Emilio, and Lázaro getting nothing but the scraps. Emilio had big dark eyes, whereas Lázaro squinted like a feral mutt ready to gnaw the hand off of anyone who got too close to him. Few people knew that Lázaro was not their brother but their cousin, and he only lived with them because his mother had died and his Anglo father had abandoned them.

As the men and boys finished, they filtered off into the grove and headed toward the barrio—some in the direction of the bunkhouse, but most to their families, where their wives waited with a warm dinner and hand-made tortillas.

Emilio buckled his bag, and as he started toward Jenny and Mariana, Lázaro grabbed hold of his arm. Emilio flashed his cousin a reassuring smile and said something Mariana could not hear. Lázaro let him go, shook his head, and stalked off toward home on his own.

Jenny, Emilio, and Mariana made their way into the grove, away from the workers. The three of them had grown up together, so nobody would question them going off.

Mariana stopped. "Do you hear that?"

At the base of a tree, a tiny brown nestling flapped its featherless wings with its mouth open and crying for its mother. Mariana crouched to the ground and scooped it up.

"Do you think it's hurt?"

"You're not supposed to touch a baby bird. Its mother will abandon it," Emilio said.

Mariana stood there with the tiny brown chick in her hand. She bit her lower lip. Why did she pick it up?

Mariana held the bird out toward Emilio. "Put it back in the nest."

Emilio backed away from her. "We don't want both of our scents on it...just in case. You need to put it back."

Mariana shook her head. She could not climb into the tree. What if she fell out? "We can't leave it to die."

"I will stand right beneath you and keep you safe," Emilio said. "The nest is just there. You can reach it from that main branch."

Above them, the tiny brother and sister nestlings called their shrill hunger cries. Mariana looked up, then to Jenny.

"Emilio's right. We don't want all of our scents on it. You can do it."

When Mariana shifted the bird to one hand and closed her fingertips over it, Emilio cupped his hands for her to step in. Mariana gave Jenny a pleading look, but Jenny ignored her.

Mariana put one foot into Emilio's hands and her free hand

on his head. She looked to Jenny, and without Mariana having to utter a single word, Jenny rushed to her side to balance her. Emilio lifted and hoisted Mariana up into the tree. She settled herself on the branch with her insides all jumbling up and her head spinning.

"Don't look down," Emilio said. "I'm right here. Can you see the nest?"

Mariana slowly looked up and raised her hand to return the bird to its brothers and sisters. She dropped it in, grasped the branch with both hands, and looked down. Instead of seeing their proud faces smiling up at her, neither of them noticed and Emilio had his hand on Jenny's lower back.

"I can't wait for tonight," Jenny whispered.

Emilio raised his eyebrows and gave her a teasing smile. "What's happening tonight?"

"You know," Jenny said.

"Every moment will crawl by until we can..." His eyes snapped onto something in the grove. Emilio yanked his hand away from Jenny then stood as stiff as an idol with eyes wide and sweat forming on his forehead.

Mariana turned to see a man glowering at them.

"We are not alone," Jenny shouted to the man, but he had turned and disappeared back into the grove.

"It will be all right," Jenny said to Emilio. "I'll talk to my father."

Without a word, Emilio jammed his hands into his pockets, hurried away, and left Mariana alone in the tree.

CHAPTER TWO

Barrio Stratton
Santiago, California

TWO SHIRTLESS AND barefooted boys raced toward Mariana. They rode a single bicycle with one boy steering and the other pedaling. The pedaler's legs pumped so fast you would think El Diablo himself chased them in the moonlight. They rode directly into her front yard and jumped off. When the bike dropped at her feet, a bouquet of peacock feathers spilled from the basket.

"Where did you get all those feathers?" Mariana asked. They had to be the very ones she and Jenny set afloat that afternoon.

The boys breathed so hard they could barely speak. Ernesto, who the other boys called *rabbit* because of his big front teeth, said, "Emilio. He is hurt."

They ran into her house without knocking. "Emilio is hurt."

Lázaro jumped up from the sofa in the living room, and Papá stumbled from the hallway in his undershirt, with one leg in his trousers, and pulling them on as he walked. "What is it?"

No, please God, no. A cold hand squeezed Mariana's heart. She should have listened to the tingling premonition she had when Emilio had dressed for the night.

The boys repeated in one voice, "Emilio. He is hurt."

"Where is he?"

"By the railroad tracks," Ernesto said. "Our papá is helping him."

Papá scowled at Lázaro. "Why weren't you with him?"

Lázaro shrugged. "He told me to stay home."

"Why is that?"

Lázaro shrugged again. He knew that Emilio had gone to meet Jenny, but he would never betray Emilio. Neither would Mariana—but what if something terrible had happened...

When Papá passed by Mariana, he frowned. "What are you doing outside?"

"I heard the boys." It was not a complete lie.

Papá's eyes narrowed and he looked from the hallway to where Mariana stood by the front door. Mariana could not tell him that she had snuck out her bedroom window to wait in the yard for Emilio. She could not tell him that he had gone to meet Jenny and that she had felt a terrible dread from the moment he left.

As Mariana followed Papá out the door, he put his hand up and halted her, then signaled for Lázaro to join him.

Ernesto picked up the bicycle, leaving the peacock feathers strewn on the ground. With him pushing, and his brother on the other side of their bike, they led Papá and Lázaro away.

Mariana lowered herself into one of the metal chairs in their yard. She should have tried to stop Emilio. She should have talked sense into Jenny. What good could ever come for the two of them? Neither family would allow it. The town would not allow it.

Jenny was not even Catholic. Papá would never give his blessing for a protestant woman to raise his grandchildren without the Catholic Church and protections of the saints.

Mamá came out of the house pinching the skin at her throat. Mariana's three sisters—fifteen-year-old Josefina, five-year-old Sofía, and three-year-old Catalina—followed Mamá out. Catalina climbed into Mariana's lap and Sofía reached up for Mamá to hold her. Josefina, far too old to sit on anyone's lap, leaned against the house, not taking her eyes from the road.

"Josefina," Mamá said, "Go get the curandera. Emilio may need a healer."

Poor Josefina. Mamá kept her running now that she no longer attended school. *Josefina, watch your sisters. Josefina, peel the potatoes. Josefina, go sit with old Señora Ortiz, she is lonely.* Josefina rolled her eyes, glared at Mariana, and crossed their small dirt yard onto the street.

Mariana felt sorry for Josefina but not sorry enough to take her place. Mariana had already taken her turn. When she had finished the ninth grade, she had to care for her three younger sisters and helping Mamá with the laundry and cleaning. Now that Josefina had finished school, she had taken on the lower work, which allowed Mariana to do more superior work like helping Mamá in the kitchen, sewing, taking care of the garden, and running to the grocery store. Tomorrow, when she started at the packing house, Josefina would be on her own helping Mamá—just like Mariana had been.

Catalina leaned back, heavy and relaxed and too young to worry. Mariana kissed her on top of the head and ran her fingers through the soft curls of Catalina's baby hair.

"Why was Emilio out at night?" Máma asked.

Mariana shifted Catalina so that her head rested on her shoulder, but she did not answer so she would not have to lie.

"Was it to see a girl?"

"Do you think he tells me anything?" Mariana asked. It was

worse than meeting a girl. He had gone to meet the only daughter of El Patrón.

Mariana stared down the moonlit street at the two lines of dark houses with their glowing yellow windows. The people of the barrio had come from all over Mexico, from the towns and ranchos of Guanajuato, Jalisco, Michoacán, and Zacatecas. The people were workers, overseers, or professionals. Many had escaped the Revolution to protect their families—just like her own papá had.

Mariana did not remember much about the hacienda where Papá had been the overseer, since they left when she was only five. Papá said it was in Jalisco, but all she remembered was their adobe house with a red tile roof, the vaqueros with their big hats, silver spurs, and guns strapped to their horses—and the thick green-gray leaves of the maguey plants that the workers climbed on like bugs to suck the honey water from its long stalk and collect in gourds.

Most of the children of the barrio did not remember much about Mexico either, but none of them could get away from the old legends of the mothers and grandmothers. The children seemed to have only one ear open to the tales, though, because they wanted to make their own stories—new stories of big houses, motorcars, and fancy clothes, just like the Anglos.

Sofía climbed off Máma's lap and made her way toward the spot where the boys had dropped their bicycle. She gathered the peacock feathers and brought them back.

"Where did you get those?" Mamá asked.

Sofía pointed. "Over there."

"They spilled from the basket of the boys' bicycle," Mariana said.

"Those are from one of Señor Stratton's birds. You cannot keep them." As Mamá reached for the feathers, Sofía stepped away.

"I found them," Sofía said.

"Put them back, they do not belong to you."

In twos and threes, the people began congregating in their yard. First, the mother of the two boys, their sisters, then the curandera and her grandchildren. Invisible cold fingers walked up Mariana's spine. People gathered for tragedies, not small injuries or broken bones.

Sofía did not obey Mamá and stood there with her bouquet of peacock feathers—with their unblinking eyes, their dilated black pupils ringed in turquoise and amber, all staring out at the people. Mamá had softened with the two little ones, letting them misbehave or requiring her or Josefina to take care of them. Maybe having five children did that to a mamá.

Josefina moved to the darkness of the side yard and out of Mamá's sight. Mariana offered her chair to the curandera and took Catalina, now completely asleep, into the house. She pulled back the covers and placed her on their bed before going out to join Josefina, who stood alone biting at her nails.

"He will be all right." Mariana put her hand on Josefina's shoulder, trying to console her.

"It's something bad," Josefina said without taking her finger from her mouth or her eyes from the road. "I can feel it."

Mariana felt it, too.

Shadowy figures finally appeared. Papá led the way with Emilio in his arms. Her brother's head hung back. His arms dangled and swayed with every step, like an overly large child being taken off to bed. Lázaro, Señor Hernández, and the two boys came behind them, followed by Jenny in a ghost-white dress.

Josefina rushed forward. Mariana paused and remembered Papá's instruction, then followed Josefina anyway.

Jenny cowered behind the procession of men, wide-eyed and dazed. Her appearance caused the people to gasp and look away as they muttered, *Santa Muerte*.

Josefina dropped to her knees before Papá and wept.

"Move," Papá said. "Out of my way."

Emilio had dark blood clotted in his ears and nose and smeared across his face.

"Move," Lázaro snapped. "Don't you see that he needs help?"

"Is he alive?" Mariana asked. He was so swollen and a strange color. A dark stain covered the front of his shirt

"We need to get him home," Lázaro said.

"Is he alive?"

Mariana looked to Jenny for an answer, but she only stared at Emilio, vacant, as if her body had no soul inside of it.

"No, no, no," Josefina wailed when Lázaro dragged her to the side of the street.

Mariana grabbed Jenny's arm. "What happened?"

Jenny turned toward her and blinked. Her face had a bewildered look, like that of a child who had awaken from a dream and had no idea where she was.

"What happened?" Mariana asked. She wanted to shake her.

Jenny opened her mouth, but no words came out. She ran her hand down her blood-smeared dress and blinked again. "He was attacked."

"By who?"

Jenny shook her head. Did she not know? Could she not say? Josefina kept wailing from the side of the street.

A door opened and a man's voice called out, "What has happened?"

"My brother, Emilio, has been…" Been what? She didn't know what to say. "He has been beaten."

Several men came toward Papá to help, but Papá kept walking and carrying his only son all by himself. As Jenny walked by, they turned their faces and crossed themselves because they all knew the stories of *Santa Muerte*, the white siren of death.

Mariana put her arm around Josefina. "Maybe he will be all right."

"He is dead! He is dead!" Josefina screamed. "¡Él está muerto! ¡Él está muerto! ¡Él está muerto!"

"The curandera will help him." Mariana grabbed Josefina by the arm and lifted her. "She is a good healer."

As they walked, more doors opened and people called out to them. All the voices jumbled together and lost their meaning.

Papá placed Emilio on the couch. Emilio's new shirt, the one he had bought with his own money and had been so proud of, was dirty and stained with blood. Jenny slipped backward and faded into the darkened hallway. All the women gathered around the curandera, crossing themselves and praying. Almost in a whisper, the curandera prayed with her hands cupped around Emilio's head. Cries and the muttering of prayers to the Father, to the Son, to the Holy Spirit, and to the *Virgen de Guadalupe* floated through the room.

A chill started at the tip of Mariana's scalp, and dragged its nails down her face, neck, between her breasts, and down her stomach, until her legs began to shiver and her vision went dark. Somewhere, far away, Papá's voice called out, "Someone get the priest."

When Father Juárez arrived, everyone moved aside to make a path. Only the curandera remained where she was. Their priest put his hand to Emilio's cheek then placed it beneath his nose and waited. The curandera whispered to him and he nodded, made the sign of the cross on Emilio's forehead, and sprinkled him with holy water.

Mamá stepped forward. She looked shaky as if she would collapse at any moment. "What about the sacraments, Father?"

Father Juárez put a hand on her shoulder, and in a tender voice said, "Sacraments are for the living. Only Emilio's soul needs our prayers now."

At that, Mamá crumpled and dropped to the floor. The people in the room crossed themselves. Josefina bolted from the house. Mariana moved forward to help Mamá, but before she could, several of the other women knelt beside her. Papá went to Emilio's side and dropped to his knees. Mariana joined Papá and the two of them recited the prayers of the Rosary even though they held no beads to keep track. While they prayed the Lord's Prayer, a tremor began in Papá's hands, and Mariana feared it would overtake him. Behind them, the people muttered their own prayers and whispered to one another.

When Mariana finally stood, most of the men and children had gone. Mamá leaned into Papá, both on their knees beside Emilio. Two Señoras stood at the window draping a black cloth over the curtain rod, while another woman hung black crepe over the door—never to be untied. She had seen them over other entryways, where they became sun-bleached and worn until they eventually fell off. She never thought they would have one on their house.

The candles flickered and cast eerie lights as they danced with Emilio's ghost. Her brother's body lay on the couch beneath an overly bright yellow and red blanket. Other than his abnormally pale skin and blue lips, he looked like he was only sleeping.

Emilio always slept warm and never pulled a blanket higher than his waist, so Mariana folded the blanket down from his chest. The dried blood on his shirt created a patch of black against the stripes. The pearled buttons glistened as they captured and held the faint candlelight in the room. Emilio had been so proud that he was able to buy his own clothes. Maybe whoever killed him would never have noticed Emilio if he had stayed in his worker clothes and never tried to be anything more than a picker.

Lázaro stood at the end of the couch filled with hate. As Mariana passed by him, she asked, "Has Josefina come home yet?"

"*Sí*, she is in the bedroom." Lázaro grabbed Mariana's arm

and pulled her toward the hallway. Jenny stood against the wall, trembling and watching from the dark.

Lázaro stepped within an inch of Jenny and hissed, "This is because of you. You are the devil!"

Jenny closed her eyes.

"She would not hurt Emilio," Mariana said.

"No? She is covered in his blood. What about her father?"

Lázaro grabbed Jenny by the arm so hard that she yelped. "Who did this?"

Jenny shook her head. "I don't know."

"How can you not know?"

"That's enough." Mariana stepped between the two of them. She put her hands on Lázaro's chest and shoved but could not budge him. All she felt was the solidness of his body and the rapid beat of his heart. "Go pray for Emilio."

Lázaro never liked Jenny or any other white person. His father was an Anglo who had abandoned his mother when she became pregnant. Since Lázaro was half Anglo, and he hated all Anglos, he halfway hated himself—which was probably why he was always so nasty.

"She is nothing but a white whore," Lázaro said. The heat of his breath dampened Mariana's face.

A loud knock came from the living room, followed by a woman's voice, "It is Señor Stratton…"

Lázaro shoved Jenny and caused her head to thump against the wall before he let go and turned toward the living room.

"Hector," Señor Stratton said, "I hear that there has been an accident."

At the sound of her father's voice, Jenny let out a gasp.

Papá turned toward Señor Stratton without rising from his knees. "My son has been killed."

"My condolences," Señor Stratton said. "I have telephoned the constable. Do you know who did it?"

Mamá let out a gasp and Papá slipped his arm around her. "No."

"Did anyone see what happened?"

Her Papá, with red-rimmed eyes and slumped shoulders, just stared toward Señor Stratton as if he did not comprehend what was being asked.

Lázaro turned around and pushed past Mariana.

"No, no, no," Jenny begged with her back against the end of the hallway. "No."

Lázaro yanked her forward. Jenny grabbed hold of Mariana's arm as they passed and their eyes met for a single second. Jenny looked terrified. "Please, no."

"Your daughter knows." Lázaro's words came out in a hiss and he swung Jenny around to face her father.

"Virginia! What are you doing here?"

"Tell him," Lázaro said.

Jenny's head hung, and she would not look up at her father.

"Tell him." Lázaro shook her arm and knocked her off balance, but she caught herself.

Emilio's knife dropped from somewhere on Jenny and clunked to the floor. The noise felt like it was the last sound on earth. It lay on their floor with its brown bone handle and brass fittings. A fuzzy ring started in Mariana's head and it grew in pitch like a bow screeching across the strings of a violin.

"Take your hands off my daughter." Señor Stratton's voice boomed through their house like the voice of God.

Lázaro's face distorted and flushed red with veins bulging in his forehead. "You murdered him." Jenny let out a yelp when Lázaro shoved her at her father.

Señor Stratton stepped forward, wrapped his arm around Jenny, and looked back at Papá. "Please tell Constable Stillwell to come to my house when he is done here."

The moment Señor Stratton and Jenny left their house,

Lázaro snapped. "Nothing will happen to her. Emilio is nothing to them. She will go home to her big house and..."

"That is enough," Papá said. "Warren Stratton is a fair man."

Lázaro's gaze bounced around the room looking for something to punch or tear to pieces. He finally crouched down on his sleeping pallet and clenched his fists. He stared at Emilio and it looked as if it took everything he had to stay in the room and not go out and kill someone.

When another knock came to the door and Lázaro started to get up, Papá gave him a stern look. "You stay there."

Papá rose to his feet and answered it. When he stepped aside, Miss Rupp, the barrio's Americanization teacher, and a man in a suit and tie walked in. His dark cowboy hat and badge left no doubt about his authority.

"Good evening. Do you speak English?" he asked.

The muscles in Papá's neck tensed. "Yes."

"I'm Constable Stillwell. I hear you have a death."

"It is my son, Emilio."

Without bothering to take off his hat, the constable pulled a notebook and pen from the inner pocket of his suit coat. Emilio's knife still lay on the floor, precisely where it fell. The constable only had half an eyebrow on the right side. He was the one the children called *El Coco*, the boogeyman, and now he stood in their living room, staring down at Emilio. He Flipped past several pages of writing and stopped on a blank page. "What's his full name?"

"Emilio Castillo de la Vega."

Lázaro rose, took a step, and placed his foot on Emilio's folding knife with the bone handle beneath the arch of his bare foot.

"Can you spell that out for me? You Mexicans have got some peculiar names." The constable's pen hovered over the tablet. "You know how to spell?"

"Yes." Papá squeezed his hands into fists. "Emilio, E-m-i-l-i-o. Castillo, C-a-s-t-i-l-l-o."

Miss Rupp, the only white person living in the barrio, taught English to the men and how to be good Americans to the women—giving classes on how to keep their homes and their children clean as if they did not already know that. Miss Rupp put her hand on Mamá's shoulder. Mamá stiffened at her touch, but she did not move away from it.

As Papá spelled out Emilio's name, Lázaro stood like a firecracker. His fuse had been lit, and with every letter, the flame grew closer and closer to his core. The only thing keeping him from shooting out the door was Emilio's knife beneath his foot.

"De, d-e. La, l-a." Papá continued while the constable put every letter onto his paper.

Mariana went to Lázaro and placed her hand on his arm.

"Vega, V-e-g-a."

"And your name?"

"Héctor, H-e-c-t-o-r." Papá slid his hands into his trouser pockets.

"Keep your hands where I can see them." The constable's thin lips snapped at Papá like a turtle.

Lázaro jerked his arm away from Mariana's touch.

Papá stood there fingering the side seams of his trousers with trembling hands. "Castillo, C-a-s-t-i-l-l-o. Díaz, D-i-a-z."

The constable finished taking down Papá's name and looked up from his notebook. "I just met with Father Juárez. Now that's a Mexican name, isn't it? Must be nice for you to have your own Mexican priest."

"Father Juárez is from Spain, Señor," Papá said with his head slightly bowed, "but it is nice to have a priest who speaks Spanish."

Lázaro's eyes glanced down at his foot, then back at the constable.

Mariana prayed, *Oh Holy Father, grant Lázaro some self-restraint for once in his life.*

The sheriff stared at Papá for a moment before speaking. "Spain, Mexico, it don't matter. You're all foreigners. Father Juárez tells me that two boys found your son. Did they see who killed him?"

"I do not know, Señor."

"Did anyone see who did it?"

"Jenny Stratton," Papá said.

The sheriff raised his eyebrows. "Jenny Stratton? Is there an association between your boy and Jenny Stratton?"

"Jenny is a friend of my daughter."

Lázaro's mouth opened, but he glanced back down to his foot and swallowed his words.

"Señor Stratton would like you to come to his house when you are done here," Papá said.

El Coco stepped closer to Emilio's body. "Pardon me, ma'am," he said to Mamá and placed his fingers on Emilio's wrist.

Lázaro crossed his arms and the veins bulged as he clenched and unclenched his hands.

"How long ago did this happen?" the constable asked.

"I'm not sure," Papá said. "Maybe an hour ago."

"Has your boy been in trouble before?"

"No, Señor. Emilio is a good boy. He went to school and he is a hard worker."

"What about you? You have any trouble with the law?"

"No, Señor. I don't make any trouble." Papá's voice shook. "I am the foreman for Señor Stratton."

Mariana wanted to scream at the constable to leave her Papá alone. He had been through enough already.

"I see," the constable said and went over to their family altar. He picked up the framed image of the *Virgen de Guadalupe*, tilted it in the light, and set it back down. He ran his hand over their wooden crucifix and fingered the locket that held several strands of Tía Carlota's hair. He put his nose to the dried flowers, lifted her grandmother's thimble from the shelf, and rolled it back and forth between his finger and thumb.

With the constable's back turned, Lázaro bent his knees and lowered his down-stretched hand toward the floor. Mariana put her hand on his back. When he glared up at her, she gave an almost imperceptible shake of her head. The constable turned back around and Lázaro straightened without the knife.

"How many of you live here?"

"Just my family and my nephew," Papá said.

"How many is that?" he asked and set the thimble back down.

"Eight."

"That's an awful lot of people for this little house."

"Yes, Señor," Papá said.

"Is there any more information you can give me?"

"No, Señor."

"Then there's not much more I need here. I'll make a report and look into it."

"Thank you, Señor."

"You ready, Miss Rupp?" the constable asked.

Once they left, and the sound of his truck faded down the street, Lázaro burst out, "He's not going to do anything. I will find out who did this and kill them!"

"Then what?" Papá asked. "What will happen to the rest of us?"

Lázaro took his foot off Emilio's knife and scooped it up from the floor. He pushed Mariana away from him and stormed toward the door. "¡Mierda! I hate gringos!"

Mariana turned to follow Lázaro, but Papá stopped her. "Let him go."

"He has Emilio's knife."

"Do you think he would be so stupid?"

Papá had much more confidence in Lázaro than Mariana

did. Most of what he did out of Papá's sight was stupid. Mamá started crying again. She rose up and put her head on Emilio's chest. Josefina appeared in the hallway. Her braid had unraveled and dark strands of hair stuck to her face. "Is Emilio still dead?"

"*Sí, mija.*" Papá held his arms out.

She went to him. "Can the curandera bring him back?"

"No, go on back to your room," Papá turned to look at Mariana. "It is time for you to go to bed, too."

Mariana followed Josefina into the hall. Catalina was in bed and still asleep with no idea that she no longer had a brother.

"Where is Sofía?" Mariana asked.

"In Papá and Mamá's bed."

In her parents' room, Sofía lay on the bed with the peacock feathers strewn all around her. The mirror had been covered with a black cloth, and the framed picture of her and Emilio when they were little hung backward, facing the wall. Mariana collected the peacock feathers from around Sofía and placed them on her parents' bureau. She carried Sofía to their room, placed her next to Josefina, and then scooted Catalina over and lay next to her. They waited for Papá to come in and bless them like he always did before they slept, but that night, he never came.

CHAPTER THREE

MARIANA AND JOSEFINA STOOD WITH THEIR BACKS AGAINST THE
wall while Mamá, two señoras, and the curandera gathered to
prepare Emilio's body. Emilio lay naked in their kitchen on top
of a table created from plywood, two sawhorses, and draped
with a tarp. Papá would not let Mariana or Josefina leave with
their little sisters, saying that they were old enough to stay and
help. But nobody was ever old enough to witness their Mamá
sponging-off the blood and dirt from the body of her son.

Years ago, Mariana used to swim naked with Lázaro and
Emilio, but now Emilio was too much of a man for his sisters to
see him without clothes. Mariana needed to move and needed
to do something, so she pulled open a drawer, took out a green
washcloth, and placed it on Emilio's private area. He would not
want her and all the women staring at his huevos.

Before leaving them in the kitchen to do the women's work
with Mamá, Papá handed Josefina Emilio's new suit. Josefina
buried her nose into the fabric and swayed back and forth with
closed eyes and an ashen face. Mariana should have begged
Papá to at least let Josefina go, but Papá's stern face made her
mouth go dry.

Mamá dipped the sponge into the basin of water. Her shoulders curled forward and she stared, unmoving, into the bottom. Josefina cried and the señoras whispered their prayers.

"Let me help you." Señora Vargas reached for the sponge in Mamá's quivering hand.

Without looking up, and in a voice barely above a whisper, Mamá said, "I gave him his first bath, and I need to give him his last."

Mamá stood at the basin, frozen in time like the black hand of a broken clock. She finally wrung out the sponge, placed it over Emilio's chest, and wiped it across the blood caked over his heart. When she dipped the sponge in the second time, Emilio's blood turned the clear water to rust.

A giant dark moth that the grandmothers called *mariposa de la muerte*, the butterfly of death, fluttered at the window glass. It whirled around and around, desperate to get out now that its work was done. Beyond the glass, *El Coco* stood outside with his hands on his hips and the fingertips of his right hand resting on the butt of his gun. Mariana watched Papá amble over to the constable with his head lowered and eyes forward. *El Coco's* mouth moved as he spoke to Papá. Papá shrugged and shook his head.

The moth landed on the sill, folded its wings back, and waited like a lump of ash. Mariana lifted the window, but it sat and did not move.

"Better keep your boy home." *El Coco's* voice drifted into the kitchen. "If he is seen lurking around the ranch house again, I'll lock him up."

Papá nodded. "I will make sure he stays away."

"See that you do. You are a guest in our country. If you want to stay, don't make trouble."

Mamá ran the sponge over Emilio again and again and tried to wipe away the clotted blood. The curandera prayed and pleaded for God and the saints to have mercy on his soul.

Outside, Papá turned his back to the constable, slipped his hands into his pockets, and walked away.

"Keep your hands where I can see them," *El Coco* called with his eyes on Papá's retreating form.

Without looking back, Papá pulled his hands out. He kept walking with his arms hanging limp and his palms to his thighs.

Once Mamá had cleaned Emilio, she struggled to get his unbending legs into his pants. She bunched and pulled as she worked the fabric over his stiffened limbs. Josefina groaned, slid down to the floor, and buried her head between her knees. Mamá eventually allowed the curandera to assist her. She lifted and tipped Emilio while Mamá pulled the clothes onto him. Mamá's hands shook so much that she could not get the buttons into the holes of his shirt. Mariana reached out and placed her hand on Mamá's.

"Let me."

Mamá looked at her with glazed and watery eyes.

"He is my brother."

Mamá nodded but did not step back. Mariana slipped one button at a time through the holes with Mamá so close, she kept bumping her with her elbow.

Once they had Emilio in his only suit and tie, Mamá clipped off a lock of his hair and placed it beneath his new harmonica in the shiny green and gold tin. It would be placed on their family altar, along with Tía Carlota's locket and her grandmother's thimble. Mamá combed Emilio's hair and slicked it back with Brilliantine, just the way he liked it. One of the señoras handed Mamá a jar of face powder to conceal the bruises on Emilio's face. It made him look unnatural and as dull and drab as a piece of cloth. Why should they mask what was done to him? The people should see what happened.

When Mariana went into the living room and pulled Emilio's box of treasures from its place beneath the sofa, Lázaro stormed into the house followed by Papá. Lázaro plopped down onto the sofa with his arms crossed and his face pinched into a snarl.

"You will stay away," Papá said. "We don't need any more trouble."

Lázaro sat without responding until Papá left the house. As soon as the front door closed, he let off a string of every curse word in the world, all tied up in knots around Jenny's name. Mariana could not blame him for his anger. Emilio's death must bring his own mother's death to his mind.

Lázaro's mother, Tía Carlota, had been kidnapped and killed during the revolution. Papá had found her in an abandoned federal camp, beaten and shot. Mariana's only memory of that time was of Lázaro sitting in a chair next to his mother's casket. He wore a black suit and shiny black shoes. His greased hair looked as slick as tar. When the first person he didn't know came up to him, Lázaro ran across the room and stuck his head in the corner with his bottom straight up in the air. He looked like a shiny black stinkbug ready to spray his rotten perfume on anyone who came near him. He has been that way ever since.

Mariana stood to leave him to his anger, but his eyes latched onto her.

"Your white whore knows who killed Emilio. Maybe she did it herself."

"Do you think Emilio stood there letting her beat and stab him? She did not have a mark on her."

"She had his blood all over her."

"You do not think much of Emilio if you think a girl could do that to him."

Lázaro never listened to any opinion or logic in normal circumstances. In his state, there was nothing more Mariana could say. All he wanted to do was snarl and snap at her or anyone who got too close to him.

"I will choke the truth out of her."

Mariana opened her mouth to tell him that Jenny loved

Emilio, but there was no reasoning with him. Any words would be no better than banging on the cage that he was trapped in.

In the kitchen, the women stood around Emilio's body and prayed. Still crouched in the corner with her arms wrapped around her knees, Josefina stared at the floor. Mariana opened Emilio's treasure box and lifted out his old kazoo. She put it to her lips and whispered the Lord's Prayer right into the mouthpiece so they would be buried with him forever. Mariana crossed herself and slipped the kazoo into the right-hand pocket of Emilio's pants, just where he used to keep it.

EMILIO'S COFFIN was not ready in time for the vigil, so his body lay on top of the plywood table, now covered in several layers of cloth and lace. Two arrangements of flowers leaned up against the rough wood and partially hid the sawhorse's legs.

Emilio had been so loved by the people of the neighborhood that their house could not hold them all. They spilled out the door and into the yard. Father Juárez wore a black cassock with a large golden cross hanging from a thick golden chain.

Once everyone settled in, and only the sound of sniffles and the innocent cooing of the babies remained, Father Juárez greeted them all and began reading from the bible. All sound jumbled together. Mariana could not breathe in the airless house, saturated with incense, sweat, and death. The Father's words billowed from his mouth like a fog that formed a cloud over her head until the words began to rain down one at a time. *Lord. Merciful. Holy.* It went on forever and ever and stretched until the end of time.

Josefina stared forward as if she could not pull her eyes away from Emilio's body. Sofía glanced around the room, looking confused, and Catalina lay asleep against Mamá's breasts. Both Papá and Lázaro stood silent and wooden.

Emilio lay with Mamá's rosary beads wrapped around his hands while his ghost drifted between the people. When his icy fingers ran up Mariana's spine, the chill sunk so deep into her bones, she felt as if she would never be able to warm them again.

When Father Juárez finished, the people moved to the back porch. They gathered around tables filled with empanadas, frijoles, arroz verde, tortillas, and stacks of mismatched plates and silverware that had come from the multitude of kitchens in the barrio. Everything had magically appeared and fallen into place, except for Jenny. Nothing had come from the ranch house, no food, no flowers, and no Jenny.

Even after the vigil, the prayers never stopped. People came and went all night and prayed in shifts. Mamá had finally collapsed and Papá carried her off to bed. Everyone wafted through, as if the house had been filled with water and they floated, slow and muffled. All Mariana wanted to do was open the windows and let it all drain out.

THE COFFIN ARRIVED in the morning and smelled of newly cut wood and wax. Papá, Lázaro, and two men on Emilio's picking crew carried the casket to the church, followed by Mamá, Mariana, and her sisters. Behind them, the curandera, and the rest of the people dressed in black suits, black dresses, and black lace veils.

Mariana carried the cross from their altar. She clutched it in both hands, for it was the only thing solid for her to grasp onto. She kept her eyes focused on Jesus, with his arms stretched and head bowed, while the dirt and gravel road passed beneath Him. *Earth to earth, ashes to ashes, dust to dust.* She heard nothing but the crunching of hard-soled shoes on the road, and a single distant scream of one of Señor Stratton's peacocks.

WHEN SORROW TAKES WING

Black bunting and incense hung heavy in the church. Mariana stood at the front with Papá and watched the pallbearers place the casket at the altar. The people knelt and crossed themselves before entering the pews. Once everyone was seated, Father Juárez presented Papá with a white cloth, which he placed on top of the coffin. By undoing each fold, Papá draped and covered Emilio's entire casket. Mariana handed Lázaro the cross, which he placed on top of the cloth, and the priest offered a prayer.

As the organ played, the notes filled Mariana's body—fuller and fuller until she felt she would burst. Every now and then, a familiar note escaped and sounded as if it came from Emilio's harmonica or his old kazoo. She could almost see Emilio lick his lips and place his harmonica to them. The thin hairs of his mustache always slipped back and forth across it as he played.

Suddenly, the church lit up in white light, as if the gates of heaven had opened for Emilio. Everyone turned toward the source, only to see the silhouettes of Señor Stratton and Jenny come in the open doorway. They closed the door and slipped into a back pew, allowing the candles to shine again in the dim and muted light.

The funeral went by in a haze: the music, the Holy Communion, the prayers, and the people responding their rote replies of *amen, Lord have mercy, and also with you*. They stood and knelt and the scent of the incense filled the church. Before she knew it, Papá, Lázaro, and the other pallbearers moved to the front and surrounded Emilio's coffin. Mariana waited for them to carry Emilio past their pew before standing with the rest of her family. She followed Papá and Mamá as they walked behind the casket of their only son.

The people stayed in their seats until they passed then joined the procession. Jenny and her father sat in the back pews. Instead of a veil, Jenny wore a tiny black hat with mesh pulled over her face that made it hard to see anything but Jenny's wide and watery eyes staring out from behind it.

A LONG LINE of people followed the family and the casket into the cemetery beside the church. Father Juárez blessed the grave before Lázaro and three other boys lowered Emilio into it with straps. The priest prayed some more, then they all recited the Lord's Prayer before Papá dropped the first handful of dirt onto Emilio's coffin. Just a few days before, Mariana had watched him fasten the pearl buttons of his new shirt while he closed it over his smooth and hairless brown chest. He was excited for his meeting with Jenny. Mariana should have stopped him. She should have begged him to stay home.

They all stood and watched the shovelfuls of dirt cover Emilio, where he would be forever trapped with no light and no air. After it was done, the people wandered out of the cemetery and headed toward the gathering at the Americanization Center.

Señor Stratton approached Papá, and Jenny slipped her hand around Mariana's. Through the black mesh that covered her face, Jenny sniffled and only managed to say, "Please forgive me." It seemed as if she could not breathe and gasped for air. "Please, Mariana, I am sorry. Please forgive me."

Mariana could not do it. The words twisted up in her throat. Before Jenny could say more, Lázaro came up to them and spat in the dirt at Jenny's feet. Mariana wanted to tell Lázaro to take his hate somewhere else before he caused them more trouble, but she could not speak. Lázaro had his own pain, and he was her family.

"I'm sorry for your loss, Hector," Señor Stratton held out an envelope. "It's just a bit of money to help get your family through this tragedy."

Papá did not reach for it. Lázaro turned his glare toward Señor Stratton and looked as if he wanted to choke him too.

"It's a gift from my family."

Papá refused to take the envelope. He stared directly into Señor Stratton's eyes. "Make sure they find out who did this to my son."

"Of course." Señor Stratton slid the envelope back into his suit pocket then looked away as if he could not hold Papá's gaze for another moment. When he motioned for Jenny to follow him, she released Mariana's hand and went to her father.

CHAPTER FOUR

MARIANA BOLTED UPRIGHT IN BED WITH HER HEART THUMPING from a nightmare. Emilio awoke in his coffin. He was panicking and pounding on the lid. Catalina rolled over and draped her tiny arm around Mariana. She was at home. In her own bed. Only a dream. Only a dream.

Someone pounded on the front door.

"Who is it?" Josefina's voice sounded sleepy and deep.

"I don't know." Mariana lifted Catalina and put her into bed with Josefina and Sofía. "Stay here."

Mariana peeked through the slit in her window curtains. Two trucks idled outside their house. She slipped into the hallway and closed the door behind her. Papá and Lázaro stood in the living room and faced the door without opening it. A single candle still burned on their altar. Papá pressed the button on the electric light switch and illuminated the room that was still cluttered with the aftermath of the vigil: black cloth, lace, extinguished candles, and flowers that had already begun to wilt. The couch had been brought back in, but several unreturned chairs and the sawhorses lined the far wall. The phantom on the other side of the door pounded again. Not sharp raps with the knuckles but the dull thud of the side of a fist.

Papá waved Lázaro to the wall behind the door and out of sight.

"Open the door." The command came in English.

"Who is it?" Papá asked.

"Open the door, Hector. It's Constable Stillwell."

Mariana slunk back into the hallway and out of sight. She heard the squeak of the hinges as the door opened.

"Have you found my son's killer?" Papá asked.

"No."

Papá backed away. Constable Stillwell, with three other men behind him, entered their home. All four of them held long rifles across their bodies and the butts of handguns stuck out of their holsters. Papá motioned to Lázaro. He stepped out from behind the door and startled one of the men who raised a barrel at Lázaro.

"I have a report that you and your boys have been smuggling liquor across the border."

"That is not true. Who has told you this?"

"It's from a reliable witness. Your bad dealings are what got your boy killed."

"That is a lie!" Lázaro said.

"*¡Tienes que estar tranquilo o lo harás peor!*"

"Tell your boy to shut up," the constable said.

"That is what I told him."

"Then speak it in English."

"We are not smuggling liquor. How would we do that? We have no motorcar. No way to do it. I am a hard-working man."

"You can claim your innocence to a judge. You and your boy are under arrest."

Arrest? Papá and Lázaro would never get out of an Anglo jail. Who would believe their word over the constable's? Lázaro looked from man to man as if weighing his options.

Please, Father in heaven, let him keep his mouth shut and his body still.

"My family needs us," Papá said in a shaky voice. "Who will support them?"

"You should have thought of that before you broke the law," the constable said. "Of course, there is one other option. I spoke to Warren Stratton before heading over and he persuaded me to not be overly harsh on you. It's your choice, Hector. Arrest or voluntary repatriation. No jail. No trial. Just you and your family going back to where you belong."

They belonged right where they were. Papá built their house with his own hands.

"Where is it we belong?" Papá asked. "Mexico?"

The constable let out a rude laugh. "Where else would you belong?"

Mariana had not been to Mexico since she was five years old. And what about Emilio? They could not leave him buried here without his family.

"When do you need my decision?" Papá asked.

"Right now. This ain't no business proposition."

For a moment, the entire house was silent except for the sound of the engines idling outside. When Papá spoke, his words came out tight and harsh. "We will go back. How long do we have?"

"I'd say you have about twenty minutes. It's a long drive and my men are tired."

"I have a wife and four daughters. We need more time."

"You have twenty minutes. I'd start getting things going if I were you."

Papá gave a single nod and dropped his head. Lázaro stood like a clay figure with his eyes fixed on the side of the constable's head.

Papá turned toward Mariana, but she could not move. He stepped into the hall and came face-to-face with her. He looked surprised for a moment, then his expression turned sad. "Go get your sisters. Have Josefina help you dress the little ones, then gather your most needed belongings. Wrap everything into your blankets and wait in your room until Lázaro or I come for you."

Mariana turned into her room at the same time Papá opened his bedroom door. She heard the soft questioning voice of Mamá and then a gasp and muffled cries.

"What is it?" Josefina asked.

"We are going to Mexico. Get dressed and then wake Sofía." Mariana twisted the knob on the lamp.

"Mexico?"

"They are deporting us. Throw as much of your and Catalina's clothes and your most important things onto your blanket, then tie it up. Make sure it's not too heavy for you to carry."

"We don't know anyone in Mexico."

"I think we have family in Guadalajara," Mariana said.

Mariana had heard that bad things were happening in Mexico. The men in the barrio had been gathering to discuss it, but nobody shared it with her.

"We only have twenty minutes. We need to hurry."

Josefina slid to the end of her bed and pulled her nightgown over her head. "Why is this happening?"

"Because of Emilio," Mariana said.

"What did he do?" Josefina asked.

"He didn't do anything. Someone wants us gone."

"Señor Stratton promised Papá he would find out who did it." Josefina reached for her black funeral dress.

"Not that one. It doesn't belong to us. Wear your church dress," Mariana said. "Emilio must have been killed by one of Señor Stratton's men or someone important."

Josefina looked confused.

"Who is more important? Emilio or a white man?" Mariana asked.

"But that is not right."

Mariana opened her top bureau drawer, grabbed her rosary, and slipped it into her skirt pocket. "Right has nothing to do with it."

The men forced Mariana, Lázaro, and Sofía into the first truck. Papá, Mamá, and Josefina with Catalina in her arms, were marched past them, toward the second one. On her way past the constable, Mamá cried, "The *novena*, the *novena*. Please let me take a candle to my neighbor." They needed to keep a candle burning and pray for Emilio for nine days.

One of the men put the butt of his rifle between Mamá's shoulder blades and pushed. She yelped and flinched in shock, or pain, and arched away from his gun. Papá turned to see what happened.

"Get into the goddamned truck," the man said.

"Mamá!" Josefina yelled and startled Catalina who looked around with wide eyes.

Papá climbed into the bed of the truck then bent, with his arms outstretched, to help Mamá in.

Lázaro stepped onto the bumper and swung his leg into the bed of the truck before turning to reach for Sofía. Mariana held her out to him and just as Lázaro had hold of her, one of the men came up behind Mariana. "Aren't you a pretty señorita?" He put his hand on her waist and ran it over her hip.

Before she knew it, Lázaro had jumped from the truck and stood before her. He put his arm around Mariana's shoulders and moved her to the bumper. "Step up here."

Once in, she took Sofía's hand and led her to the cab of the truck. She lowered herself, sat down, and leaned her back against the cab. Sofía climbed into her lap and Lázaro dropped down beside her and whispered, "I'm going to come back and slit their throats. Starting with that gringo and ending with Jenny the white whore."

The truck's engine rumbled and ground into gear before

they pulled away and left behind all that Papá had worked so hard for. What about all their furniture, dishes, and the children's toys? And worse of all, what about Emilio and the spirits of the memories that had filled the walls of their home?

Lázaro pulled a baseball bat from his bundle of blanket. "I could smash the window and crack their heads open right now."

"You could," Mariana said, "and they could stop the truck and shoot all of us dead."

Lázaro lay the bat next to him and kept a grip on the handle. He and Emilio had saved their money for that bat and two baseball gloves so they could play on the barrio baseball team. That would be another thing taken from them. Mariana would never again pack a picnic lunch to watch Emilio taunt the pitcher and always try to steal the next base. Emilio had more stolen bases than any other player on the team.

As they bumped down the unpaved street, Mariana felt the helpless eyes of her neighbors peek out their curtains at them. She knew there would be hundreds of prayers said for her family that night in the barrio, but there were not enough prayers in the world to stop a powerful man from covering up his own evil.

Mariana clutched Sofía tight. She leaned against the cab of the truck, unable to see where they were going, only where they had been—and hoping the two trucks did not become separated. Sofía lay wrapped in her blanket and drifted in and out of sleep. Thousands of stars blinked overhead and the dingy yellow moon sat low on the horizon. They drove through the lonely land that had become nothing but road and the silhouettes of scrub and cactus.

Papá rode in the truck in front of them with no power over his own fate. Or the fate of his family. Lázaro clutched the handle of the bat and stared with unblinking eyes at the heads of the men in the cab.

Mariana shifted Sofía, adjusted her blanket, and noticed

something dark against Sofía's chest. Mariana lifted the edge of the blanket. Peacock feathers! A bouquet of bad luck, loss, and misfortune clasped in Sofía's tiny fist. Her hand twitched and her eyes opened when Mariana slid them out and dropped them over the side of the truck.

"No…" Sofía cried. "Those are mine."

For the first time since they left the barrio, Lázaro took his glare off the men and put it on her. "Hasn't she lost enough tonight?"

Sofía put her face against Mariana and wept.

"Peacock feathers are bad luck."

"That is only a superstition."

"We cannot risk inviting any more misfortune." Mariana pulled the blanket up to Sofía's chin. "God has forsaken us."

Lázaro said nothing about God or about Him forsaking them because he knows. They all knew.

The truck slowed and inched forward to a railroad crossing lit up by an oncoming train. The sound felt as if it came from within Mariana's chest and pounded against her ribcage.

When the train finally passed and the truck began to roll forward, Lázaro scooted up into a squat with his head snapping from side to side. Before she had a chance to utter a word, he placed one hand on the truck bed and leapt over the side. In the grimy moonlight, she saw him roll on the dirt, spring to his feet, and scamper off into the scrub like a jackrabbit. The baseball bat caught the light twice before he disappeared into the night. They bumped down the crooked and narrow dirt road for hours, right through the middle of nothing—just her and Sofía in the bed of the truck.

CHAPTER FIVE

THE KNOBS OF MARIANA'S SPINE TAPPED AGAINST THE CAB OF THE truck as she curled around Sofía and tried to keep her warm. How could Lázaro abandon them like this? He left her and Sofía to nothing but their own fates. What if the trucks separated and each one entered Mexico at different locations? She could not care for herself or for Sofía.

With one arm around her sister, Mariana placed the other hand onto the dry wood of the truck bed and scooted toward the edge, again and again, until she could lean over and peer around the cab. The front headlamps caught nothing but a bit of road ahead of them. No other truck. No Papá. No Mamá. No Josefina or Catalina.

Mariana tipped her head back and tried to swallow down the lump in her throat. Above them, stars shone like a million shards of broken glass. Sofía let out a sleepy whimper, shifted, and nuzzled into Mariana's arms. Poor little Sofía stuck with Mariana, a girl who brought nothing but misfortune and bad luck. She had been born on the day Halley's Comet passed over Mexico, which everyone knew was a bad omen—and Mariana's spirit had ridden in on it.

43

The truck bumped down the dirt road for hours, right through the middle of nothing. The slight glow of morning had come when they finally slowed and stopped. The truck jostled as the men climbed out of the cab. Mariana held tight to Sofía, closed her eyes, and pretended to be asleep.

"What the…"

"Hey." Something knocked against the truck bed. "Wake up."

The man wore his hat low over his eyes and a shadow of beard covered his jaw. He dropped the tailgate.

"Where is he?" He raised his gun with the barrel pointed directly at Mariana and poor little Sofía.

"I don't…" Mariana's voice shook. "…know. I fell asleep."

Sofía began to whimper.

Another man appeared at the side of the truck. "What's wrong."

"The goddamned boy escaped."

"How far back?"

"Don't know. The lying bitch says she was asleep."

"Is that so?"

Out of the corner of her eye, Mariana saw movement, then felt something hard press against the side of her head. The man pushed a pistol against her temple and clicked it. She flinched and pulled Sofía against her. Her heart pulsated up her neck and beat through her ears.

"When did he jump out?"

Mariana squeezed her eyes shut and waited for the blast. The man pushed the gun harder into her head and almost tipped her over.

"I…I was asleep." She lied and she did not care. God would forgive her.

He moved the gun and relieved the pressure. Mariana gulped in air, over and over, unable to control it. He put the gun at Sofía's tiny head. "Did you see your brother jump out?"

Sofía looked up at Mariana with eyes as big as walnuts.

WHEN SORROW TAKES WING

"She's...five...years..." Mariana could not stop choking on the air.

"What's going on?" A deep voice came from the other side of the truck. The man pulled his gun away. Mariana turned to see the big hat and mustache of *El Coco*. He drove the truck with Papá and Mamá. Her family was here. Praise the Lord and the *Virgen de Guadalupe*.

"The boy is gone."

"How far back?"

"Don't know."

"What do you mean you don't know? How long has it been since you checked on him?"

The men did not respond.

The man with the pistol put his hands in the air. "I was driving."

"Shit," the constable said. He took his hat off and ran his fingers through his thin brown hair. His half an eyebrow made his face look unfinished—like God had rushed the job and tossed him from heaven like that.

"Get them out of the truck."

The man at the tailgate raised the barrel of his shotgun again. "Out."

"That is not necessary," the constable said. "They're only girls."

Mariana scooted to the edge of the tailgate and felt the slivers of wood snag in her skirt and several splinters poke through into her flesh. Sofía raised her head and looked up with red-rimmed eyes. Mariana kissed the top of her head. "It's all right."

Just then, the fourth man came with Mamá, Papá, Josefina, and Catalina before him, all of them clasping their bundles of bedding wrapped around all they had in the world. Papá's face had no color and two big furrows formed between his brows, but he said nothing—their guns robbed her Papá of his manhood, shamed him, and made his family know that Papá could not protect his own family. His eyes scanned the area, then met Mariana's with a questioning look.

Josefina stepped forward and held an arm out for Sofía. As soon as Mariana let her go, the morning cold washed over her body and filled her with shivers that she could not control.

"Mamá!" Sofía cried and held her arms out, unsatisfied with Josefina.

Mamá held Catalina in one arm and her bundle in the other. "I cannot take you, *mija*." She kissed Sofía on the head.

"Your boy escaped," *El Coco* said to Papá. "You better hope he finds his way to Mexico. If I find him anywhere near Stratton Ranch or Santiago, I'll personally drive him to San Quentin until he hangs on the gallows or rots in a cell."

Papá gave a nod of understanding, but could not say a word.

El Coco looked at his wristwatch. "It's about time. Earl and Stuart, you two walk them in. We'll head back to find that boy. Goddamnit."

Mariana grabbed her knotted lump of blanket. When she reached for Lázaro's, Papá grabbed her wrist. "Leave it. We will not carry his load."

Mariana lowered it to the ground and left everything precious to Lázaro behind her. She hoped he had not been stupid enough to put his mother's locket into it.

Papá took the whimpering Sofía from Josefina's arms and lifted her onto his shoulders. He turned, and with the face of a wooden idol, started toward the border station. For as far as Mariana could see, a line of parked motorcars waited to get into Mexico. All the Anglos stared at them being forced across the border, while they sat preserved behind glass and driving in at their own wills—and when they were done, they would safely return to their homes. Mariana's cheeks burned, and with every step, she felt the prick of the wood slivers in her behind.

Josefina peered into each motorcar she passed—as if begging

them to help her family. Mariana put her arm around Josefina's shoulders. "There's nothing they can do. Don't degrade yourself."

About halfway down the line, the motors started coming to life. Papá kept walking and leading his family right up to the United States Immigration and Customs station with the American flag on one side and the Mexican flag on the other.

The line of motorcars coughed out smoke and burned oil as they slowly inched into Mexico like a string of black beetles. The guards simply glanced into the windows with disinterested faces and let them pass by.

The cars on the other side, the ones coming back into the United States, were directed, one by one, into an inspection station where the drivers and passengers stepped out. Anglo guards patted them down and forced men to hold open the lapels of their jackets while agents checked beneath them. Guards lifted off people's hats to look inside while others combed through their cars, opening trunks and hoods, pulling off caps in the engines, and inspecting luggage and ladies' purses.

"What are they doing?" Mariana asked.

Papá glanced back at the men behind them before speaking. "Checking for liquor. And migrants."

"Migrants?"

Sofía put her hands on top of Papá's head and lay one cheek down to rest her head. "This is the new border patrol."

"What are they doing with migrants?"

"Stopping them from going into the United States illegally."

"People like us?"

The cords in Papá's neck flared out and his voice turned sharp. "When we came, I paid a four-dollar tax for each of us."

Mariana looked back. The men were far enough back that she could speak. "Can we pay it again and go back?"

Father turned away from her.

"It's different now," he said. "The tax is so high that people cannot pay it, and they cannot pass the new reading and writing tests that are in English. If they want to cross, they have to do it like jackrabbits and risk being shot."

"We could pass the reading and writing tests. We went to school and Americanization classes."

"They can have their country. I'm done with it," Papá said. "I'm tired of putting my sweat into a country that's not mine."

Her family walked beneath an archway with *Mexico* painted in big black letters on one side and *United States* on the other. And that was that. They would never again see the home Papá had built in Stratton barrio or the friends and neighbors they knew. They were now Mexicans in Mexico—a country Mariana barely remembered and a country Sofía and Catalina never knew.

The moment her family had cleared the station and were out of the border guards' hearing, Papá stopped and turned his red face to Mariana.

"What happened to Lázaro?"

"He jumped out when we stopped for the train..."

"You didn't stop him?"

"How could I? He just jumped without a word to me."

Tears slipped down Mamá's eyes, and she began to pray. Everything would be on Papá's back with Lázaro gone. Poor Papá with nothing left but a wife and four daughters.

Just inside the border, they walked alongside the road, past a horse racing track, and a whole complex of white buildings with green trim. Mexican flags fluttered from every peak and corner. A long fence had *This is the Famous Belvedere Hotel and Casino* painted in letters as tall as Catalina. They were written in English even though they were now in Mexico.

"Can we stay there?" Josefina asked. "I'm tired."

"That is not a place for my family," Papá sounded as if he were spitting the words from his mouth.

WHEN SORROW TAKES WING

"What is it?" Mariana asked.

"It's a casino."

"What's a casino?"

"It's where people gamble with cards and slot machines."

The boys in the barrio gambled with their ragged decks of cards, and bet pennies, sticks of gum, or rocks when they had nothing better. It had seemed only an amusement and not anything bad.

A covered boardwalk crossed a river that connected the racetrack and casino with the city on the other side. Next to it, the line of motorcars rumbled over a rickety bridge with ties so loose they played a ceaseless dull and discordant refrain. Mariana could not look for fear the ties would collapse and send the cars straight into the water.

Mariana had not known what to expect and had imagined that Tijuana would be a small village surrounded by ranchos—not a busy, overcrowded city packed with Anglos and motorcars, telephone lines, and lampposts. It would have seemed like any other city in California if not for all the bars and cantinas with signs and flags advertising Cerveza, Vinos, Whiskey, and Tequila. Armed soldiers in high boots walked the streets beside the tourists.

Anglos posed for pictures as they leaned against motorcars or buildings with bottles of liquor tipped to their lips. They skipped around laughing and drinking like naughty children set loose away from the prohibition laws in the United States. Of course, they could enjoy their visit because they knew they could jump in their cars or board the train and pass right back into California any time they wanted—welcome in both countries.

A group of young Mexican girls, dressed in scanty dresses that showed the swells of their tiny breasts, stood in a small cluster outside a seedy building and talked to lone men as they passed by. Dirty children milled through the streets lugging wooden boxes and calling out to the Anglos in accented English, *Shoeshine, señor?* A sad-looking burro, led by a man who looked to be a hundred years old, clip-clopped down the street pulling a cart loaded with handwoven blankets and pottery. They moved slow and were victim to the tourists who stopped him to take photographs.

Papá found them rooms in a hotel with dirty blankets on the beds and only two cold-water showers for the entire hotel.

That night, with no candles for Emilio's *novena*, Mamá knelt by the window. With her face to the glow of a lamppost, she prayed for Emilio's soul and ignored her hungry family—and the dreadful moans and squeaking bedsprings that came from the next room.

With all four girls squeezed into one bed, Papá reached from one forehead to the next, traced the sign of the cross, and recited, "May almighty God, Father, Son, and Holy Spirit bless you for all time and eternity. May this blessing remain forever with you."

At least Tijuana had not taken Papá's nightly blessing away from them. And maybe Papá did not believe that God had completely forsaken them.

Mariana barely slept. The room had thin curtains that barely blocked the light from the lamppost just outside the window. Sofía cried for her Yasmin doll they had accidentally left behind. And from the streets, the blare of never-ending jazz, mariachi music, horns and drums, exploding fireworks, loud drunken voices, laughter, screeching women, and the rumble of motorcars and buses with squeaky brakes came in through the window all night long.

Warren Stratton had not sent them *back to their country where they belonged.* He sent them straight to hell.

CHAPTER SIX

MAMÁ MARCHED ALL HER GIRLS, ROSARIES IN HAND, TO FIND A church while Papá went to look for work. Mariana held Catalina while Josefina gripped Sofía's hand and yanked her down the street. Mamá had seven more nights to pray for Emilio and needed to light a prayer candle. After lighting the candle, she would find them breakfast, not before. Mariana tried to keep a happy face even though her stomach cramped. Sofía and Catalina whined, but they were little and knew nothing but their own feelings.

It did not help that they all awoke that morning with itchy little welts all over their bodies. Like the rest of Tijuana, the bedbugs had caroused all night long. The inexcusable one was Josefina. She had a sour expression on her face and took it out on Sofía by grabbing her by the arm and snapping at her.

The morning streets lay quiet. Only a few taxis lined the sides with their drivers sitting on back bumpers and smoking cigarettes. Street dogs, with dusty coats and tucked tails, scurried around sticking their muzzles into discarded paper sacks and upended garbage cans. They passed a bakery window filled with shelves of sweet breads: pink, brown, and yellow conchas,

51

coyotas, and fruit-filled empanadas. Mariana's stomach growled from the warm scents of cinnamon, cardamom, and baking bread.

Catalina reached her hand toward the window.

"I'm hungry," Sofía said.

"Can we get some?" Josefina asked to the back of Mamá's head. "Please. We are starving and can eat it while walking."

Mamá stopped and turned toward them. At first, Mariana could almost taste the sweetness of the concha—but then she noticed Mamá's eyebrows and lips pinched together. "You are worried about your stomachs while Emilio's spirit is wandering around not knowing where his family went? He has nobody praying for him."

A tear slid down Sofía's cheek. "I prayed for him."

Mamá turned away and continued toward the bell tower and cross that rose in the distance behind the saloons, restaurants, and curio shops of downtown. She led them down an alley lined with garbage bins, for right at the end of the alley stood a white-washed church with large wooden doors.

Dust and windblown debris covered the church courtyard, and the husks of dried weeds sprung from cracks in the paving stones. Mamá reached into the bag she had worn across her body and pulled out a handful of folded black lace. She handed both Mariana and Josefina a veil, then draped her own over her hair.

Of course Mamá had packed their veils. Instead of her own clothing, she probably packed everything from their family altar. The rest of the family grabbed their personal belongings and their practical things, but Mamá brought their history and their faith—she had climbed into the truck with her blanket stuffed with the framed image of the *Virgen de Guadalupe*, wooden crucifix, Tía Carlotta's locket, and Emilio's harmonica case.

Mamá stopped at the steps of the church, where a notice,

printed in large black letters, was nailed to the massive wooden doors. Catalina wiggled and wanted down. "Not right now," Mariana whispered and kissed Catalina on the side of her head.

As they ascended, the words on the notice became clear: *DEATH TO THE CHURCH. CLOSED BY ARTICLE 27 OF THE CONSTITUTION OF MEXICO.*

"What does it mean, Mamá?" Josefina asked.

"The government has closed the church."

"Maybe there is another one," Josefina said.

"It is all the churches, *mija*." Mamá's resolute shoulders drooped down. "Word went around the barrio that President Calles had closed the churches. It seemed so ridiculous that I did not believe it. Who would take religion from the people?"

Mamá put her hand on the door as if feeling for a heartbeat. She pushed and the door swung open. Mamá peeked her head through and listened before stepping inside and waving her girls in behind her.

Mariana dipped her fingers into the font by the door. It was dry, but she crossed herself anyway. Her eyes adjusted to the dim light shimmering in through the stained glass windows. Beams of sunlight glowed through the robes and faces of angels and saints except where the pieces of stained glass were broken out, leaving gaps of bright white emptiness.

The church had been ransacked. Pews lay on their backs or at odd angles and the altar was riddled with bullet holes. Upon the altar sat the bottom quarter of a cross with Jesus' feet still nailed to it, but the rest of him missing. It looked like it had been used for target practice. They stepped up onto the sanctuary and Mariana crossed herself for treading on a sacred space. Fragments of figurines, glass, and wood littered the floor. The heads had been shot off of what appeared to be statuettes of Saint Francis and Saint Teresa. Most of the pieces were unrecognizable and shot to oblivion. Catalina squirmed and wanted down, but Mariana held tight and shushed her.

"Who would do this?" Josefina asked.

Mamá groaned. She dropped to her knees upon all the broken pieces of ceramic and glass and chanted her prayers so fast that Mariana could only catch some of the words. *Lady of Guadalupe, Mystical rose, hear my prayer, Queen of martyrs...*

Mariana balanced Catalina on one hip, swept a space clear with her foot, and knelt beside Mamá.

"I'm scared," Josefina said. "I want to go home."

Mamá did not answer, she just kept chanting her trance-like prayers with her head to her fingertips.

"The church is closed!" Booming like the voice of God, the sharp words reverberated through the empty church.

Catalina whimpered and wrapped her arms around Mariana's neck. The silhouette of a federal officer stood in the doorway.

He came toward them and Josefina backed away, toward the altar where Mamá had not paused in her prayers.

"You are in violation of the law." He raised his rifle, placed the butt of it to his shoulder, and pointed the barrel toward Mamá. "Stand up and turn around."

Mamá kept praying and did not acknowledge his presence until she finally crossed herself. She placed her hand on the altar for balance, and as she rose, she closed her other hand around a fragment of ceramic that looked like the hand and sleeve of a saint. She slipped it into her skirt pocket before fully standing and turning toward the man. Catalina buried her head into Mariana's neck.

"We didn't know," Josefina said in English. "We just got here from the United States."

"*Silencio.*" He cocked his rifle with his fat thumb and moved toward them. He had a bloated baby face and bushy black eyebrows over tiny eyes that sunk deep into their sockets.

All Mariana could hear was the pounding of her own heart

and the creak of the man's leather boots and holster with every one of his steps.

"I apologize," Mamá said in Spanish. "We have just arrived from the United States."

"There is a notice on the door," he said. "Don't you read?"

"Yes," Mamá said. "We will leave."

His eyes caught Mariana and he cast them over her breasts and hips. A bubble of fear started in her chest and expanded with every second his gaze lay on her. *Oh please, God of mercy...*

"You will not leave before paying the fine."

"I don't have any money." Mamá's voice trembled.

"That is unfortunate for you." He answered Mamá without taking his eyes from Mariana. "People who cannot pay go to jail."

Mamá stepped toward the officer and blocked his view of Mariana. "It is my fault. Let my daughters leave."

When the man didn't answer, Mamá unfastened her hair and let it cascade past her shoulder and over her breast. The soldier looked up and down Mamá's body. Seeming satisfied, he jerked his head toward the door indicating the rest of them could leave.

"Mamá! No!" Mariana clasped Catalina tight.

Mamá shot Mariana a steely look. "You will leave, and you will take your sisters with you."

"No, Mamá. Please."

Josefina shifted Sofía to her other hip. "My Papá will pay the fine. Please let her go."

He reached out and grabbed Mariana's arm. "Can he pay for two of his women?"

His touch made Mariana's skin burn as if her flesh bubbled beneath his grasp. He had black eyes, tiny square teeth, and the skin of his neck bulged over his tight collar.

"Go," Mamá said. "Go straight home and wait for me."

Home? They had no home. On her way out, Josefina grabbed

one of the few unbroken votive candles below an empty alcove. Her face was ashen, and her hand shook when she dropped the heavy glass candle inside her shirt.

"Mamá," Sofía cried and reached her arms back into the church.

They all paused by the door.

"Go," Mamá said.

Mariana was unable to move and unable to think. Josefina looked at her as if she should know what to do.

"Come on," Mariana said and slid out the door with her sisters.

They needed help. Mamá needed help. On the street, a long-skirted Indio woman walked by with four children behind her. Two men casually strolled by in business suits, immersed in conversation. A group of men in cotton pants and huaraches stood on the corner waiting for work. Children trolled the streets with their shoe shine kits, sticks of sugar cane, or candies. A few tourists staggered around, still woozy and wrapped in ponchos and giant sombreros. Who could they ask for help? Who would stand against a federal officer?

"Take the girls to the hotel to wait for Papá," Mariana said. "I will stay here and follow them to make sure we know where he is taking Mamá."

"Mamá said..."

"I don't care what she said. We cannot leave her."

"Should I go look for Papá?"

"No. Stay in the room until I return."

Josefina took Sofía's hand.

"You stole that," Mariana pointed her chin toward the candle hammocked in Josefina's shirt. "From a church!"

"God will not mind." Josefina started untucking her blouse. "You take it. I will have the girls."

"We will be in more trouble for stealing."

"We need it for Emilio's novena."

"It's probably cursed now," Mariana said.

"If anything is cursed, it is our family," Josefina said. "We came for a candle and all this would be for nothing."

"Don't say that in front of the little ones."

"God will not mind a candle." Josefina dropped the heavy glass votive into the neck of Mariana's blouse and took Catalina from her.

"I will get the girls safely back to the room. Come back as soon as you can."

Josefina gave Mariana a reassuring smile before striding off with Catalina balanced on one hip and pulling Sofía by the hand.

Josefina was too young to know that the *federale* would not take Mamá to the jail—at least not yet. Mariana glanced around the street looking for someone to help, but this was not their barrio, and she saw nothing but strangers. Mariana trembled. Emilio or Lázaro always saved her—but they were not coming. Nobody was coming.

Poor Mamá only had her, and she was a cowardly daughter who could do nothing. It felt as if a cold hand squeezed her chest and prevented her from breathing. Mariana crossed herself and prayed the Hail Mary as she made her way to the entrance *Hail Mary, full of grace*. She dropped to her hands and knees and slipped into the partially open door. *Holy Mary, Mother of God.*

She could not see Mamá or the soldier, but she could hear him grunting like an animal on the other side of the altar. *No! Not her Mamá. Please, God.*

Mariana hugged the wall as she crawled around the pews and passed by the confessionals. In an alcove, a wrought iron stand was filled with broken shards of devotional candles with all the prayers shattered and lying in pieces on the floor of the church.

Before she reached the railing of the sanctuary, Mariana

crawled between two upright pews, toward the central aisle, and toward his feral sounds. The candle hung low inside her shirt and swayed with every move. She kept her lips squeezed tight, afraid to make a sound, and afraid the pounding heartbeat in her throat would burst out of her.

When she reached the end of the pew, she peeked around to see the back of the man kneeling between her mamá's bare legs with his pants down and boots still on. Mamá's knee was flecked with red droplets of blood, probably from kneeling on the broken statuettes of the saints. The *federale's* flabby flesh pumped and pumped on her poor Mamá right there beside the Lord's altar. Right there, where priests, in their holy vestments had sung their Offertory Chants over the bread and wine of the Blessed Sacrament.

Poor Mamá. She just lost her son, all she wanted to do was pray for him. Mamá lay there, unmoving and silent and absorbing the abuses of the man.

Mariana slipped the thick glass votive from her blouse. While he was distracted, she could pound him on the back of his greasy black head. She needed to rescue her Mamá. Mariana was all that she had. What if the animal killed Mamá when he was done with her? Mariana peeked over the pew with the candle grasped in her hand. She rose and took a step into the aisle. *Holy Mary, Mother of God...*

Mariana's arm began to shake and she could not breathe. Her chest felt like it was collapsing from within. The man was an animal. A wild beast. Mariana could not will herself to take another step. The *federale* let out a brutal roar and collapsed on top of Mamá and pinned her to the floor of the sanctuary—suffocating her with his massive flesh.

Mariana's feet would not step forward. Poor Mamá had nobody but her, a daughter who had been born on the tail of a comet—a daughter who brought bad luck to their family. Mariana dropped her arm, lowered herself into a heap on the floor, and backed herself into the crook of an overturned pew. Mariana lay there, unable to breathe and smothering in the scent of incense and dust with the useless candle still in her hand. God had abandoned them.

The sound of shuffling, along with the clink of a belt buckle and the squeak of leather, resonated in the hollow church.

"You are a whore and the mother of whores." The *federale's* words echoed through the hollow church. It sounded as if he spit on the ground…or on her Mamá. His steps beat hard on the floor and made Mariana flinch when a big black boot hit the ground a foot from her head. His leather holster creaked with every step. Mariana lay still and listened to the tap of his boots fade as he marched away, then out the door.

Mariana waited and heard nothing but her own heartbeat in her ears. Mamá? Why was she so silent? Finally, Mamá let her anguish out. Her wails pierced through the sanctuary, echoed through all the brokenness, and resonated deep into Mariana's chest. Her cry was so strong that another piece of glass dropped from a window and onto the top of the confessional.

Mariana stepped into the aisle. Mamá lay there and curled herself in like a baby. With her knees up, she pulled the fabric of her black skirt over her legs.

Mariana approached the sanctuary with shaky steps. "Mamá…"

Mamá flinched.

"Are you all right?"

Mamá turned toward her and gulped down her cries. Her entire chest heaved as she tried to contain them. She pushed herself up and sat with her chin to her chest.

"It's all right, Mamá. You can cry." Mariana stepped up onto the sanctuary, knelt, and wrapped her arms around her Mamá.

Mamá shrugged her off. "How long have you been here?"

Mariana could not bear to give her mamá any more shame. "Just now. I came in when I saw the *federale* leave the church."

"Nothing happened." Mamá ran her hands down her skirt as if she was plastering it to her legs.

"But, Mamá…"

She looked up and stared hard into Mariana's eyes. "Nothing happened."

Mamá's small shoulders were curled forward and still wrapped in the black mourning clothes for her son. Once out of the church, Mariana turned to pull the door shut. She caught one last glimpse of the stained glass saints with rays of bright light piercing through them like knives.

Mamá hobbled back toward the hotel and would not allow Mariana to help her. When they arrived, Josefina was sitting on one of the beds, wide-eyed, with Catalina and Sofía asleep beside her. She jumped up and wrapped her arms around Mamá.

"Everything is fine, *mija*," Mamá said and pushed Josefina off.

"Has Papá come back yet?" Mamá asked.

"No, and I was getting worried. I didn't want to sit here doing nothing. I'm so glad you are back. Papá is going to be angry at that man for pointing a gun at us."

"We are not going to tell Papá," Mamá said.

"But…" Josefina started to say.

Mamá pressed her finger to Josefina's lips. "This will only upset him. We do not need any more trouble. Nothing happened and no good will come from telling."

When Mamá gathered a change of clothes and asked Mariana to come stand guard at the hotel shower, she realized that Mamá was right. This was something that Papá could never live with.

Once they stepped into the hall and shut the door, Mariana reached out to wrap her arms around Mamá.

Mamá stiffened and pushed her away. "I told you nothing happened."

Mamá moved through the grimy hallway with her back

looking as fragile as a bird's, like it could snap at any moment. All of this was Mariana's fault. She was the one who had made friends with Jenny, she kept bringing her around Emilio, and she was the one the *federale* had wanted—until Mamá offered herself in her place.

When Mamá stepped into the shower and shut the door, Mariana knelt down and rested her head against the cracked wood. *Oh, most gracious Virgin, you have promised to show compassion and pity on all who love and trust you. Please have mercy on my mamá and help her through her suffering. Please do not allow the seed of that nasty federale to take root. I beg you to intercede and remove the curse from our family.*

Mariana remained with her head pressed against the door as she prayed and listened to the shower run. She did not stop until she heard the creak of Mamá's hand turning the doorknob.

When they returned to the room, Mariana removed the votive candle from her shirt and held it out to Mamá like an offering. "For Emilio's *novena*."

At that, Mamá finally allowed herself to cry.

CHAPTER SEVEN

THE CURSE REMAINED ON THEIR FAMILY FOR A WEEK. POOR MAMÁ sat in the room with a vacant stare and ignored her children. Papá needed to get them out of the hotel and into a house before Mamá lost her will to live and became nothing but a dried-up husk in that chair. All Mariana could do was pray that Mamá did not carry the seed of that *federale*—for if she did, that would be something Mamá could not live through.

Papá found work behind a wheelbarrow, where he pushed loads of brick to build another Tijuana bar. He rose early, dressed in the dark, and tried not to wake his family. The first two mornings, Mamá had risen with him, but they had no kitchen for her to cook him breakfast or to pack him a lunch, so she sat on the edge of the bed, useless to her husband. On the third day, Mamá did not bother to get out of bed.

They still had no word about Lázaro. All he cared about was revenge, not thinking once about their family. Papá had taken him in and raised him like his own son and what did Papá get for it? Nothing. They needed the wages of two men.

Sofía and Catalina did nothing but whine that they were hungry. They always asked for Papá or Emilio, never being satisfied with either of their big sisters. Mariana and Josefina bickered and fought about every little thing. They argued about whose turn it was to distract the little ones or whose turn it was to empty the bucket where they all went pee. With only Papá brave enough to tolerate the cold water showers, they all began to smell.

Other than their fateful trip to the church, Mariana had only left the hotel once with Papá to get food for the family. Papá passed by all the Anglo shops with their bright colored awnings and flapping flags and took her to one of the Mexican-owned businesses off the main boulevard. It was brightly painted, but dingy and only attracted the poor workers, who, like Papá, had to haggle about the price in order to feed their families.

Mariana sat at the window and passed the hours by watching other people live their lives. A line of parked taxis and motorcars always lined the street in front of the hotel. The taxi drivers, dark skinned and lanky, leaned against their cars calling out to the tourists, *Need a ride, señor? Cheap travel price. Best service in town. El Toreo, Belvedere Hotel and Casino, anywhere you desire.*

Barefoot children worked the streets with their shoe shine kits, race forms, sugar cane, newspapers, pork rinds, or oranges. Street solicitors followed tourists dressed in brightly colored serapes and sombreros to offer them cheap marriages or quickie divorces. They lured men to a place called the Moulin Rouge with *girls for every taste*, the racetrack, the bullring, or cockfights. Old women sat against walls with tiny wide-eyed children nestled in their skirts or blankets and sold trinkets to tourists as they passed by.

"I think I should try to find a job," Mariana said. "I am capable of working."

Mamá did not respond.

"Every day I see girls my age going to work in the hotels and the restaurants."

Mamá's face twitched as if she wanted to speak, but her mouth no longer worked.

Above the constant tunes of mariachi and jazz coming from the bars, a car horn blared up the street, then another.

"What is happening?" Josefina sat down beside her.

A few blocks up, a skinny man with a knapsack thrown over one shoulder stood in the street with several taxis stopped at odd angles. Moving out of the road with one hand up and head down, he looked like a coyote who had suddenly found himself in civilization.

A familiar coyote.

The man moved to the side of the street and the taxis continued past him. It had to be Lázaro. Who else would wear such an ugly white hat?

Mariana leaned out the window. "Lázaro! Lázaro!"

Josefina pushed against Mariana's shoulder. "Where?"

"I think that's him." Mariana pointed to the man.

"It is!" Josefina began to yell with her. "Lázaro!"

He did not look up. One moment Josefina was next to her, the next moment, the door slammed shut and Josefina was gone. Both little ones sat on the bed with eyes wide and staring at the back of the door.

Mamá looked up, finally with some life in her eyes—even if it was a red hot glare. "Go get your sister."

A woman, dressed in a bathrobe and smoking a cigarette, sat in a chair outside an open door in the hallway. On the bed inside, a man lay sprawled and asleep and completely naked. Mariana gasped.

The woman shrugged her shoulders when Mariana hurried past her. "Just as God made him," she laughed.

Mariana crossed herself and hurried down the narrow wooden stairs. Music from a player piano rose up from the lobby. Please let them find Lázaro. In a fog of cigarette smoke, a line of people crowded the front desk and tried to get a room.

They were mostly Anglo men of lower class or young men with brand-new sailor haircuts.

"*Hola, señorita,*" one of them said with a slow and horrible accent. "How much? *Cuánto dinero?*"

Mariana ignored him and kept her eyes on the door. Lázaro could disappear down any alley or any street and they would never find him.

A man grabbed hold of her arm. She turned to see the face of a brutish man with red hair and a wispy mustache. "I'm not a...I am not for sale."

"Of course you are. Everyone has a price."

"I don't." Mariana tried to pull away. Her heart quivered in her throat and all she wanted to do was get out the door.

"You may not have a price now," he said, "but you will."

He released her and Mariana darted for the door with a chorus of raspy deep laughs ringing behind her.

On the street, the wind whirled up a thin layer of dust and whipped the flags. She searched the street for Lázaro's white hat or Josefina's white blouse among a sea of white blouses. People moved all about, selling, buying, or begging—everyone wanted something from someone else.

On the other side of the street, she spotted Lázaro with Josefina closing in on him. She called out and waved her arms. He caught sight of Josefina and smiled his tightlipped coyote grin that Mariana usually wanted to wipe from his face—but at that moment, it was the best face she had ever seen. Josefina made it to Lázaro and threw her arms around him.

Mariana waited for a taxi loaded with Anglos in sombreros, brim to brim, to pass by before crossing the street. Lázaro stood stiff and leaned his head away from Josefina, who wrapped herself around him and sobbed.

"Where have you been?" Mariana asked.

Josefina let go and eased herself away from him. He looked

different. His shoulders sagged, and his eyes had no fire in them.

"I went back to kill Warren Stratton and burn his house down."

Mariana crossed herself. "*¡Dios mío!* Tell me you didn't do it."

He shook his head before finally saying, "He hired armed men to watch the ranch."

"You are lucky they did not shoot you or throw you in jail."

He stared at Mariana for a moment before squaring his shoulders. "They could not catch me. I am too cunning for them. I was right under their noses the whole time and they did not even know it."

"Then you got your revenge?"

He narrowed his eyes at Mariana. "I got what I wanted to get." He swung the knapsack from his shoulder, which turned out to be a pillowcase—one of Mamá and Papá's pillowcases with the red and green embroidery. She remembered watching Mamá make those very stitches.

"What's in there?" Josefina asked.

"Take me to your Mamá, and I will show you."

The moment they opened the door to the room and the two little ones caught sight of Lázaro, they jumped up and down on the bed. They squealed with their arms out to him. Mamá lifted her head and stared at him with dark eyes. As Lázaro dumped the items from his sack, all their treasured belongings spilled onto the bed. When Sofía's Yasmin doll tumbled out, she grabbed it up, clasped it to her chest, and sobbed.

Lázaro stepped over to Mamá and stood before her with his head bowed in shame. She slowly rose to her feet. At her full height, she only came up to his lowered chin. Without saying a word, she reached her arm back and slapped him across the face so hard it knocked his hat from his head. Then, she began to cry in a long and wailing lament. She finally released some of her grief.

CHAPTER EIGHT

AFTER TWO WEEKS IN THE HOTEL, PAPÁ FOUND THEM HALF-A-house outside of town. They left the hotel, excited to have their own home, but their spirits drooped with every step they took through the dirt streets filled with stray dogs, barefoot children, and houses repaired with tin and tar paper. Papá stopped before a two-story house with more bare wood than blue paint.

Another family lived on the top floor—along with half a dozen cages of screeching canaries, in as many colors as you can imagine, on their balcony. Two children, wearing nothing but their underwear, peered through the railing at them and waved down at Catalina and Sofía.

Mamá stopped before the white iron gate that led to the courtyard. She refused to move forward and clogged their procession.

"It is better than the hotel," Papá said. "We will have a kitchen and our own bathroom."

Mamá turned to stone. No words could move her. Not even Papá's hand on her lower back could nudge her forward. They all stood outside with the neighbors wandering out their doors to stare at the strange people blown like tumbleweeds against the courtyard gate.

"It's only temporary." Papá stood beside her with rounded shoulders and sad eyes.

Did Mamá think standing there would change anything? All that her stubbornness did was make Papá feel more ashamed. Papá should pick her up and move her aside. They must all look destitute, moving in with all their belongings wrapped in nothing but their bedding.

They waited like that until a pack of skinny dogs came nosing toward them. Sofía reached out to one. It growled, bared its yellow teeth, and melted Mamá's obstinacy.

They rushed through the white gate into a dusty brick courtyard with dirt so hard that nothing but weeds could ever grow in it. They all stood at the front door waiting for Papá to put the key in the lock. Mariana and Josefina stepped before Mamá so they did not have the same problem getting through the door. The inside was furnished and smelled of old cooking oil and cigarettes, but it was better than Mariana had expected.

Even after they had scrubbed every surface of the house and aired out the couch and mattresses, Mamá's heart would not soften to it because they still lived beneath the feet of another family. The Padilla's lived in the top half of the house with a grandmother and five young children who tromped across their ceiling all day long. The house was also wrong because the front door lined up with the back door, which allowed spirits to move straight through the house.

Lázaro found daywork. He carted wheelbarrows of adobe bricks or dug trenches, but the work was not steady. Every evening, after a full day's work, he headed into the city supposedly looking for some night work but more likely to carouse and get away from the horrible melancholy that suffocated them all in the walls of their new house. It made Mariana angry, but she did not blame him. If she was a boy, she would do the exact same thing.

Mamá faded into the family. She let the little ones run around and get into things, which left it to Josefina and Mariana to mother them. What would become of her little sisters? Would they turn feral like the neighborhood children who ran barefoot through the streets and played with sticks and rocks and fought over half-broken toys?

If not for the cooking, Mamá would be no more present than the furniture. She spent most of her time praying or staring about their cluttered house with soulless eyes. Catalina kept eating chunks of plaster that had broken off the wall, but Mamá did not seem concerned about it.

One morning, not long after they had moved into the half-a-house, Mamá stood crying in the kitchen as she dropped little squares of stale tortillas into a pan of sizzling oil. The crying seemed better than the nothingness, at least it showed that her Mamá was still in there—and that her soul still inhabited her husk.

"What's wrong, Mamá?" Please do not let it be the unthinkable. What would it do to Mamá if she was carrying a child? Would she know if it came from the seed of that foul *federale* or from their own beloved Papá? What would it do to Papá if the baby came out looking nothing like him?

Mamá wiped her eyes on the back of her hand and took on a stern expression. "You will find out soon enough. Set the table."

At breakfast, Papá chewed his chilaquiles with a grave look on his face. Mamá sat at the table and poked her fork into the tiny bit of food she had put on her plate, but not bringing any of it to her pinched lips. Once the family had eaten, Mamá rose to clear the table. Mariana and Josefina stood to help her, but Mamá held her hand up. "Papá has something to tell you."

They lowered themselves into their chairs and Mamá disappeared into the kitchen with the dirty plates.

Papa pressed his lips together and crossed his arms. He did not look either of them in the eye. "I will be leaving in the morning."

Josefina jumped to her feet. "Why?"

Had Mamá told him what happened? Was he abandoning them? No. Papá would not do that.

"We have family in Guadalajara, and I'm going there to look for work."

"We're not coming?" Josefina asked.

"Lázaro will stay and take care of you."

Josefina glanced over at Lázaro, then back at Papá with a horrified expression on her face. "Don't leave us!"

"*Mija...*" Papá put his arm out for Josefina. She stood beside his chair and he wrapped an arm around her hips. "If it is safe, I will send money for all of you to join me."

"Safe?" Josefina asked. "Why wouldn't it be safe?"

Mariana had seen the newspapers. "Rebels are fighting against the government for closing the churches. Priests are being murdered and whole villages attacked by federal soldiers."

Papá looked surprised that Mariana knew.

"Will you be where the fighting is?" Josefina asked.

"I don't think so," Papá said. "My cousins are seeking a peaceful resolution with boycotts and petitions."

"Please," Mariana said. "Stay here where it is safe and we can escape back across the border if we need."

Josefina's face turned red like it always did before she bolted off.

Papá took a deep breath. "During the revolution, I fled to safety across the border. I did it to protect my family. This time, I'm staying in my own country. For good, or for bad."

"Who will tuck us into bed at night?" Josefina asked.

"Your Mamá can bless you. Or Lázaro."

Josefina shot Lázaro a hateful look before running from the

room in tears and shouting at him. "I wish you never came back to us."

Papá must have already discussed this with Lázaro because he did not seem surprised by the news. He just sat there like a stone with no feelings. Mariana did not have the same amount of confidence in Lázaro that Papá had.

Not too long ago, Lázaro had wrapped the tips of his old toy arrows with gasoline-soaked rags, shot them through the air at night, and caught the dry grass next to the barrio on fire, which threatened the entire neighborhood. The burnt field of ashes blackened the bottoms of the children's feet for months. Another time, he tried to charge a battery by putting wires on each end and sticking them into the electrical socket. The barrio had gone without electricity for three days after that.

Their family was crumbling apart. First Emilio, then Mamá, and now Papá was abandoning them. If Mamá had not been so unhappy, if she could only try to start a life here, Papá would not need to look for a better place.

PAPÁ'S CHAIR did not have time to cool before Lázaro proved himself a poor choice to protect the family.

Mariana sat on the edge of their bed telling Sofía and Catalina their favorite bedtime story, *Pedro Urdemales and the Giant*.

"And so, taking the four thousand pesos from the giant, Pedro went happily on his way, proving once again that he was the best mischief-maker in the world."

"I want Emilio," Sofía said when Mariana finished. She should not have told them that story. It was their favorite from Emilio. He would act it out for them as he told it and take on the character of Pedro.

"He is in heaven with God."

71

"I want to go to heaven with Emilio. I don't like it here."

"You need to stop asking for what you cannot have."

Sofía's face pinched like she was about to cry. All the tears, the unhappiness, and the complaints weighed on Mariana. She could not fix a thing. She could not make Mamá happy and she could not produce Emilio or bring Papá home—but her sisters kept whining and expecting her to change things beyond her control.

Mariana slipped out the bedroom door. Within a few steps, she heard Sofía behind her.

"You better get back in bed before *El Coco* comes to get you," Mariana said. "He eats up little girls who will not go to sleep."

A look of terror came to Sofía's eyes and she dashed back toward the bedroom. She should not have said that. *El Coco* was real to them. He had come to their door with guns and took all of them from their beds in the night. She was a horrible big sister.

Mariana followed Sofía back in, pulled the blanket up to her chin, and traced the sign of the cross on her forehead, "May almighty God, Father, Son, and Holy Spirit bless you for all time and eternity. May this blessing remain forever with you." At least she could offer them Papá's prayer.

"Go to sleep. *El Coco* cannot get you now."

When she finally closed the door, Lázaro called to her, "Come outside. I need to talk to you."

She followed him out into the night. Dogs barked in the distance, and a glow of light and distant mariachi music came to them from downtown.

Lázaro led her out of the tiny bricked-in yard and into the street. Mariana leaned back on the low wall and caused several bricks on the top to shift. She wasn't surprised. The entire house seemed about to crumble and bring the entire Padilla family down on their heads.

"I'm in charge of the family now and I need your help."

"You need *my* help?" Mariana did not trust any man who asked for her help. It usually meant her doing all the work and them getting all the credit.

"You know I'm trying to support this family, but I only make a few centavos a day," he said.

Lázaro had mistakenly thought he would make a fortune in Tijuana. Because of the no drinking, no gambling, and no cabaret laws in California, the Anglos swarmed into town. True to their nature, though, the Anglo businessmen followed the money. They set up shops, hotels, bars, and restaurants to keep the money going from one Anglo pocket to the next.

Since Lázaro was half-white and half-Mexican, just like the town, he thought he had finally found a place where he could prosper, but all he found were men who kept pushing his nose to the dirt doing day-jobs: cleaning floors, hauling away garbage, delivering goods to the back doors of shops, or hauling wheelbarrows full of bricks.

"You need to start helping me earn money," Lázaro said.

"I can do that. I will inquire at the shops tomorrow." Of course she would. She could get out of the house *and* do more to help her family.

One of the Padilla children began to cry, and someone strummed on a guitar down the street. The cool night air felt good after the hot day. Mariana twisted her hair off her neck and glanced up at the stars.

"That will not do us much good. We will both work till our deaths and barely make enough to survive," Lázaro said.

"Then what are you asking me?"

"Do you want to give Josefina, Sofía, and Catalina a better life? Look around."

Their barrio was filled with stray dogs and barefoot children who ran around in mismatched clothes or in last year's pants with their ankles showing.

"This is all your sisters will ever have," Lázaro said. "These empty-handed people will be their friends and their future husbands unless we do something."

"What trouble are you trying to get me into? I will not go to jail for your stupid ideas."

Lázaro stepped close, and with a shifty look in his eyes that she knew very well, he whispered, "Gringo men will pay a lot of money to spend a few hours with a beautiful señorita. I would do it myself if I were a woman."

"You are asking me to be a prostitute?" Mariana's face instantly turned hot.

Lázaro clasped his hand over her mouth and said, "You will wake the babies."

Mariana's throat stung with tears. She closed her eyes and he let go of her mouth.

Lázaro softened his voice like he would do to coax an animal or a child. "You are a beautiful woman. We could make a lot of money, especially for the first time. Men will pay much money for a virgin."

"*We* could make a lot of money? *We*? Even if I did it, what makes you think I am a virgin?"

Lázaro laughed. "You are a virgin."

"You are a dog!" Mariana said. "My papá trusted you and you act like a dog."

Lázaro grabbed ahold of Mariana's arm and dug his fingers in so hard that tears came to her eyes. "Your papá put me in charge. It is up to me to feed the family and you will do what I tell you."

"Get away from me."

Lázaro let go, backed away, and smirked at her. "If you don't, Josefina will."

Mariana slapped Lázaro. She missed his cheek and hit him on the side of his head so hard that her hand stung.

Lázaro howled and clasped his hand over his ear. "You'll be sorry when you watch your sisters starve."

"Burros know more than you do! What would Emilio do to you if he were alive? What will my papá do when I tell him?"

Lázaro strutted off down the street like a mad rooster, cursing Mariana and kicking at the dirt.

The words of the man who grabbed her the day Lázaro returned came back to her. *You may not have a price now, but you will. Everyone has a price.* The words felt like a curse put on her.

Mariana took a deep breath and looked up toward heaven. A falling star streaked across the sky. One of the grandmothers in the barrio had told her that a falling star was a sign that someone had done an awful thing, but Jenny had told her they were for wishing. She tended to believe the grandmothers, but it could not hurt to make a wish on top of it. She closed her eyes and wished she could leave Tijuana for good.

CHAPTER NINE

MARIANA HAD NOT BEEN ABLE TO FIND WORK IN THE SHOPS OR restaurants. She found a notice in the newspaper that the Hotel de Obregón needed maids, so with Josefina watching the little ones, she pulled her shawl over her head and stepped out of the safety of their house.

She had learned not to walk the streets of Tijuana with her hair down or uncovered. She had made that mistake on the first day she went looking for work. Wearing her finest dress, and with her hair cascading down her back, she had made her way downtown, alone and not thinking—not realizing that she was no longer living in the barrio surrounded by neighbors who cared for one another.

The first man she had passed on her way to town was a gray-haired and slight grandfather leaning against the wall of his adobe house.

"*Mi princesa*," he called out.

At first Mariana thought he had mistaken her for one of his granddaughters—until he licked his lips with half-lidded and amorous eyes in his liver-spotted face. Her smile faded and a sick feeling washed through Mariana's body.

As she got closer to town, men lined both sides of the street. They sat on walls or gathered in packs on street corners smoking cigarettes and stopping their conversations at her approach. Some of them made kissing sounds and called to her.

"*Mí diosa.*"

"I must be asleep to dream of such beauty."

"You must be an angel who has escaped from heaven to steal my heart."

Others swayed their shoulders or thrust their hips at her.

"Come here my queen, I have a surprise for you."

Mariana had walked faster, afraid to meet their eyes. Afraid to encourage them and terrified of being grabbed and pulled into one of the filthy doorways.

Downtown, shop owners loitered outside their shops and muttered under their breath at her. White men had approached and whispered to her in Spanish with their terrible Anglo accents, "*¿Cuánto dinero, Señorita?*"

In the shops where she had applied for work, where the men seemed eager to hire her, their women quickly stepped in with bitter words telling her they were not hiring. They glared at her with raised eyebrows and tight lips and let her know that even if the men offered her a job, they would make her life miserable. One woman had waited by the door to whisper to her that they did not hire whores.

Now, even with her shawl over her head and hair tied up, men called to her, whistled, or solicited favors—but less often than that first day when she had ignorantly strolled into town like she was on her way to a fiesta. It was not only her. She noticed they did it to all young girls who walked on their own or in groups without a male. It made her heartsick to think that in a year or two Josefina would suffer the same fate—and eventually Sofía and Catalina.

Mariana passed by Nero's, the restaurant where Mamá had found work in the kitchen. When she was first offered the position, Mamá had thought she would be the main cook, but on her first day found that they had no cook. They had a chef. An Anglo chef trained in France.

Lázaro had finally found steady day work in another restaurant. It was his first day, and he made sure to tease Mariana that he had found work before her, but he still went out at night, doing who knows what.

An Anglo man with a Mexican girl, young enough to be his daughter and wobbling in her high-heels, came toward Mariana. The girl looked no older than Josefina and wore stockings and a low-cut blouse that showed the slight swell of new breasts. She had a false smile stretched across her face and had her arm looped through the man's.

Mariana crossed herself and pulled her shawl tighter. She kept her eyes on the pant legs and shoes of the people around her. Lázaro had given her a knife and she held it under the fabric of her shawl. She wondered if she would be able to use it on someone if she had to. More likely, they would just pull it from her hand and slice her up with it.

"You too ugly to show your face, *niña?*" a man called out to her. "Come here and I will give you my opinion."

Mariana ignored him.

A skinny street dog rummaged in a garbage bin behind Restaurante Paraiso Chino and pulled the skeleton of a large fish from the waste.

"Maybe you are too ugly for her," one of the men laughed.

"Do you think my friend is ugly, señorita?"

"Idiot!" an Anglo voice yelled from the alleyway and caused the street dog to scamper off with the fish remains. A man stumbled from the back door of the restaurant as if pushed through it. "You're fired, and don't come around for your pay."

"*No hablo Inglés,*" the man said. The voice sounded familiar. Mariana looked over and saw Lázaro standing with his head down and pretending not to speak English to another man dressed in the white clothing of a chef.

"Fired. You understand fired? *Usted está despedido,*" The chef said. *"¡Idiota! No dinero. Comprendes? ¡No dinero!"*

"Sí, entiendo Señor." Lázaro sounded so defeated that Mariana felt sorry for him. She hurried past and turned down the next street to let Lázaro keep what was left of his pride.

THE HOTEL DE Obregón was much nicer than the one they had stayed in when her family first arrived. It took up half a block and was a creme-color plaster building two stories high with red and yellow striped awnings. Maybe the hotel would have manners and money rather than sailors or cheap Anglo men hoping to get as much pleasure from their dollars as possible—if she was lucky enough to get the job.

Well-dressed men and women in hats, gloves, and furs sat on pretty little sofas and high-backed chairs in the lobby. Potted palms, cut flowers, and rugs of orange and yellow brought color to the white-washed walls and thick wooden beams. Mariana felt out of place and shabby—a dirty local girl who was nothing more than a shadow drifting through all the brightly dressed women.

The clerk at the front desk wore a suit with a vest and a red bowtie. He stood with his head down, writing in a ledger. Mariana approached the ornate, highly waxed counter, afraid to disturb him. Behind him, rows and rows of boxes lined the wall —a few with keys hanging in the openings and many with slips of papers in them. The clerk looked up with a pleasant face, but it quickly changed the moment he met eyes with Mariana.

"I am here about a maid job," Mariana said.

His eyes dulled and his lips pursed together as if he just

tasted something foul. "Around the back and through the alley," he said before dropping his head back down and ignoring her.

She should leave. If only she could go home, back to Santiago. Back to where she was a person. Mariana pulled her shawl further over her face and slipped out the front door into the brightly lit street filled with tourists and peddlers and taxis. At least the hissing and whistling local men did not gather in that section of town.

She walked around to the back of the hotel to an alley that stunk of garbage and urine. A line of at least thirty girls stood down the center to keep away from the doorways and garbage bins. All eyes turned to her and looked her up and down when she joined them, then pointedly turned their backs to her.

The girls with the longer skirts held them up from the sludge of the alleyway and whispered in groups of two or three. It seemed as if she was the only girl who had come alone. They spoke in Spanish and a few in an Indio language she did not understand. They did not seem much different than some of the Anglo girls in Santiago who told her to go home where she belonged. This was not her home, and this was not where she belonged, but just like in Santiago, she was here—like it or not.

A back door opened and an Anglo man in a light gray suit and tie stepped into the alleyway in polished leather shoes. All the girls stopped talking when he walked the line. He slid the shawls off their heads and lifted the chins of the girls who did not meet his eyes.

Being the last girl in the line, Mariana let her shawl drop back and held her head high. She flinched when he put his hand on her lower back, but she smiled at him.

"Follow me," he said.

As she followed him back up the line, he pulled out every tall, lighter-skinned girl. He opened the door he had come through, let the chosen girls in, and left the rest behind in the alley. Mariana half-felt as if she should apologize to them and half-felt like shooting them a self-satisfied grin. She did neither, not wanting to curse her luck.

Mariana and four other girls entered the back of the hotel. The man put them in a line and led them through the kitchen, where every worker stopped their dish washing, chopping, and grilling to stare at them filing through.

He took them to a hallway and told them to wait along the wall before disappearing into a doorway with a plaque on it. The women lined up and shouldered one another to get closest to the door, pushing Mariana to the end once more. The first girl, dressed in a white blouse and skirt with bright colored embroidery and her hair up in an intricate bun, came out ten minutes later with a blank, unreadable expression. The next, a much prettier girl wearing a store-bought dress with her ankles showing, beamed on her way out. As Mariana got closer, she could read the name plaque: Wm Swanson. The two others, who were pretty in a plain sort of way, looked apprehensive when they exited. Maybe he had hired the first two and did not need any more girls.

At her turn, she walked through the door into a hotel room that had been converted into an office. Instead of a bed, it had a large desk with a ledger and a stack of important papers on it. A large white statue of a topless woman, with no left arm and a stump on the right, sat in the corner of the desk.

The man who sat behind the desk rose to his feet when she walked in. A big smile came to his freshly shaven face and crinkled his gray-blue eyes. He was not old but had dark brown hair streaked with silvery gray. He wore a light creme-color suit and vest with a yellow, gray, and red tie. Mariana felt dull—like a little gray and brown house sparrow standing before an elegant white swan.

He came from behind the giant desk and towered above her. He stood taller than Emilio, by at least five inches. "I'm William

Swanson, general manager of Hotel de Obregón." When Mariana did not respond, he asked, "And who are you?"

She gave a slight, embarrassed smile. "Mariana Castillo."

His eyebrows pinched together, but his smile did not fade. "Where are you from, Mariana Castillo?"

"I am from Santiago, California."

"That would explain it. Your English is outstanding. How is your Spanish?"

"*Tan bueno como mi inglés.*"

He nodded. "What brings you to Tijuana?"

She should have thought through what she would say. Deported at gunpoint did not seem the right thing to tell this man. "Family."

He stepped closer and held his hands out to her. "Let me see your hands."

When she held them out, he took hold of her wrists. His touch surprised her and her reaction seemed to amuse him. "I'm not going to hurt you."

His nails were clean and perfectly trimmed, unlike the hands of any man Mariana had ever known—except for Jenny's father, Señor Stratton. He rotated her wrists until her hands turned palm up. Mariana's stomach fluttered with hundreds of moth wings that made her feel light-headed and nauseous.

He slowly ran his fingertips over her wrists and palms before he let go, stuck his hands into his pockets, and backed away. Once he got to his desk, he leaned back, half-sitting on the edge of it. "Have you ever worked?"

"Yes, I have worked."

"Where?"

"I worked in the Santiago Packing House, packing citrus." It was not a complete lie. She did get the job...she just never showed up for her first day because of what happened to Emilio.

"How long did you work there?"

"A little over a year." That was a complete lie, may God forgive her.

"You are too pretty to be a maid," he said, "but that is all I have now."

"Oh, please. I can do it. I will work very hard."

He let out a laugh. "I will hire you."

"Oh, thank you. I will work hard and you will not regret it."

With an amused smile, he looked Mariana up and down. "Maybe you can work your way up to something better."

She wanted to ask what would be higher, but she did not want him to change his mind. Maybe a waitress or manager of the maids.

CHAPTER TEN

LÁZARO HAD SURVIVED HIS HUMILIATION AND FOUND ANOTHER JOB making more money than her—but he was a liar, and even when a liar tells the truth, you cannot believe them. Six days a week, Mariana dressed in her black and white maid's uniform, twisted her hair up, and tucked it beneath an ugly white cap. Dressed in such unsightly clothing, she thought the street harassment would end, but it did not. Every day she walked the line of men who taunted her, blew kisses, or told her that they had houses she could clean.

Even with Lázaro, Mamá, and her working, they could barely pay for the rent and food. Josefina began taking Sofía and Catalina into town to peddle bracelets to the tourists. Ever since the Padilla's grandmother taught Josefina how to braid the brightly colored bracelets, Josefina spent the evenings with her fingers working the threads and her days trading them for pennies or centavos. The tourists could not resist the dark and pleading eyes of the two beautiful little girls.

With Lázaro hardly ever home, Josefina had rigged up a line with tin cans attached that she stretched across their walkway every evening before bed. On a few occasions, Lázaro had forgotten about it, raised the alarm, and came into the house facing three frightened women armed with a baseball bat and knives.

After the third time he tripped over the wire, and almost got beaten and stabbed by his own family, Lázaro dragged in one of the mangy dogs from the street.

They named the mutt Feo because he was the ugliest dog they had ever seen, with a wiry dirt-brown coat covered in fleas. The moment Lázaro had stepped into the house with the thing on a rope, Mamá shooed him back out and sent Josefina and Sofía behind him with soap and a bucket of water. It surprised everyone that Mamá let them keep the dog at all. She did not like animals in the house, and it would be another mouth to feed. Fear had a way of wearing down anyone's standards.

Mariana hoped her sisters would not get too attached to it, because the moment Papá returned, Feo's ugly behind would be right back on the street.

Feo howled at the door the entire first week, mourning his freedom—but he settled into it and looked forward to table scraps and playtime with Josefina, Sofía, and Catalina.

The next thing to be dragged into their home, this time by Josefina, was Salbatore Sotelo. He had arrived in bare feet and dirty trousers. His mop of curly black hair made him look like a Mexican Harpo Marx—nothing but a clown to entertain and distract them. He carried a guitar and had a big toothy grin that made Mariana want to scream, not because of his friendliness or his obvious talent on the instrument, but because Mariana wanted to keep her sisters safe. He was a boy with no future.

Every day that Josefina took the little ones to sell their bracelets to the tourists, Mariana wanted to cry. If only she could keep her sisters in cages like the Padilla's canaries—safe from all the stray cats mewling at them from the street below.

Josefina had met Salbatore in town, both intent on separating the tourists from their money. Salbatore strummed his guitar, singing love songs and crooning like some heartsick peasant. Tourists paid him to jump into a taxi with them and serenade them all the way to the racetrack or casino.

Josefina fluttered to Salbatore like a moth. The day she brought him home, she sat next to him on their couch mooning to the point that Mariana thought soon she would need to swat them apart with a broom. She had sent Lázaro to scare him away, but he could not bring himself to do it.

"When I began to threaten him," Lázaro said, "he looked at me with those bewildered eyes, like he had no idea why I would be angry with him, and I couldn't do it."

"You have no trouble threatening me," Mariana said.

"It never does any good."

"You're right. You are terrible at it."

Being that Josefina was about to turn sixteen, and that was a dangerous age for such feelings, Mamá forbade Josefina from bringing Salbatore to the house. As a result, Josefina stayed out later and kept the little ones from coming home. Mamá eventually relented and tried to talk some sense into the girl by asking her what sort of a life she would have with a street boy. If only Papá were home, he would get rid of him.

Mariana's dreams for Salbatore's disappearance began to fade when the ridiculous boy began showing how resourceful he was. He cemented the loose bricks in their wall, knew the town, the people, and where to get things. His grandmother was a curandera and he brought them herbs and cures. One day, he showed up with an aloe vera plant for burns and insect bites. His grandmother prescribed tobacco smoke blown into Catalina's ear to relieve her earache, and Salbatore helped Lázaro get a permanent job with his uncle cleaning out the horse stalls at the racetrack.

Except for Mamá, Salbatore became the boy they all hated to

love—just like their nasty stray mutt, Feo. Mariana did not want to like either of them, but she could not resist. Even with the rest of the family softening to him, Mamá always made her feelings well known by grumbling about Salbatore the moment his long and floppy feet stepped out their door.

CHAPTER ELEVEN

FINALLY WITH A DAY OFF FROM WORK, MARIANA SAT ON THE couch sewing up the holes in her sisters' socks, determined to keep them in shoes as they peddled their bracelets to the tourists. The day they ran around barefoot, with all the other street children of Tijuana, would be the day that she knew their family hit the bottom of the bucket. For the last three months, ever since getting her job, she spent more time in the hotel than she did in her own home, caring for strangers more than her own family.

Every Friday and Saturday night, an endless stream of motorcars rattled into town and turned Tijuana into a crazy house—a commotion of motorcars, honking horns, shopkeepers, and street solicitors offering to shine shoes, or selling roasted corn, sugar cane, pork rinds, or clay figurines. Photographers draped tourists with bright colored ponchos and sombreros to take pictures of them sitting in carts strapped to white burros painted with zebra stripes. Public taxi drivers called out destinations and packed their motorcars with tourists. And her poor little sisters were out there, trying to get their little crumbs to bring home for the family.

The United States closed the border from six in the evening until eight the next morning. Trapped in Mexico for the night, the tourists had no choice but to find lodgings, bringing even more money into Tijuana and more filth for her to clean from the rooms.

On the weekdays, the Hotel de Obregón had the higher class tourists, but on weekends, sometimes four to six people packed a room—with all the trash and filth that went with it. For four pesos a day, Mariana cleared the rooms of dirty sheets, empty liquor bottles, vomit, blood, racing forms, betting slips, plates of food scraps, forgotten souvenirs, underpants, and occasionally a woman's high heeled shoe or a man's hat.

Often, men pretended not to hear her tap on the door and she would walk in to find them lying naked on the bed. Wide awake—every part of them. Anglo men frequently groped her in the hallway, thinking that everything in Tijuana existed solely for their entertainment or for their pleasure.

It was nice to finally have a day off. Mariana knotted the thread and snipped it from the sock.

Feo growled, deep back in his throat. With the sound of the gate latch, he leapt to his feet and started barking. Mariana set the sock beside her and rose to get the bat. She relaxed when she heard the sound of a key in the door and Mamá's voice saying, "Shut up *estúpido*. This is my house. You are nothing but a guest."

Feo had not yet learned the difference between one of the family members coming home and a stranger approaching. Mamá looked gaunt with the bones in her cheeks more pronounced and her eyes sunk back.

"You need to start eating more," Mariana said. "Papá wants to come home to a healthy wife, not a scarecrow."

Mamá took a deep breath and lowered herself onto the couch.

"What's wrong?"

Mamá shook her head and started to push herself back up.

"What is it Mamá? Please." Her belly did not protrude, so she was probably not with child, but maybe she was and she starved herself to get rid of it.

Mamá shook her head. "I am tired. I need to go to bed."

"I'm not a little girl anymore. You can tell me," Mariana said. "You need someone. Another woman."

Mariana took a firm hold of Mamá's arm. If she let her go, Mamá would shut herself into her room with Mariana imagining the worst. Mamá sat back down and closed her eyes. The seconds stretched out, becoming minutes. Mariana waited.

She knew better than to ask twice. Mamá never gave in to nagging. Never. The more her children begged her, the more she refused to budge.

Mamá took another deep breath and pulled an envelope from her pocket with Papá's tight handwriting. "Your Papá is staying in Guadalajara to fight for our religion, and we cannot join him."

"Why not?"

"It's not safe." Mamá covered her face with her hands and shook her head. "The devil has our family by the throat. What will we do if anything happened to your papá?"

Mamá placed her hand on Mariana's, and they both sat in silence listening to the resonant voice of Señor Padilla above them. The constant sounds of living beneath their feet made Mariana want to scream. On her days off, all day long, she had to listen to the frantic padding of children's feet, running wherever they went, and the slow shuffle of their grandmother's steps. In the evening, especially the evening, the sound of Señor Padilla coming home to his family, when they did not have their own Papá, was more than Mariana could bear. They needed to get out of Tijuana.

Curse Warren Stratton! He had done this to her family. What was his daughter doing? Riding through the orange groves on her Arabian horse without a worry? Jenny would never have to work so her family could eat or have a place to sleep. Warren Stratton remained free while her papá risked his life in Guadalajara and her family wandered through the streets of Tijuana like little black ants, searching for crumbs to carry back. If God was just, it would be the other way around.

That night, Mariana dreamt of Papá sitting beneath a mesquite tree and whittling a piece of wood with his knife. He wore white cotton pants and a hat woven from cactus fibers, instead of his dark trousers and plaid shirt. He wore huaraches instead of his leather boots. Mariana sat next to him picking up each sliver of wood as it fell to the ground and placing them in her lap. An orange-yellow sky lit the pointy silhouettes of blue maguey plants, and the earth had a strong smoky scent. She watched Papá's hands and tried to discover the shape he was carving into the wood. In the dream, she felt a sense of serenity and calm while she waited. Her father turned to her and smiled. When the sun finished setting, she could no longer see him or the carving in his hand.

Mariana woke from the dream with a sense of loss. She wanted to be back beside Papá, but instead, she was in their tiny half-a-house in Tijuana with Sofía next to her, scratching at flea bites in her sleep.

CHAPTER TWELVE

WHEN MARIANA WENT TO THE LAUNDRY ROOM TO EMPTY HER basket of linens, she turned to see William Swanson standing in the doorway watching her. She had not spoken to him since the day he had hired her, but she had noticed him watching her in the distance many times. Whenever she saw him, her belly would flutter, worried that she was not doing a good enough job. Her family needed her income. If she made enough, she could get her sisters off the street.

Mr. Swanson leaned against the frame, cool and confident in a light gray linen suit. She gave him a quick smile, then turned back to her task.

"I have heard wonderful things about you," he said.

Heat rose in Mariana's cheeks. She glanced toward him. "I am a hard worker and I like my job here."

He came into the laundry room. As he stepped closer to her, the hard soles of his shoes tapped on the cement floor. He came up behind her, so close that she breathed in his scent. He smelled of expensive things and exotic places that she could never have.

"You do not have a ring on your finger. Are you not married?"

Her words caught in her throat and she could not get them out. Looking down into her empty basket, she shook her head. A tingling sensation, half-fear, and half-attraction to this man, tickled every one of her nerve endings.

"Have you ever hoped for more than this?" He put a hand on her shoulder. "You are a beautiful woman."

"Has another position opened up?"

"What?" His eyebrows pinched together.

"You told me that there may be a better position for me."

He paused and stepped back from her. "Turn around so I can see your face."

Mariana turned, unable to look up at him. He put his smooth fingers under her chin and lifted her head to meet his gaze. He was a refined and handsome man with gray-blue eyes that peered deeply into hers.

"A much better position has opened up. Can you read and write in both Spanish and English?"

She nodded. "I always got top marks in school."

"How would you like to work for me? As my secretary? You would no longer need to touch other people's soiled sheets and towels."

Mariana could not believe her good luck. She worked hard in school and hoped one day it would raise her up in society. How should she respond? She needed to know how much more money it would pay, but if she asked, would she seem greedy? Would it cause him to take it away?

"I would like that very much," she said. "When will I start?"

"You can start tomorrow." Mr. Swanson reached down and slowly peeled her cap from her head. Mariana stood stiff and frozen. He unpinned her hair until it fell and cascaded down her shoulders and back.

Mariana had a hard time keeping his gaze.

"I'm not going to hurt you."

He reached into his pocket and pulled out a wad of money held together with a golden clip with his initials on it, WJS. He unclipped the bills, fingered through them, and pulled out a fifty pesos note.

He held out the bill, ornate and crisp, with the face of a man with a white bandana on the front. "Here's some money for some new clothes. You cannot come in your maid uniform."

Mariana took the bill and stared down at it. She had never seen such a large amount. The bill was imprinted with *Banco De Mexico* and *50 Pesos*. Would he take this out of her pay?

She moved the bill back toward him. "I have some other clothes."

"Don't be silly. You need nice clothes to be my secretary. You will not be required to pay me back…as long as you get some pretty dresses. Your ankles need to show and none of those high-necked and matronly blouses. I need something pretty to look at every day."

Mariana's hand began to shake. She nodded and slipped the bill into her apron pocket. He reached out and scooped up a section of her hair. "And wear your hair down like this. It is too beautiful to hide."

Mariana smiled with shaky lips. "All right."

Mr. Swanson turned around and walked toward the door. Before leaving, he turned. "Your pay will be doubled to start, with more opportunities to better yourself."

She did it. She was finally going to make something of herself.

MARIANA STEPPED from the back alley of the hotel with the fifty pesos bill tucked in her pocket. She did not say goodbye to her fellow maids, since she would still be working in the same hotel, but mostly because she was afraid to tell them. She did not want to see their knowing glances or the resentment for her moving above them.

On the way home, Mariana passed by an open cantina door that reeked of cigarette smoke. Inside, people stood in front of metal slot machines. They dropped their money in and hoped to win, even though the odds were against them. She would never put her hard-earned money into one of those machines even though her luck was changing. The odds had been against her ever finding a job with good wages, but here she was with a great opportunity and fifty pesos in her pocket.

She needed to shop for some clothes before tomorrow, but what if someone took her money or gave her the wrong amount of change? She had never held this much money in her life and everyone in Tijuana worked hard to take from others to fill their own pockets.

"Mariana," someone called from behind her. She turned to see Lázaro coming up the walkway. She slipped her hand into her pocket and squeezed the bill tight into her fist. She would not allow him to touch her money.

He had dirt smeared on his face and across his shirt and trousers. She glanced back at the hotel, looked into the windows, and hoped that Mr. Swanson or any of the workers could not see her with Lázaro.

"You stink," Mariana said. Lázaro called himself a groomsman when all he really did at the racetrack was shovel manure and feed the horses—taking care of both ends of the animals.

"You know what this smell is?" Lázaro squinted at her. "It is the smell of money. One day I will own my own racehorse while you, dear cousin, will still be nothing but a maid."

"Would you like to make a bet on that?"

"A bet? Since when do you gamble?"

"Since I am sure that I will win." Mariana stopped at a shop with a window filled with beautiful dresses, hats, gloves, and high-heeled shoes. Maybe Lázaro could be a blessing for once in his life. If he accompanied her, the shop owners would make sure to give her the correct amount of change and nobody would rob her of her money or her purchases. Of course, she would not put it past Lázaro to take her money himself, but she could tell Mamá or threaten to write a letter to Papá. She had a much better chance with him than a stranger. "I have made something of myself."

Lázaro gave a derisive laugh. "Oh yeah, what have you done? Are you the head maid now?"

Mariana pulled her hand from her pocket, unfolded her fist, and showed him her fifty pesos bill. She quickly closed her fingers when he tried to snatch it from her and hid her hand behind her back.

"You finally took my advice?'

"What advice?" He always tried to take credit for anything anyone else had accomplished.

"To earn your money on your back."

Heat rose into her cheeks, and before she knew it, she slapped him across the face with her closed fist still gripping the money.

He grabbed her wrist hard and brought tears to her eyes. "Don't you ever…"

Before he could finish, a sailor had his arm around Lázaro's throat and pulled him away from Mariana. Another sailor with him, glassy-eyed and unsteady, punched Lázaro in the stomach.

"You bothering this señorita?" the sailor with his arm around Lázaro's throat asked.

Lázaro's face turned red and he could not speak.

"It's all right," Mariana said. "He's my cousin."

"Cousin or not…" He swayed and pulled Lázaro with him. "…that is no way to treat a lady."

"Thank you for helping," Mariana said. "Please let him go. It was my fault. I slapped him."

"I'm sure you had a perfectly good re…" he breathed out a hot breath, reeking of booze, "…reason."

"It was my fault. Thank you," Mariana said.

He let go and shoved Lázaro off the walkway. Lázaro stumbled but steadied himself on a parked car.

"You're welcome. If he gives you…any…trouble, you just let me…" He slapped his friend on the shoulder. "…and my mate here know."

His friend nodded in agreement before the two of them stumbled away.

Lázaro, completely red in the face and looking like a mad rooster, shot her a nasty look.

"I'm sorry, but you deserved it."

Lazaro took a deep breath. He probably would have strutted off with his chest all puffed out if not for the money in her hand. Lázaro would never turn his back to a single centavo. After a few breaths, the red faded from his face.

Mariana finally said, "I need to get some new clothes. Will you help me?"

Lázaro stood there breathing hard and not answering. "I got a new position as a secretary at the hotel. They gave me money for some clothes."

After a few more breaths, Lázaro's expression began to soften. "Money that you will have to pay back?"

"No. I do not have to pay it back."

"Nobody does that. Nobody gives money for nothing. And who would hire a girl with no experience?"

"I…I was educated in California. I can write in both English and Spanish."

Lázaro narrowed his eyes. "Nobody does that unless they want something from you."

Mariana clenched her fist again. How dare he try to take the excitement from her? He was only angry that nobody would do it for him. "Will you help me or not?"

"I'm right. You will see." He paused as if turning it over in his head. "I'll help you if you treat me to a pulque on the way home."

"What is that?"

"It's a drink. Nothing but a drink."

Mariana agreed and they stepped into the shop.

AFTERWARD, they exited with armloads of boxes stuffed with stockings, a new pair of heels, and dresses of silk, wool, and velveteen—nothing longer than mid-calf. She also bought her sisters two pairs of new socks each and Mamá a pair of new stockings. Lázaro got nothing since he would be drinking his share.

Lázaro led Mariana to a cantina in an alley where Mariana would never think of stepping her feet. A mangy dog sniffed at a drunk Anglo snoring in the dust by the front entrance. Two Indios in army uniforms hunched over the bar with placid smiles and hooded eyelids, drinking from glasses filled with a milky liquid. The men would have seemed harmless if not for the ammunition belts strapped across their chests—filled with long and dusty bullets.

On the other side of the dance floor, a quartet in rumpled morning coats were just preparing for a break. People, in singles or pairs, slumped over their drinks smoking cigarettes or running their hands up the dresses of young girls who looked to be only fifteen or sixteen years old—and already worn-out. A drunk old man in huaraches and cotton pants perched on a barstool and looked about to tip over any minute.

"You are bringing me here?"

"It's my favorite place." Lázaro led her to a booth next to three slot machines. The barman came around and limped over to them. His left foot was twisted in at a peculiar angle and dragged along the floor. He stopped at the end of their table with the face of a wooden frog.

"*Un pulque por favor,*" Lázaro said.

As soon as the barman limped away, Mariana asked, "Why you would you bring me to a rat hole like this?"

"It's better than drinking in a tourist bar where all the gringos treat you worse than burro shit, because at least the burro shit could fertilize their gardens."

By the smell of Lázaro, he could fertilize their gardens just as well. The barman returned with a glass of milky liquid and plunked it down on the table.

"What is that?" Mariana asked.

"Pulque, the drink of the Aztec gods. Take a sip."

Mariana took the glass. It smelled terrible—like a mix of yeast and something from the outhouse.

"Go ahead," Lázaro said. "It tastes better than it smells."

Mariana put the glass to her lips and took a sip. It was room temperature and felt like she was drinking someone's spit. The foul taste caused her throat to close up and she could not swallow it down. Mariana let the liquid dribble back into Lázaro's glass.

"*¡Que demonios!*"

"It tastes like spit anyway," she said.

A drunk in the booth next to them groped the girl with him, manipulating her breasts as if they were tiny lumps of bread dough.

"That poor girl," Mariana said.

"He does not have a gun to her head."

"No little girl dreams of being a prostitute when she grows up. No papá hopes that is the fate of his daughter."

Lázaro shrugged.

"You are a pig."

Lázaro took his time drinking the foul pulque, making

Mariana watch the poor girls, not any older than Josefina, with grown men. How would they feel if those were their daughters? Would they allow other men to put their hands all over them?

They finally walked home with their packages—past half-naked children, and past the clusters of men with their long necks and dark suits who lingered outside buildings and watched them like buzzards. The staring didn't stop when she walked with Lázaro, but at least they did not click their tongues at her, whistle, call her *mi princesa,* or try to call her over to them.

Mariana had complained many times to Lázaro about how the men taunted her. He had no sympathy, telling her that they were harmless and he wished women would give *him* compliments like that. He said that it should make her feel good about her beauty. He did not understand how creepy and disgusting it felt to have strange men, many of them old men, look at her and lick their lips like she was some delicious morsel of cake.

CHAPTER THIRTEEN

MARIANA WAITED BY THE WINDOW WATCHING FOR JAVIER, THE driver William sent every morning to pick her up for work. She wore one of her new rose-color silk crepe dresses, silk stockings, and white gloves. Her hair, mostly down but with the sides twisted and pinned back, hung over one shoulder, just as William liked it.

She had shown up for work her first day with a twisted ankle, winded and disheveled from scurrying past the gauntlet of men on her way to town. It alarmed William, and unlike Lázaro, he worried for her safety. That evening, without asking Mariana's opinion, he sent her home in a motorcar with the hotel's driver. The entire way, she wondered if she should lead him to another house so he would not see the condition of her home, but he did not seem bothered by it.

Lázaro was disgruntled that he had to walk to work and his employer did not arrange for his transportation, so he narrowed his eyes at Mariana and mumbled, "A monkey in silk is still a monkey," before slamming the door shut behind him.

Her sisters still slept, tangled in their blankets with their hair unbraided and grimy. They were all dotted with red bug bites, and above the levels of their socks, they had rings of dirt around their ankles. That night, like it or not, she would fill the tub and scrub Sofía and Catalina clean—and insist that Josefina do the same.

Mamá sat on the sofa and glared at Mariana. "A tree that grows crooked can never be straightened out."

Mariana opened her mouth to defend herself and ask Mamá why she was not taking care of her own children—to ask her why she had left the little ones to be cared for by her or Josefina. But, seeing Mamá as thin and dejected as she was, she swallowed her words.

William had been nothing but good to her. Other than giving her compliments and innocently brushing up against her, he treated her with respect. He had the hotel florist bring fresh flowers for her desk every three days and had the old ones taken away before the heads even began to droop.

She had her own desk in an adjoining room to his office with her own typewriter, filing cabinet, and telephone. Her lunches at the hotel were free. Since William lived in the hotel, he ate every meal in the dining room with nothing more than a signature on the bill. For the last month, she had eaten lunch with him. Even when he was out, and she ate alone, they accepted her signature for his account.

"You are doing well for yourself, wearing your fancy dresses and riding to work like a princess," Mamá said in a tone that sounded bitter.

"I give you every cent I earn. I'm doing this for our family. I am tired of seeing the little ones dirty and peddling on the streets. I'm afraid that they will end up on the arms of Anglo men who pay them for their services."

The driver pulled up to the crooked brick wall of their courtyard.

"So you are selling yourself instead?"

Mariana turned toward her mamá. She was only the shell of

the mamá who had raised her. The mamá who had kept an immaculate house and cooked big meals for her family. The mamá who used to smile and laugh and take pleasure in braiding the hair of all her girls. The mamá who used to have a husband who cared for her. The mamá who had never been forced to the ground and raped.

The driver honked his horn with three short and friendly beeps. Mariana's throat closed up and stung as she tried to swallow her tears.

CHAPTER FOURTEEN

WILLIAM WAS NOT IN HIS OFFICE, BUT HIS HAT HUNG ON THE rack. A small blue box with a white bow rested on Mariana's desk and a new arrangement of flowers sat in the corner. Instead of the usual cheery arrangement of daisies and sunflowers, it was a dozen red roses accented with long stems of eucalyptus leaves. She looked around, peeked back into William's office, then sat down at her desk.

She didn't know if she should open the gift or wait for him. If William wanted her to wait, he would have handed it to her instead, wouldn't he? She untied the ribbon and lifted the top to reveal a velvet box imprinted with *Maxwell and Sons Jewelers*. Mariana looked back toward William's office. The sound of a couple laughing from a private room drifted from their open window into hers.

Lifting the lid of the box, she found the most spectacular ring she had ever seen in her entire life. A silver ring with a large center stone that looked like a real diamond, surrounded by smaller diamonds, sat on a pad of blue velvet. Mariana stared down at it. She could not breathe. What did this mean?

"Are you going to put it on?"

Her skeleton about jumped out of her skin. William stood in the doorway with one hand in his pocket. He let out an endearing laugh. "You look like a child caught with her hand in the cookie jar."

"Is this for me?"

"Are you surprised?" He stepped closer and sat on the edge of her desk.

"Yes." Mariana cradled the open box like a palmful of water. "Are they real diamonds?"

"Do I look like a cut-glass sort of man?" William reached his hand out. "May I?"

Mariana lifted the box and he took the ring from it. She had never seen anything so beautiful in her entire life. William took the wrist of Mariana's left hand and slid the ring onto her finger. Onto the finger only reserved for a wedding band.

As Mariana twisted her hand, the diamonds caught the light and sparkled on her finger.

"You have no idea what you do to me." William took her hand and brought it to his lips. "I am in love with you, Mariana Castillo."

The wanting in his eyes made Mariana feel like the most beautiful woman on the earth.

"Tell me that we have a future together."

She looked up at him, but her words caught in her throat. Could this be happening to her? Why would this man, a man who had everything, want her?

"We need to keep this quiet for a while. It's against the company fraternization policy."

Mariana nodded, not sure exactly what a fraternization policy was, but figured it had to do with intimacy between the two of them.

"I have a special treat for you." He held his hand out for her to take it.

What could be more special than a dozen roses and an engagement ring?

William gave her a conspiratorial wink. "Wait for five minutes, then meet me at the hotel motorcar."

As soon as William left their offices, Mariana checked the clock. Nine twenty-five. She had arrived at work at nine o'clock, and within twenty-five minutes, her entire life had changed course. The ring sparkled on her finger. Never in her life would she have imagined wearing a ring with diamonds in it. Never in her life would she think that she would be engaged to a wealthy Anglo businessman.

At nine-thirty, Mariana stepped into the hallway. One of the maids came from the laundry room with a cart of freshly laundered sheets. Mariana smiled at her, but the woman narrowed her eyes and looked away.

Javier opened the car door the moment Mariana stepped from the hotel lobby. Inside, William waited with his arm across the back seat. When she slid in, his hand caressed her shoulder and sent a wash of warm tingles down her body.

As soon as Javier climbed into the driver's seat, William leaned forward. "The Belvedere, please."

"The casino on the other side of the river?"

"Yes," William said. "Have you been there before?"

"No. I have walked past it, but have never been." Mariana forced a smile. It was the casino her family had walked past on their way into Tijuana—the one Papá said was not a place for his family.

They would have to cross that frightening and rickety bridge —the one with no side rails and loose ties that banged as motorcars drove across it. The thought of the slats of wood disappearing beneath them as they rolled over the river made Mariana shiver. She could almost feel the icy water in her bones —a bad omen.

"Do we have to take the bridge?"

"I don't think this motorcar can float," William said, "so it is our only choice."

"What about the walkway?"

"Are you scared?"

"Yes," Mariana said. "It looks and sounds like it will collapse at any moment."

Mariana crossed herself when the first few planks and the dark line of the river came into view.

"We'll be fine," William said and pulled her closer to him. "They call the bridge *La Marimba*. Listen to the wheels on the cross-ties. They'll play you a song."

Mariana closed her eyes and William took her hand. He held it and rubbed his finger over the top of her ring. "If we go over, I'll save you."

She had never held a man's hand before—except for Emilio's or Papá's.

"We're halfway over," William said.

The *thump-thump, thump-thump* of the wheels reverberated over the boards. She did not belong on this bridge or with this man, but she did not want to ruin her opportunity. When they made it to the other side of the river, they drove down the road, past the horse racing track where Lázaro worked, and along the fence with *This is the Famous Belvedere Hotel and Casino* painted in giant letters. What would Papá say if he knew she was not only going to the casino but with an Anglo man twenty years older than her?

The casino was a maze of tables with card games or spinning wheels and rows of slot machines. The upbeat sounds of jazz music, the *click-click-click-click* of spinning wheels, and coins dropping into slot machines overwhelmed Mariana.

Women in heels, furs, and gloves up to their elbows strolled around with amber, gold, and rose-color drinks. Men kissed some sort of a talisman or the woman next to them before rolling dice across a green velvet table.

"How do people have so much money to throw away?"

William laughed. "They're not here to throw it away. They're here to win more."

"Do they?"

He laughed. "Their odds are not good."

William placed his hand on her lower back, then slipped it around to her waist. Her entire body tingled from his touch. She felt like melting into his arms and letting her fears and burdens float away.

He guided her through the crowds to a cashier standing behind golden bars. William pulled out a wad of money, counted out a bunch of bills, and traded them for a stack of chips.

He ordered her a cocktail that tasted like apricot and then another. Even with all the beautiful Anglo women in short dresses that showed their knees, he only paid attention to her. He whispered flattering words about Mariana's beauty and called her his *Lucky Lady*.

They gathered around a table with four other people and a man in a tuxedo, who seemed to be the person running it. Everyone placed their chips in different areas and cheered or groaned when the dice hit the back wall and came to a stop. Mariana sipped her drink, unable to figure out the rules of the game.

When William finished gambling and cashed in his chips, he slipped a twenty-pesos note into her purse.

"What's that for?"

"My *Lucky Lady*." He lifted her hair and kissed her on the back of the neck. "I usually walk out lighter than I came in."

Tingles went down Mariana's neck from the spot his lips had touched, all the way down her spine to the spot between her legs. Her head felt warm and fuzzy from the drinks, the lights, William's touch, and all the fancy people moving around them.

CHAPTER FIFTEEN

EVERY DAY SINCE WILLIAM GAVE HER THE RING, THEY SLIPPED OUT of the hotel for a couple of hours of gambling at the Belvedere. They would work in the morning, have lunch together in the hotel dining room, then cross the dreaded river to gamble for a couple of hours at the Belvedere. Once they returned to the hotel, they worked until six o'clock in the evening when Javier would drive her home—but today, William said he had a special surprise for Mariana's eighteenth birthday.

Some days, William had Javier drive through the nicer neighborhoods with fancy gated drives and flowering bougainvillea climbing up the walls. He would ask her opinion about which houses she preferred and if she would like to have a swimming pool or an atrium.

They still had not yet set a date or talked about their wedding because of the fraternization policy. William had not met her family and asked her not to tell them about their relationship until it was time for her to stop working. She slipped her ring off and put it into her pocket every day the moment Javier dropped her off at home.

The sun was high and hot and tourists crowded the dusty streets, half drunk and stumbling about in sombreros and brightly colored serapes. William's arm rested on the window frame and he loosened his tie. "Roll your window down, will you? We need a cross breeze."

When Mariana rolled her window down, she noticed three girls and an ugly Mexican Harpo Marx boy with a guitar. "Pull over," she said. "Want to meet my sisters? They will keep our secret."

"Keep going," William directed Javier. "It is too hot to stop."

"But…" Mariana's stomach felt queasy, "you have not met any of my family yet."

William's eyes followed her sisters. As they passed, his head turned, keeping them in his view with a wrinkled nose and curling lip. "How many siblings do you have?"

"Three sisters." How could he not know that? She had told him about her sisters and her cousin, Lázaro.

"Is that your brother?"

"I told you my brother died."

William took his eyes from the group and turned his head to look out the front window. "Yes, I remember. But you have a… someone who works at the racetrack."

"My cousin, Lázaro."

"Yes, that's it." William said and swallowed hard like he was trying to get a terrible taste from his mouth. "Was that him?"

"No." Mariana's stomach turned. She could not picture her family intermingling with William. She could not imagine Lázaro able to hold his tongue or Mamá softening her glare. Out of all of them, Josefina, Sofía, and Catalina would be the most palatable—but the look on William's face…

"Hey there," William took her hand. "I'll meet them next time. I'm just grumpy and hot. Let's get a drink and relax at the casino."

After William bought drinks, he led her to a carpeted stair-well instead of to the gaming tables or slot machines.

"Where are we going?"

They climbed to the second story and turned down a hallway with nothing but doors on either side. Mariana stopped.

"It's a surprise."

Mariana's heart caught in her throat. This did not feel right. Her instincts told her to turn around and go back downstairs.

William took her hand and kissed the ring he had given to her. "Do you trust me?"

She did trust William. After all these months, he had been nothing but kind and generous to her. They had kissed passion-ately, at first with excitement from William, but more recently she sensed his frustration. She nodded, but could not step forward.

"Then come and see my surprise."

"I think we should go."

"I have been planning this for a long time." William's jaw clenched, causing the cords in his neck to stand out.

Was she about to lose him? Did he think her a ridiculous child? With a swarm of butterflies in her stomach, Mariana took a step down the hall with him, and then another and another until they stood before a door with the number 222 on it.

William slid a key into the lock and swung it open. The room was larger than the ones at the Hotel de Obregón. Someone had sprinkled bright red rose petals from the door, over the dark wooden floor, and all the way to the bed where they lay splattered like blood across the white bedcover.

William closed and latched the door. Through the window, she could see the horse racing track with multi-colored flags waving in the breeze. Somewhere out there, Lázaro was working.

He took her hand and led her toward the bed. The velvet petals beneath her feet made it all feel unreal, like a restless dream. William took off his jacket and draped it over a chair next to the bed.

He dropped to his knees before her. "I love you, Mariana."

Was this it? Would he officially propose to her? Would he actually speak the word *marriage*? He had been talking about their future and they had been looking at houses, but he never did actually say the word marriage or wife.

William lifted her hand to his mouth and kissed her ring finger again. Then he kissed up her arm, slowly rising, planting kisses until he stood before her. "You have no idea how much I have wanted you."

He reached around to unfasten her dress.

"I don't know if I'm ready," Mariana said.

"You're just nervous." William kissed her neck. "It will be all right. Trust me."

The back of her dress came loose and he slid it off her shoulders. Mariana looked back at the uncovered window. "Can we close the curtains?"

"Nobody can see in and I want to have the light."

He lifted off her camisole and stepped back to look at her bare breasts. She fought to not cry and cover herself with her hands. William reached out and ran his fingers over her breasts. Her nipples tingled and it radiated all the way down her stomach and between her legs. Oh God, what was she doing?

William slid her bloomers over her hips and down to the floor. He slipped off her heels and tossed them aside. He unclipped one stocking and slid it down her leg. Once both stockings were off, he unclipped her garter belt, and she stood there in nothing but her own shame.

"You are even more beautiful than I imagined." He pulled her toward him and kissed her with urgency, pressing his fully clothed body against her bare skin. His lips pushed hard and his tongue thrust about in her mouth while he pulled off his tie and unbuttoned his shirt.

He finally pulled away to take a breath and unfasten his belt. His chest was pasty white with a carpet of brown hair—nothing like the cinnamon brown and hairless chests of Emilio and Lázaro.

When Mariana crossed her arms over her breasts, William reached out and took her wrists. "I want to see you."

She had seen boys' private parts, and had brief glances of men's when she was cleaning the hotel rooms, but never so close to her—except for Emilio's when the women were preparing his body. She had covered him with a green wash-cloth and that was all she could think of as William stood there in nothing but his underpants. When he pulled them off and stood with his private part erect before her, her entire body began to shiver.

"I will be gentle." He guided her backward, onto the bed.

Mariana breathed in the slight scent of bleach mixed with the roses and William's aftershave. The mixture made her sick to her stomach. William lay next to her, running his fingers over her breasts, down her stomach, and into her privates. She flinched, pulling her legs tight.

"It's all right," William assured, rising up on an elbow and kissing her.

"What if I get pregnant?"

"You won't. I will pull it out in time."

Mariana's body ached for his touch, but at the same time, she wanted to cover herself back up and run home. The gentle touching and kissing made her body warm and desire engulfed her. She kissed him back. She wanted to melt into him and let him take her. Suddenly, an urgency overtook him. He climbed on top of her and his weight pressed the breath from her lungs. He pushed inside her, tearing her and piercing her with pain.

Mariana gasped.

"That was the worst of it. I'll hurry."

Afterward, she lay with her cheek against William's bare chest. "Next time, it will be better. The first time is the most painful."

Loud and laughing voices came from the hall, only feet from where she and William lay naked. All around them, bruised rose petals lay on the sheets with their edges curling up and turning black. This was only supposed to happen on her wedding night.

"I need to get home so my mother doesn't worry," Mariana said.

"You would still be at work. Why would she worry?"

Mariana's throat tightened and she could not answer. The thought of her mamá made her want to curl into a ball and cry.

She watched William button his shirt, tuck it in, and buckle his belt. When he finished, he leaned over and gave her a kiss on the cheek. "I'm going to use the restroom. I'll be back."

Once the door shut behind him and she had her privacy, Mariana got up and noticed blood smeared on the bed, even brighter red than the rose petals.

She had stripped off countless bloody sheets when she worked as a maid at the hotel. Had that many girls lost their innocence? She didn't want to think about it. No, the blood could have been from other things. Mariana pulled the blankets over the spot, covering her shame and quickly dressing before William could return.

In the car, on the way back to the Hotel de Obregón, William still did not speak a word about marriage. He was affectionate and pulled her toward him when they crossed the dreaded bridge, but this time, she did not worry about falling into the river. She twisted the ring around her finger remembering what the soldier had yelled at her when they had first arrived, *Everyone has a price.* Was this her price? No, she and William would be married.

Back at the Hotel de Obregón, and in their offices, William pulled her chair out for her. When she sat, he kissed the top of her head. "I have some work to do downtown. Have Javier take you home when it is time."

When his footsteps faded away, it felt as if she were drowning. Water filled her lungs, spilled out her eyes, and down her cheeks.

Who was she upset at? William? Lázaro, for predicting this? Warren Stratton for sending them there? God? All of them? Or just herself? She had willingly gone to the casino and placed herself into William's hands. He would marry her. William was a good man.

WHEN JAVIER PULLED up to their house, Mariana could not move. William's scent lingered on her and she stared at the crooked wall with the white gate and peeling paint.

"Are you all right?" Javier asked with tenderness in his voice.

Oh, God…did he know? He had been driving them to the casino for months. Did he notice that this time had been different? All he had to do was look in the mirror to see her and William in the back together. Tears came to her eyes again. Mariana slipped the ring from her finger, like she always had to do when she got home, dropped it into her purse, and reached for the door handle.

Feo barked ferociously as if she was a bandit come to rob the house. Mariana put her key into the lock and waved to Javier that all was well and he could leave. As soon as the door cracked open, Feo darted through into the courtyard and lifted his leg on a tall weed. Inside, two lines of string with handmade paper flowers hung from wall to wall. A cake with eighteen candles sat on the table. Pain started at the back of Mariana's throat, expanded, and filled her chest until she could not swallow or breathe.

"Hello, is anyone home?"

With no answer, Mariana headed straight to the bathroom and filled the tub with water.

CHAPTER SIXTEEN

No matter how much poison Mamá put down, the ants kept coming, marching in lines across their floor, up the cupboards, and along the counters—a full procession hungry and searching for food like everyone else in Tijuana. Mariana swept the ants into a dustpan while Josefina and Salbatore sat on the sofa. Josefina had been teaching him to speak English.

"Listen closely and watch my lips," Josefina said. "Excuse me, sir. It seems your huaraches are on fire."

They both giggled and his lips stretched across his big teeth in a ridiculous grin. Why should Josefina have so much time with the man she loves? Especially since he is so unsuitable and Mariana cannot even bring her fiancé to meet her family?

Mariana opened the front door and hit the dustpan against the wall. A few of the ants fell into the dirt, but most of them still clung to the metal pan. She knocked it against the wall again and again. The infernal things would not let go. Dammit! She threw the pan into the courtyard and sent it cartwheeling across the dirt.

Back inside, Salbatore's lips formed into an odd oval shape. "Ess ques me, sir."

Josefina giggled at his pronunciation.

Mariana could not get away from their affection, their laughter, or their tenderness. She had complained to her mamá that the boy should not come around as much, but now, no matter how much Mamá or Mariana wanted him away from Josefina, they relied on him. He kept their girls safe in the streets. Every night, Salbatore strummed on his guitar and sang his silly *corridos*—his stories of love and oppression, while Josefina snuck lovesick glances at him behind Mamá's back.

He was such a ridiculous boy, unaffected by Mariana and Mamá's poisonous words or the evil eyes and curses they put on him. Mariana did not know if he was too stupid to understand that he was not wanted or too stubborn to care. They had all made too many concessions. They needed Papá to return home and put an end to the disorder.

Mariana went to kneel before the altar in Mamá's bedroom. Ever since she gave herself to William, she had about wore down the beads of her rosary, praying for forgiveness. After two months of going to the Belvedere and lying with him, she could not put a stop to it now. If she did, he may not marry her and make this all legitimate.

There were no priests in Mexico to offer her absolution—if absolution for such a sin existed. She thought that she could hide what she had done, but the truth was that she knew, William knew, and most of all—God knew. The thought that William had seen her naked, explored her, done *THAT* to her over and over again made her unable to sleep at night.

The day after it had happened, she promised God that it would be the last time. Maybe Salbatore's Uncle Umberto knew where to find a priest in hiding. If not, William could fly them to California to be married by Father Juárez—just like she had always dreamed of when she was a little girl.

She did not even know if William was Catholic, Baptist, or any religion at all. Every time he took her to the casino, her resolution weakened and she would accept anything William had to offer, just to keep him. She loved him and could not imagine having a life without him. She had given her entire self to him, body and soul.

Whenever Mariana heard a motorcar rumble up the alley, she would run to the window to see if Javier had come to pick her up for William. Every time Feo barked, she peeked out of the kitchen or the window—only to be disappointed at the ugly face of Salbatore coming in or someone walking by their house. In the evenings, she tried to imagine what William was doing, what he was eating, thinking, and feeling.

Every evening that she climbed into bed with Sofía, waves of disappointment tumbled over Mariana. She began creating excuses for William. Maybe he was afraid to lose his job. Maybe the thought of her needy family was too much for him.

What had she done? She had sinned against her own body for a man who had not even met her mamá. Maybe God had tested her and she had failed. When she was angry, she resented Josefina and felt like smashing Salbatore in the face.

LÁZARO SAT at the dinner table, all washed up and waiting for his dinner. Lázaro wanted to eat the moment he got home, but Mamá always made him clean up. She refused to allow him to sit at the table, stinking it up like horse manure.

Mamá sent Mariana out with a plate of *Mole De Iguana Negra* that she had brought home from the restaurant. They had trouble selling all the Iguana meat the chef had bought because the Anglos did not want to sit there picking out all the tiny bones.

Mariana set the plate in front of Lázaro. He eyed her when she lowered herself in the seat across from him.

"What do you want?" Lázaro asked.

"Maybe I only want to sit with my cousin."

Lázaro pulled off a piece of his tortilla and dipped it into the mole sauce.

"How is your work going?"

"Work is work." He stirred the crumbly white cheese on top of his mole, and let it melt into the sauce. Of course he had nothing to say about shoveling manure, and he still resented her for her easy job.

"How is your work going?" he asked with a tone of disgust and narrowed eyes.

"It is going well. William is good…"

Lázaro stopped chewing. "You are in love with him!"

"No!" Mariana said, louder than she had intended. "I mean, Mr…"

"It is obvious!" He squinted at her. "The chauffeur who picks you up…the way you dress and act like you are better than the rest of us…"

"I do not…" Mariana's throat tightened.

"Don't get your hopes set on him. An Anglo will never make a wife out of a Mexican woman."

Without thinking, Mariana shoved his plate, toppling the food off the table and into Lázaro's lap.

He jumped up from his chair and let the plate clank to the floor. "Idiot!" he yelled at her. "You are as stupid as a dog."

Black sauce dripped from the crotch of his pants and onto the cement floor. Mariana ran to her room and slammed the door before he had a chance to get his hands on her or Mamá made her clean it up.

"What's wrong?" Josefina sat on the bed digging through the bin where they kept the cotton cloths for their monthly *la vergüenza*, the shame.

"Is it that time?" Mariana asked.

"I couldn't wait to be a woman and now I am already tired of it."

Mariana usually started a day or two before Josefina, but she had not.

CHAPTER SEVENTEEN

MARIANA HAD NO IDEA HOW TO TELL WILLIAM THAT SHE WAS going to have their child. Their lovemaking had become routine, leaving for lunch, going to the Belvedere, and then back to the Hotel de Obregón for the second half of their workday.

William sat on the edge of the bed slipping on his socks. He seemed distracted the last few days, with extra trips into town and not having the staff bring fresh flowers for her desk.

"When would you like to meet my mamá?"

He straightened up with his sock only halfway onto his foot and hanging off the toes. "Where is that coming from?"

"I thought, that since we will be getting married, you would like to meet her."

"Married?" He appeared to be completely taken by surprise.

Mariana held up her finger with the ring on it. "You said you wanted a future."

"A future, not a marriage."

Mariana could not breathe. "Aren't they the same?"

"No."

"What about the houses we drove by. You asked me which ones I liked."

His brows pinched together. "Oh, here it is. I knew this time would come. It always does."

Without another word, he finished pulling his sock on. With jerky and angry movements, he shoved his feet into his shoes.

Mariana opened her mouth to tell him that she was pregnant, but the words would not come out. She did not want to tell him here, with his anger. Instead, she finished getting dressed and silently followed behind him through the casino with all the fancy women with bobbed hair and wrapped in furs. What ever made her think that she could be one of them?

When they drove across the bridge, with its ominous *thump-thump, thump-thump, thump-thump* of loose boards, Mariana knew that this was the end for her. This would be the last time William would take her to the Belvedere. He would probably tell her to pack her things the moment they got to the Hotel de Obregón. In the middle of the bridge, before they had a chance to get to the smooth road into Tijuana, Mariana leaned over and whispered, "I am pregnant."

All color drained from William's face and he sat there in silence for what seemed an eternity. Then he began shaking his head. "What do you want?"

"Us." Tears welled up and spilled down her cheeks. "I love you."

William looked up at the back of Javier's head. "We will talk when we get back to the office. There are people who can... doctors who can..."

Mariana closed her eyes. She felt sick and unable to breathe in the hot and dusty motorcar.

They rode the rest of the way in silence. When Javier pulled around to the side of the hotel, she followed William into the front doors, through the lobby, and past the front desk. The front desk clerk looked uneasy when they passed him.

"Mr. Swanson," he said.

William held his hand up, stopping him. "Not now."

"But…"

William kept going. At his office door, his body stiffened.

"Daddy!" an excited little voice called, then two tiny arms and an entire little blond girl with ringlets and a lace dress with a blue sash jumped into his arms. She looked to be five years old.

After a moment of stunned silence, William said, "Julia, what are you doing here?"

A woman's voice came from inside the office. "We thought we would surprise you."

William turned and faced Mariana with a pleading look of frozen shock. A woman stepped from his office and turned to face Mariana. She was a tiny blond woman with bobbed hair and a perfect little pixie face. Her effervescent smile turned sour and she pursed her lips at the sight of Mariana.

"Are you surprised to see us, Daddy?" The little girl took his face into her tiny hands and turned his head toward her.

Mariana left without grabbing anything from her office. There was nothing in there that belonged to her.

CHAPTER EIGHTEEN

MARIANA HAD NOT HEARD FROM WILLIAM IN FOUR MONTHS. THE same evening his family had shown up at the hotel, Javier had come to the house with an envelope with a short note of apology, a fifty-pesos bill, and the name of a doctor who could *take care of her little problem.* She could not kill what God had given her, whether she wanted it or not. She could not place sin upon sin, so she gave the fifty pesos to Mamá and told her that she had lost her job.

Just as Lázaro had predicted, an Anglo man wanted nothing to do with a Mexican woman. Her belly had become round, and she didn't know how much longer she could hide it beneath her skirts.

Unable to find another job, Mariana worked at keeping their house clean, cooking dinners, and caring for her sisters. At least with her at home, the little ones did not need to go out into the streets with Josefina. With the money tight, she went to a jeweler to sell the ring William had given her. As if God could not punish her more, she found out that William was a cut-glass sort of a man and they were rhinestones instead of diamonds. Mariana was apparently even cheaper than she had thought.

Mamá's spirits briefly lifted when Mexico elected Álvaro Obregón as the new president. She hoped he would reopen the churches and Papá would come home to them—but she sunk back into her darkness when someone assassinated him before he could take office. Even if he had not been, Salbatore said that he had already been president before President Calles, and the two took turns to keep the power in their own pockets.

It was Mamá's day off from the restaurant, so they decided to have a nice dinner. Mariana peeled the papery husks off the green tomatillos, exposed each sticky fruit before dropping them into the colander. Once it was full, she rinsed them off and dumped them onto a dish towel next to the cutting board.

As Mariana cut the tomatillos into wedges, Josefina came in, quiet and not her usual self. She scooped up a handful of poblano chiles, set them next to the stove, and lit the gas burner. With a set of tongs, Josefina began to char them. She placed the bright green chiles on the grate with the flame on high to blister and blacken the skins.

"Is something wrong?" Mariana asked.

Josefina shook her head and focused on the chiles.

Mariana placed another tomatillo on the cutting board, sliced it in half, and exposed the dense white core. She cut it in half again and again. Mamá came into the kitchen, slow and hesitant. When Mamá stopped next to Mariana, she looked over. Mamá had a grave look. Papá? Had she heard news of Papá?

"What is it?" Mariana asked.

Mamá reached out and put her hand on Mariana's belly. Her eyes narrowed and she slapped Mariana across the face. "When were you going to tell me?"

Mariana put her hand to her stinging hot cheek and looked over at her sister. Josefina's eyes grew wide. She turned off the burner and slunk out of the kitchen.

"I don't know, Mamá." Mariana had hoped that William

would come around and change his mind. Maybe he would start sending her money and they would figure out a solution together.

"How could you do this to our family? Don't you think we have suffered enough?"

"I'm sorry, Mamá."

"Sorry won't fix it. You should have told me sooner—when a curandera could fix it."

"But, Mamá! I could not kill my baby."

"What about your Papá? You have shamed our family."

"I loved William. I thought we were going to be married."

"You *thought* you were going to be married? *Thought?* Men will promise anything to get what they want. Until the day you stand before a priest, you cannot count on anything." Mamá had never looked at her with such hatred before, and it was worse than the slap. "I told you that something was wrong with him buying you clothes and sending a chauffeur to pick you up. Did you listen to me? Does anyone listen to me? No. And now, look what he has done to you."

"I'm sorry, Mamá."

"It's better to eat the dirt than to spread your legs for a piece of bread."

"Mamá!"

"What are you going to do about it now?"

"I don't know."

"Did you learn nothing from your Tía Carlota? Look what happened to her. This family has been cursed with stupid women."

"I'm sorry, Mamá."

"*I'm sorry, Mamá, I'm sorry, Mamá.*" She mocked Mariana and sounded like a crazy woman. "Sorry does not fix anything. When your baby is born and wants a father, will you say *I'm sorry, bebé, you have no father.* When your baby needs to be fed and needs a house, will you say, *I'm sorry, bebé but you have no father to feed you or to give you a roof?*"

The sound of Feo barking stopped Mamá's tirade. She scowled at Mariana in a look that no Mamá should ever give her daughter—then she spat at Mariana's feet, missing her shoes and leaving a blotch of wet cement on the kitchen floor. "Go. I don't want to look at you."

Mariana ran out and into their bedroom. Josefina perched on the edge of their bed, sitting on her hands and looking up at Mariana with watery eyes and a quivering chin.

"I'm sorry," Josefina sobbed. "I didn't know. I was worried. I saw your belly and you hadn't said anything. I didn't know. I only asked Mamá."

"Leave me alone and go help Mamá in the kitchen." Mariana lay down and turned her back to Josefina. She should have told Josefina that it was okay. She should have told her that she didn't blame her, but she couldn't. Josefina had the man she loved.

CHAPTER NINETEEN

ONE WEEK LATER, MARIANA STOOD AT THE TRAIN STATION WITH
an address written on a slip of paper and a used cardboard suitcase that Lázaro had found in some cheap shop. The suitcase
had someone else's dirty brown stains across the fabric on the
inside lid. One spot was in the shape of a rabbit—just like the
rabbit in the moon.

Mamá had sent a letter to Papá, telling him everything and
that it was up to him to care for his disgraced daughter. He may
or may not have received the letter before she arrived, but like it
or not, Mariana was on her way. Lázaro had given her a small
pouch of money and told her to pin it inside her waistband so
nobody could steal it. The dark train, filled with strangers,
huffed alongside the platform.

"I'm scared," she told Lázaro.

"I know. Maybe now you can talk to your papá and bring
him back—or have him send extra money for the family. Maybe
now he will realize that, even though there is fighting in
Guadalajara, it cannot be worse than what is happening to his
family in Tijuana."

Mariana held onto Lázaro's arm. His muscles tightened and

he squeezed her hand against his ribs. Did he feel the same bad omen that she did? Josefina had cried for days after Mamá had told them that she was sending Mariana to Guadalajara. Sofía and Catalina begged her not to go, but she kept a brave face, telling them she was going to find Papá. At first, Mariana had thought they would be too young to understand, but both Emilio and Papá had gone away. In their little lives, when somebody left, they did not return.

"What if I can't find him?" Mariana asked Lázaro.

"You have the address."

"It is a big city. What if I get lost?"

"Then you will ask for directions."

She had never spent a single night away from her family, and now, here she was at the train station with nobody but Lázaro to say goodbye to her. She did not want to leave him. Mamá would not let her sisters come to the station, so she had to say goodbye to them at home—all of them sobbed while Josefina clung to her and begged Mamá to change her mind.

Mamá ignored them and looked through Mariana like she was already a ghost. A ghost woman with a tiny ghost baby.

The engineer blew the whistle, and people shifted toward the cars. He blew it again, but Mariana's feet would not move. Lázaro peeled her hand off his arm. "It's time."

With one hand on her back, and the other holding her suitcase, he led her to the steps. She climbed up, feeling like someone had filled her shoes with cement.

Lázaro lifted the suitcase to her. "I'm sorry."

Mariana took it and turned. The dark round faces of the Indio passengers stared forward with weary eyes as they clutched their bundles and baskets. She wondered if they knew the dangers they could encounter riding into the belly of the rebellion. Just last year, a group of Cristeros, led by a warrior priest, attacked a train and set fire to it—burning the passengers alive and shooting people who tried to escape through the windows.

The inside was all wood and dust and packed with foul-smelling strangers. She passed a man who stank of pulque and had a rooster beneath his coat. The bird's head poked out and twitched from side to side. She took the only empty seat in front of a barefoot man in a big straw hat. She slid next to the window and placed her suitcase beside her to deter anyone from sitting there.

Lázaro stood on the platform with his hands in his pockets and his head staring down the tracks. Mamá had been furious with him and blamed him for Mariana's disgrace. Papá had put Lázaro in charge of the family and he had failed them. Now, he had to take her to the station, and he had to be the one to put her on the train.

The whistle screamed and a bell clanged. The train lurched and squeaked when it began to roll forward. Lázaro looked up and their eyes met for a moment. Mariana wondered if that would be the last time she would ever see her cousin. Whether she believed in superstitions or not, all the grandmothers' predictions seemed to be true. Her spirit had ridden in on Halley's Comet and she had brought nothing but bad luck.

Her baby fluttered in her stomach like a little moth beating its wings. Not Mexican, not Anglo—a little gray nothing fluttering around unwanted and unloved.

The train moved and took her away from her family. As the hours ticked by, the car rocked back and forth, back and forth, and hot air blew in through the open windows. Every now and then, a whirlwind of dust moved across the land. The telegraph poles slid by at regular intervals—measuring the distance like tally marks on the landscape.

Most of the passengers in her car were Indios, small and dark, and speaking languages she did not understand. When she boarded, she noticed most of the Anglos, Spaniards, and

Mestizos getting into a different car. She was Mestizo, part Spaniard and part Indio, and should be with them—but she had disgraced herself and was worth nothing but a dog-cheap ticket in a third-class car.

The train skirted the border between the United States and Mexico. It stopped at Tecate and Lindero before crossing into California, where the Anglos were the only ones who entered or exited the cars.

It was dark when they pulled into the Calexico station. Across the border, back in Mexico, a giant electric owl glowed high above the buildings with its neon light blinking across the night. Who would make such a thing? Everyone knew that owls warned of bad luck, sickness, and death. A bad omen for everyone who passed by. A bad omen for her.

Mariana had not eaten any of the food Josefina had packed for her. Josefina pleaded with her to eat it, if not for herself, then for her baby. She took out one of the waxed paper bundles and unrolled it.

A slip of paper with black lettering fell from the cold bean tamale and onto her lap. Mariana held it to the window, trying to catch some of the moonlight. *I am sorry that I told Mamá. Please come back home.* Poor Josefina. Mariana had told her a dozen times that it was not her fault. Josefina would nod at the reassuring words, but it was apparent that she did not believe them.

Mariana slid the note into her skirt pocket. Anything from her family, even this note on a torn strip of paper, seemed precious now. Ever since Mamá had put her hand on Mariana's belly and looked at her with shame, nothing tasted good.

Two small forms climbed onto the seat with Mariana and sat on top of her suitcase. They had appeared out of the dark like two coyote pups sniffing at the air. The children looked to be the same ages as Sofía and Catalina and looked up at her with big dark eyes.

She asked them if they were hungry, but they did not answer. The youngest one, a little girl in a plain cotton dress and bare feet, reached her tiny hand toward Mariana's tamale and wiggled her fingers. Mariana wrapped the tamale back up and handed it to the oldest girl. The girl said something in a language that Mariana did not understand before she helped her little sister off the seat, took her by the hand, and steadied her while they made their way back to their mamá. She should have given them two tamales so their mamá could also eat.

She pulled out another bundle, unwrapped it, and removed another note from Josefina. Mariana read the second slip of paper with Josefina's messy handwriting scrawled across it. *I am a terrible sister. May God forgive me.*

As the night wore on, the Indios slept, wrapped in their blankets and leaning against one another. Mariana had nobody to rest on, so she put her head against the window and listened to the occasional cough or the whine of a child.

With every tie in the tracks, her head bumped against the glass. Papá had taken this same journey alone. Mariana wondered which seat Papá had sat in. It could have been the same one, and he could have put his head to the very same window as the landscape slipped by and put more and more distance between him and his family.

Mariana wished she had brought a blanket because the coach had turned into an icebox in the night. She took her extra dresses from her suitcase, draped them over herself, and curled up on the bench seat. Outside, the stars blinked like thousands of tiny ice crystals. Far off across the darkness, a campfire glowed, and Mariana imagined a group of vaqueros sitting around it eating from tin plates while the silhouettes of their horses shifted behind them.

Mariana got little sleep. In the morning, they passed through miles and miles of dry arroyos and canyons with nothing but mounds of rocks with crosses on top or an occasional team of burros led by men ambling along in dirt-red serapes.

In the distance, a small cluster of mud huts and trees appeared. They grew larger and larger as they approached until the train slowed and stopped at a dusty village. Round-faced women worked outside thatched-roof houses made of sticks and clay or outside single room adobes.

Chickens, mangy dogs, pigs, and small children wandered in and out of open doors. An Indio papá walked barefoot toward the train with his little girl on his shoulders. Her papá used to carry Mariana that way until she got too big and then Josefina took her place, then Sofía, and Catalina. Mariana could still remember the feel of Papá's hair in her fingers as she held on.

Quiet and sullen Indios from the village came to the train windows with scant trays of onions, oranges, tamales, corn tortillas, or sweetbreads for sale. A few of the passengers in her coach bargained with them, not accepting the stated price, and finally trading the goods for their centavos. Most of the vendors gathered around the windows of the first-class car, eventually straggling off with empty trays.

Some of the villages were larger, almost small cities—filled with people, goats, skinny dogs, and burros clopping along with droopy heads. Women in cotton dresses draped blue rebozos over their heads or used them as slings to tie their babies to them while they sat behind vegetable stands or wandered the streets. Boys in cotton pants and bare feet carried large baskets on their heads filled with woven cloth or corn. The buildings were whitewashed or had pink-tinged plaster with faded murals painted on them, and almost all were riddled with bullet holes.

No matter how tiny, each village had a church in the heart of it. Their bell towers, some with one bell and others with three or five, and each topped with a cross, rose higher than any other building. Several had long planks of wood nailed over the doors and all of them had paper notices tacked to them.

At every stop, young boys swarmed to the windows with trinkets, sugar cane, and woven blankets for sale. Women offered tortillas, tamales wrapped in cloth, fruits, or candies. Dozens of hands reached up, offering something to sell. Dark eyes glanced into the windows and moved on when they noticed the car filled with peasants—moving to the first-class compartment where they called out, "caña de azúcar, tortillas, papayas," and jostled one another to get to the windows. Mariana unwrapped the last of her tamales. After that, she would have to take some of the money from her waistband to buy herself some food.

All day long, the train swayed, creaked, and thumped as it took Mariana deeper and deeper into the desert, past nothing but dry land, scrub, and cactus—where it looked like nothing but lizards, rattlesnakes, and coyotes could survive. But somehow, they still came across dusty villages filled with people. How did they survive so deep in the nothingness?

At dusk, groves of orange trees slipped by the windows. Mariana thought she was dreaming of the green trees with their bright orange fruit and could almost see Emilio and Lázaro when they were boys hiding in the branches. She imagined Jenny loping through on her pony and all of them dropping dusty-gray eucalyptus leaves and pods into the water, pretending they were launching fleets of miniature boats. Mariana blinked, but the groves were still there drifting by the window.

The train crawled into the city of Hermosillo with fortress-like stucco walls painted in faded red, yellow, and green. Instead of vendors swarming the train, young men in trousers and caps leaped aboard the first-class cars. They emerged with passengers and luggage and led them to dusty old motorcars or wagons tethered to mules. All the Indios in her car gathered up their belongings and their children and moved to the door.

Outside the window, vendors sat at small tables with sweetmeats and pyramids of oranges while the young men spirited away all the Anglos, Spaniards, and Mestizos. At least a hundred federal soldiers in high boots, with rifles and hostile dark eyes, crouched on top of wooden crates and piles of sandbags. Three large-wheeled cannons stood with their barrels pointed down the railroad tracks. One of them could be the dog in the church who had raped her mama.

"Is this the end?" Mariana called out to blank faces. "I need to get to Guadalajara."

Nobody answered back.

"*Por favor*," Mariana stood at her bench seat. "Please. Does anyone speak Spanish?"

A man with a bushy mustache and straw sombrero stopped next to her. "It is only for the night."

"The night?" Mariana had not planned to leave the safety of the train car until she had reached her destination. "I am going to Guadalajara."

"We cannot cross the Yaqui desert in the dark," the man said. "It is for our safety."

Lázaro had told her that Yaqui warriors had attacked a train a few years back. The conductor had been so frightened that he disconnected the engine and left the passengers stranded to their own fates. Many were still missing and others were found half-buried in the sand. That had been this railway? How could Lázaro put her on a train that went through the Yaqui lands?

Mariana felt a hand on her arm. "In the morning, you will be back on your way to Guadalajara."

"Where will I sleep?"

The man in the sombrero said something to the woman with the two little girls she had shared her tamales with. The woman listened and nodded. The man asked her something else. With a soft voice and no expression, she replied, "Palma."

The man turned to Mariana. He had red-rimmed and watery

dark eyes that looked tired but kind. "This is Palma. She will take care of you for the night."

The little girls peeked out from behind their mamá and reminded her of Sofía and Catalina—who were probably having their dinner back in Tijuana, eating food made by their own mamá's hands. Mariana picked up her suitcase and followed the woman out of the train car.

People blocked the platform as they greeted one another or waited for porters to take their luggage. Mariana followed behind the woman. The youngest girl held onto her mamá's skirt, and the older one clasped her sister's hand. Mariana felt like a giant standing among the Indios. Some of the men were as tall as her, but most were not. Once they cleared through the crowd, Mariana could see that the city had been through tough times. Bullets had scarred the colorful stucco walls and dimpled the dusty trucks and motorcars.

Palma turned to her and asked something that Mariana could not understand, other than it had been a question. Mariana shrugged. She led Mariana past women selling bouquets of yucca lilies, sweetbreads, and stews of meats boiling in cooking pots, to a vendor with a stack of woven blankets. Palma pointed at a blanket, then at Mariana's suitcase.

"No," Mariana said. "I do not have one."

Palma spoke to the vendor, a beautiful woman with coffee-color skin and a black eye.

The vendor translated, "You need a blanket to sleep on."

Mariana hesitated. She needed her money to last. "How much?"

The woman evaluated Mariana. She ran her eyes up and down Mariana's dress, her stockings, and her shoes. "Two pesos."

Palma erupted into a string of words. She and the vendor went back and forth until the vendor finally turned to Mariana. With a look of disappointment, she said, "Fifty centavos."

Mariana unpinned the money pouch from her waistband and dug out a silver fifty-centavos coin. Palma inspected the blankets. She ran the fabric through her fingers and held it up to the light. She chose a white blanket with blue and black bars and a white fringe.

Mariana followed Palma and her girls through narrow streets with iron-barred windows and balconies. They passed a palm-lined plaza in front of an old white cathedral. A fat woman in black lace rode by on the back of a small burro and looked like a character who should be in the funny pages. Palma came to a stop at a tiny house fenced in by scrap lumber and barbed wire. One chicken and three skinny dogs lay in the shade and did not move when Palma lifted a wire and swung the gate open. She motioned Mariana and her girls to step through.

"Nina," Palma called through a thick red blanket that took the place of a door.

A woman in a white cotton dress and no shoes stepped out.

"Palma!" As they embraced, a girl who looked to be about seven came out, holding the hand of a three-year-old boy wearing a striped shirt and no pants and no underwear. Palma spoke to the woman while she occasionally turned her hand toward Mariana. The tone of their voices made Mariana aware that she would be a burden for both of them, but they seemed resigned to do it.

Mariana spent the rest of the daylight on a stone bench in front of the house. She watched the children play and pet any one of the mangy dogs that had the courage to slink up to her. The little boy ran around the yard and only paused to pee on one of the dogs or through the sideways slats of the fence. Her own little ghost-baby fluttered in her belly. She put her hand to her stomach. Because of her sin, her baby would have even less than these children. She was worse off than they were with no house, no papá, and no yard to pee in.

At dinner, Mariana sat in the one good chair in the house and ate from one of the three spoons the family owned. The papá and two boys had come home, sweaty and dirt-stained from a day's labor. With Mariana, Palma, and her daughters, there were ten people eating beans and tortillas meant for six. Mariana's plate was the only one with an egg on it and she didn't deserve it. She held her plate out to the papá and offered it to him.

"No señorita," he said. "You are our guest. It is our pleasure."

Out of respect, she ate the egg, feeling more and more guilty with every bite. This family needed every resource they had, and here she was with a pouch full of money that could feed this family for a long time. She should pay them for their kindness, but who knew what would happen as she rode deeper and deeper into the desert.

That night, Mariana slept on a mat stretched across their dirt floor. She covered herself with her new blanket and breathed in the smell of the wool and hard earth. She had become a woman of the dirt.

CHAPTER TWENTY

THE SOUND OF THE TRAIN WHISTLE WOKE HER THE NEXT morning. At first, she lay there listening to it, like she always did in the barrio, until a dog started licking her face. A dog? Mariana jumped to her feet. The train! She needed to get to Guadalajara. The whistle blew again. How far had they walked? What if she missed it? How could she be so stupid to fall asleep? She should have been watching the windows for morning light.

Mariana wrapped her blanket around her shoulders and grabbed her suitcase. Even though she might need it, she placed two pesos on the family's table before slipping out their blanket-door. The sky glowed orange and purple as she hurried past the tiny houses, the plaza, the cathedral, and through the narrow city streets. The whistle blew again, and she could hear the train huffing like a beast.

When she rounded a corner to the platform, Mariana stopped. Soldiers had piled all over the train cars. They crouched on the roof behind sandbags, sat on crates, and leaned against cannons, now loaded onto the flatcars. All of them had their rifles slung over their shoulders with the barrels aimed straight up to heaven. Most of the passengers had boarded and filled the windows with worried faces.

An Anglo in a cream-color suit and hat stepped from a dusty black car and waited while the driver waved down two porters with ropes wound across their bodies. They unlashed a trunk from the back of the motorcar and carried it behind the man. Mariana rushed over to him.

"Excuse me, sir," she said.

The man turned to look at her. She realized what a sight she must be wrapped in the blanket and rising straight from bed.

"Are the soldiers there to protect us from the Yaquis?"

He let out an amused laugh. "Half of them are Yaquis."

"Why are they on the train?"

"Have you not heard about the rebellion? The Cristeros who call themselves men of God, but are nothing more than thieves and murderers are robbing the trains."

"They are there to protect us then?"

He let out another laugh and made her feel like a child with stupid questions. "They are on their way to fight. If the train is attacked, they will lose their transportation, so yes, as a consequence, we will be protected."

The whistle blew again and the man looked at his watch. "Twenty minutes behind schedule. Pretty good for this railway."

Mariana climbed back onto the third-class car and recognized some of the faces.

The whole way through the Yaqui desert, the people sat, stared out the windows, and didn't speak. Gullies from dry arroyos cracked the land, and Mariana could see nothing but an endless expanse of brown sand, dry and parched, with an occasional cactus or scraggly mesquite.

The train stopped at a poor village of adobe huts with hairless dogs and barefoot children in ragged clothes. Like usual, vendors and beggars swarmed the train. The vendors here had measly wares of cactus fruit and greasy meats of questionable origin. The beggars pleaded, "One centavo, for the love of God."

Small children stood staring at the train, their eyes wide black orbs and watching like scared deer. Were they afraid of the train? Or of the soldiers piled all over it like buzzards? Had *federales* marched into their village with squeaky leather boots and holsters, threatening the people with their guns and searching for Cristeros? Or women?

At one stop, an old woman in a skirt and *huaraches* cleared tumbleweeds away from the front of a white plastered church. She moved slow and hunched and dragged away one sticker ball at a time with her bare hands until, suddenly, gunfire cracked from the train roof and a harsh voice yelled for her to cease and go home. The woman ignored them and kept at her task, either deaf or trusting in God to redirect the bullets.

The Indios dropped to their knees beneath the windows. Women shielded their children and the men's hands suddenly became armed with rusty pistols and knives. Mariana crawled over to them. She ignored the pain in her knees from the hard wooden floor and hoped their silent prayers could stop the bullets. People inside the first-class cars screamed for them to stop, to have mercy. Mariana did not want to witness the wickedness, but she could not take her eyes away from it.

Finally, a voice with authority yelled from above, "Cease!" The people held their breath when the sound of heavy boots stomped across the roof of the train. The old woman took hold of the stem of another tumbleweed and dragged it away from the wall of her church. The soldier in command must have been reminded of his own grandmother, for they finally let her be.

The train started moving away from the village, leaving the vendors with their unsold wares and their church scarred with even more bullet holes than when the train pulled in. The desert went on forever, desolate and parched. The train swayed back and forth and rattled along the rails with everyone quiet and watching.

Mariana relaxed when they began to pass by large ranchos with grand houses, huts, and corrals. Vaqueros, in wide-brimmed hats, rode horses or perched along fence rails, and they stared at the train with their lizard eyes. They must have made it out of the Yaqui lands. Mariana could not tell if the vaqueros gave their evil looks to the soldiers, the people in the cars, or the train that brought them all across the land.

Long-ago, she, Emilio, Lázaro, and several other children on the hacienda would run up to the vaqueros and ask to touch their horses or run their hands over the embroidered saddles to feel the flowers, snakes, or geometric patterns stitched into the leather. One of them let Mariana spin the wheel of his spur. She could still almost hear the metal clink as she spun it around and around with her finger.

At Guaymas, the train rolled into a great mist of sea fog. The vendors sat wrapped in their blankets behind little tables, each with a candle lit and flickering. Mariana climbed out of the car because she needed to get herself some food. She could not bring herself to buy any of the meats, so she purchased a mango, several oranges, and sweetbread. The train whistled and the passengers climbed back on. At one station, men loaded several stretchers with injured soldiers into one of the boxcars.

At some point, she had fallen asleep because when she opened her eyes, the faded blue light of morning had filled the coach. The Indios knelt before the windows and recited their morning prayers. Something seemed off with them, because their prayers had the tone of fear and mourning. Maybe something happened to one of the small children. Maybe someone was sick.

Over their dark heads, Mariana saw a dead man hanging by the neck from a telegraph pole. His form slid from window to window, bobbing as the train swayed down the tracks. He had a distorted face, dirty white peasant clothes, and bare feet. Once his form passed by the last window, another body appeared at the front one. And then another and another.

Mariana crossed the aisle and knelt before an open window. Men hung by their necks as far down the tracks as she could see. Black crows perched on the wires above the bodies and watched the train pass by. Mariana crossed herself, pulled her rosary beads from beneath her shirt, and placed the cross to her lips.

As the Indios uttered their prayers, Mariana realized that she understood, "Yea, though I walk through the valley of the shadow of death, I will fear no evil." They spoke in their own language, but they prayed in Latin. It was their people hanging and their religion that had been stolen as much as—maybe even more than—her own.

All of a sudden, a gun fired from the roof of the train. People screamed, ducked below the window rims, and pulled their children beneath them. One of the crows dropped from the line and the rest took to the air, followed by more gunfire. Was it out of respect for the dead? Or were the soldiers only entertaining themselves and using the crows to practice their aim?

In her dream, just after Papá had left for Guadalajara, he had been dressed in the white cotton clothes of an Indio—just like the men dangling before her. Mariana forced herself to look into their gruesome faces and make sure none of them was her papá. Even if she did see him, would she recognize him? Suddenly, the image of what he had been whittling in her dream became clear. It was Christ dressed in robes with outstretched arms—straight out, like the beam of the cross he had been nailed to.

CHAPTER TWENTY-ONE

THE TRAIN SCREECHED INTO THE OUTSKIRTS OF GUADALAJARA, past miles of broken-down shacks and streets filled with poverty. Small children roamed around naked from the waist down or in tattered clothes. One little girl lifted her dress and squatted in the street to pee while a group of boys chased a skinny dog with a stick. In the distance, two white spires rose up, each topped with a cross.

Deeper into the city, the streets became paved and lined with shade trees and lampposts. The train passed beautiful parks, statues, plazas, and monuments. The two and three-story ornate buildings had flat roofs and shuttered windows with iron bars. A soldier on one of the rooftops shifted his weight like a vulture —while his black eyes tracked the people down below.

After days of nothing but dry desert and dusty villages, the city seemed almost blasphemous in its extravagance. Men in derby hats and tight black suits strolled by with women in pretty chiffon dresses—right past Indios in white cotton pants and huaraches, and stately women in lace shawls and mantillas. Taxis swerved through traffic and barely missed motorcars and burros that plodded down the street with overloaded carts.

She had been here before. Most of her memories of Mexico were on the hacienda with vaqueros, pomegranates, and the giant maguey plants that were taller than a man and had arms that reached out like an octopus—this was familiar. She had a flash of a memory here in a park. Emilio was pushing her on a swing. No, it was another boy because Emilio and Lázaro swung next to her. They pumped their legs, but she needed to be pushed. There were three cousins. One pushed her and the other two climbed into a tree. One fell out and broke his ankle.

The train inched into the station and she needed to get off. As long as she was on the train, she was heading in the right direction. The moment she stepped off, she would be lost in this gigantic city.

Mariana clutched her suitcase. She touched her rosary beneath her blouse, felt the beads, and followed them down to the crucifix. With a lurch, the train came to a complete stop. The heavy sound of boots stomped overhead and the dark forms of soldiers passed by the window, one by one, crawling off and dropping into the city.

The Indios gathered their belongings and their children. Her stomach churned. She did not know where to start. The car emptied, and she rose, touched the money pouch pinned to her waistband, then took hold of her suitcase handle. What if someone robbed her? What if she could not find her cousins?

Without direction, she headed toward the cathedral and its twin towers. She passed through a plaza filled with thick-leaved palm trees, a bandstand, and a promenade packed with peddlers squatting on the ground in serapes and sombreros. People stopped to haggle with them and bargain for flowers, shark's teeth, prickly pears, stuffed birds mounted on sticks, or live green parrots that flapped their wings against bamboo cages too small for them.

When Mariana reached the cathedral, a side door flew open. Instead of the friendly face of a priest or an altar boy, a line of soldiers, strapped with guns, burst through. They marched out with golden candlesticks, a crucifix, and what looked like the embroidered vestments of a priest.

A soldier stopped a man, spoke a few words to him, patted the man's pockets, and took his money. One of the soldiers' eyes latched onto Mariana. His body became alert and she imagined him dragging her inside the cathedral to do whatever he wished to her. She should have known better than to stare—or to do anything that would bring attention to herself. Her hands began to sweat and tremble when the soldier started toward her.

A well-dressed couple with two girls came up the street. Mariana slipped into step beside them, swallowed down the lump in her chest, and began a conversation with the woman.

"*Hola, Señora.*"

The woman gave her a polite smile but did not respond.

"I am sorry to bother you, but I am lost."

The woman nodded, as if giving permission for Mariana to continue walking with them, but they did not pause. She must look a terrible sight after days on the train without a bath and carrying her cheap cardboard suitcase.

Once they rounded the corner, they stopped, and with the two little girls tucked between them, they turned to Mariana. "Where are you headed?"

"I am new to the city and cannot find my way." She pulled the slip of paper with her cousins' address from her skirt pocket. "I am looking for this address."

When the woman took the slip from Mariana, it caused a wash of panic. Mariana should have memorized the address. What if she did not give it back? The woman held the paper out to her husband. For all she knew, the man might be a government official and have her arrested.

He pulled a pair of spectacles from a breast pocket and put them on. She listened for footsteps coming from behind and wished they would keep walking and get as far away from the soldiers as possible. The little girls hid halfway behind their parents and peeked out at Mariana.

The man read the address, then stared into Mariana's eyes. He appeared serious and intent. With a nod, he pointed down an avenue. "Three blocks that way, then turn left. You will see it."

The man held the paper out to her.

"*Gracias.*" Mariana took it in her hand, but he did not let go.

"*¡Viva Cristo Rey!,*" he whispered. "Good luck and God bless."

Mariana was afraid to respond. His words could be a trap, so she only nodded and hurried off as soon as he released the paper.

A block away, Mariana came across a group of peasant women in cotton dresses and shawls. They squatted along a sidewalk under gunpoint. Soldiers moved through the women taking pamphlets away from them and throwing them onto a newly lit fire. The smoldering papers read—*¡Viva Cristo Rey!, Live Christ the King,* and *What is the Union Popular?*—the papers turned as black as the words printed on them before crumbling to ash.

Mariana altered her path, took a right down the next street, and prayed to God that she would not get lost and need more directions. She traveled two more blocks before taking a left, then another left, hoping to end up where she needed.

When Mariana rounded the corner, it felt as if someone had stuck an invisible arm out, halted her, and cemented her feet to the sidewalk. Seven life-sized figures in dirty cotton clothes and red armbands hung like ornaments in a park tree. People knelt on the sidewalk and tossed flowers beneath their dangling feet as they wept. At first, Mariana thought it was some local tradition, like the burning of Judas at Easter, but the smell of death confirmed the horror. A shrill scream boiled up in her chest. Her entire body shook as she tried to contain it and melt into the people.

Instead of effigies stuffed with straw, they were real men. One of the bodies had a note pinned to its leg, *This is the fate of fanatics and bandits against the government.* An armed soldier stood between the people and the tree to prevent them from cutting the men down. His eyes were so dark that they had no center to them—just two black holes. One of the hanged men had a scrap of blue fabric tied around his wrist. Maybe it had been part of his wife's rebozo that he had worn for good luck.

A wiry-coated dog crossed the line of mourners and sniffed at the stained dirt below the bodies. As he raised his nose toward the flayed and bare foot of one of the men, a woman screamed and tossed a rock at the mutt. It fell short and landed in a damp spot on the dirt. Behind the tree, a little boy sat on an iron swing in the play yard pumping his legs back and forth, like a pendulum measuring the time. The dog nudged the foot of the man with the blue fabric and caused his body to rotate and slowly unwind on his rope.

Mariana forced herself to move closer and drop to her knees beside the mourners. Their weeping wove in with all the other city noises—the rattle of motorcars and the sounds of the street vendors calling out or ringing their bells. Mariana looked at the faces of the dead men and prayed that she would not see her father in them, but felt guilty for wishing to find some other family's father or son. The eyes that looked back at her were open and crawling with flies. Two of the men's ears had been cut off, leaving nothing but coagulated dark holes on the sides of their heads.

Within all the noise, something was missing. It took a moment to realize that there were no prayers. No rosaries. No priest. No comfort for the people—only an armed soldier standing in the center of their grief.

Mariana put her hand to her heart and felt for the rosary beneath her shirt. She found the small lump of a bead, said a silent prayer, and slipped her finger along the string to the next bead. She repeated her prayers again and again: "Hail Mary full of grace, the Lord is with thee…"

After completing the rosary on as many beads as she could touch beneath her blouse, Mariana rose. Her legs stung from lack of circulation as she made her way along a plastered wall with numbered doors and barred windows. Armed soldiers patrolled from the tops of the buildings and she could feel their eyes upon her.

She found the address she was looking for in a row of cream-color houses. A fancy number fifteen was painted on a square of black tin. Mariana's hand trembled when she lifted the iron knocker and hit it against the door three times.

She waited. Nobody came. She knocked again and waited. Nothing. The sun was getting low and this was her only hope, her only connection to the city. She knocked again. If nobody answered, should she check at the neighbors? Did people have neighbors when they had no yards? In the center of the door, a small window finally opened. The dark eyes and brows of a woman stared out at her through an iron grille.

"I am looking for my papá, Hector Castillo," Mariana said.

The woman's eyes softened and Mariana heard the scraping of a metal latch. The thick door swung open barely wide enough for her to slip through.

"Are you Mariana or Josefina?" The woman bolted the door behind her.

"Mariana." Her knees began to tremble and she wanted to drop to the floor and kiss it.

The woman looked to be the same age as Mamá, but more proper and elegant with her dark hair pulled into a tight bun. She wore big golden hoop earrings and a ruby-color dress of lace and silk. "I am your cousin, Carmina."

Mariana wanted to hug her, to fall into her arms and cry, but she just stood there, unable to speak and trembling.

The entry chamber had dark orange tiles, white plaster

walls, and large wooden beams across the ceiling. Directly in front, an arched double door with iron latches stood shut, making Mariana feel like a goat being herded from one pen to the next.

When Carmina opened the second door, Mariana caught a whiff of burning sage before she entered a living room filled with dark leather furniture. Another woman, dressed in a modern emerald dress and a flowered shawl with golden fringe, stood behind the door with her long pale fingers holding onto the edge of it.

"This is Mariana," Carmina said. "Our cousin. She's looking for her papá."

Their grim expressions gave Mariana a bad feeling. Her heart hung by a single string within her ribcage and she prayed that these women would not clip it.

"I'm your cousin, Celia," the other woman said. By the facial features, Mariana could tell they were sisters. Carmina appeared to be the younger of the two and not as delicate as Celia. She had not expected such beautiful and elegant cousins —with finely shaped features, like the porcelain dolls in the curio shops.

"Is my papá here?"

"No," Celia said. "Come in and have a seat."

Mariana's heart pounded. She had come all this way.

"Socorro," Celia called.

A dark Indio woman, who looked no taller than five feet, came in from an archway next to the fireplace. She wore a white cotton dress with red embroidery and black patent leather shoes that looked unnatural on her. "Please, get Mariana something to eat and then get the Rose Room ready for her."

Carmina gave a worried look to Celia.

"It will be fine," Celia assured her.

Mariana lowered herself onto the couch. The fireplace was not lit, but candles burned with their tiny flames flickering all around the room. Her cousins sat down on either side of her and didn't say anything.

"Where is my papá?" Her voice came out childish and on the verge of tears.

Carmina put her hand on top of Mariana's, but it was Celia who spoke. "Does your Papá know that you are coming?"

Mariana felt sick to her stomach. Why were they not telling her? Her cousins began talking, but their voices tangled together and Mariana's vision began to fade. "Is he alive?"

"Oh, yes. Poor child. Yes, he is alive."

Her vision turned dark and their voices faded into the distance. *Help her to lie down. Socorro, bring a wet towel. The poor girl must be exhausted.*

Thank you, Father in heaven. Papá is alive and she had found him. The sound of shoes tap-tapped on the floor and she could not tell if they came from inside the house or out. Maybe soldiers on the roof. A cool cloth touched her head. And then a hand on her belly.

"You are with child?"

"Where is your husband?"

Mariana shook her head.

"You do not have a husband?"

Mariana shook her head again.

"You came here alone—and in your condition?"

The room had no natural sunlight, only the glow of candle flames. "Is my papá here?"

"No," Celia said. "But he should be home tomorrow."

Papá must not have received Mamá's letter. He does not know of her disgrace yet. The Indio woman shuffled in with a tray of food, and her eyes fixed on the glass of swishing orange liquid as if at any moment it might slip off the tray and spill to the floor.

"You should try to eat something."

Mariana pushed herself up. "I'm afraid I will get sick."

"Eat for your baby."

Mariana took a bite of bread and chewed.

Her cousins fussed over her and forced her to eat more bread and swallow sips of mango juice. Afterward, they took her upstairs to a room with a bed so tall that it had its own step-stool beside it. A painting of the Virgin and Child surrounded by roses hung over the night table.

"You are allowed to have this painting? And I saw the crucifix and the statuettes of the *Virgen de Guadalupe* and *San Miguel* downstairs."

"The soldiers will have to kill us to take them." Carmina raised her chin and exposed a long and elegant neck. Carmina set the remainder of the juice and the plate of bread and cheese on the bedside table.

Her cousins showed her the lavatory with shiny red and blue tiles and a giant bathtub. All this time, she had pictured Papá living in a hut and sleeping on a mat, not in a grand house.

"With this big of a house, why didn't my papá send for us?"

Celia stared at her for a moment before answering. "This is not your papá's house to invite anyone."

Mariana's chest felt as if it were filling with water and drowning her from the inside. "But you are my cousins."

"*Ay, niña,*" Celia said and placed her hand on Mariana's shoulder.

Mariana's chest rose up and down. She breathed deep and tried to keep herself together.

When they returned to the bedroom, Socorro sat like a wooden idol in a chair next to another door, and a small bundle of sage smoldered in a ceramic bowl.

"Where does that door lead?" Mariana asked.

Celia seemed hesitant, but answered, "To a rooftop patio."

"You can see it in the morning," Carmina said. "It is not safe at night."

A large iron sliding bolt kept the door latched from the

inside. They were on the second floor and Mariana could not imagine why it would not be safe, until she remembered the soldiers on the rooftops and imagined them walking outside the bedroom and peering in through the gap in the curtains. Mariana peeked through, but all she could see was an iron grille and the moon casting a silver light on the silhouettes of potted palms and a water fountain.

Her cousins left her with Socorro, who sat in the chair stone-faced with her slanting and watchful eyes. Mariana could not change clothes while the woman sat there like that, so she went back to the bathroom and stripped down.

The tiles felt cold and smooth on her bare feet—nothing like the coarse cement floor at their half-a-house in Tijuana. The reflection in the mirror that stared back at her seemed like a different girl. This one had swollen breasts and belly. She was a girl who meant nothing to anybody. Her own mamá had sent her away to a papá and cousins who did not know she was coming. She slid her white nightgown over her head and looked more than ever like the ghost she had become.

When she returned to the room, the bed was turned down, and Socorro still sat in the chair. Mariana slid her dirty body beneath the smoothest sheets she had ever felt.

"You can leave when I fall asleep," Mariana said.

Socorro did not answer. Mariana wondered how much Spanish she understood and could not imagine the woman sitting there all night staring across the darkened room at her. A slice of moonlight peeked in from a gap in the curtains. Mariana watched for it to turn black, blocked by the body of a soldier with a gun slung across his body.

When she finally slept, she dreamt of the seven men in the tree, with their spirits rising like giant white moths tethered to the branches and unable to ascend.

CHAPTER TWENTY-TWO

MARIANA AWOKE TO THE SOUND OF A ROOSTER CROWING AND AN empty chair where Socorro had been sitting. The scent of sage still hung in the air. She peeked through the curtain to a terra-cotta patio with potted palms and a bougainvillea with splotches of papery red flowers that crept up one of the walls. A small dirt-color bird splashed around in a clay fountain. It dipped into the water and shook tiny droplets into the air. Even such a small and insignificant bird still desired to care for itself.

Mariana slid open the bolt and stepped out onto the cool tiles into a wash of morning light. The sound of chickens clucking came from several directions and was mixed in with street noises below. She could see across all the flat rooftops with their clotheslines and potted plants. Sagging telephone wires connected all the buildings as if they were strung for a fiesta and waited for someone to add brightly colored paper flowers along them.

The house wrapped around three sides of the patio. The fourth side was a cream-color wall at least six feet tall—tall enough to divide the house from the neighbor's but not tall enough to keep a soldier from dropping from a rooftop into the patio.

"I was hoping to talk with you before the men get home," a soft voice said behind her.

Mariana turned to see Celia standing in one of the other doors facing the patio. It stood open and exposed an unmade four-poster bed. Celia pulled her shawl tighter around her shoulders and stepped barefoot to a chair facing the fountain.

She sat and watched as another tiny brown bird land on the edge. "It is not safe for you here. You need to go home to your mamá."

When Mariana lowered herself into the chair opposite of Celia, her movement caused the bird to flutter into the air. "She sent me away."

"Maybe she did not know of the danger."

Mariana shrugged. "Or maybe she did."

Celia's eyebrows pinched together, and she probably wondered about the depth of Mariana's depravity for her own mamá to not want her.

"Have I been here before?"

Celia nodded. "Just before your family left for the United States."

"I remember this patio and some cousins who were the same age as Emilio. Were there three cousins?"

A sad smile came to Celia's face. "My sons, Leon and Lorenzo, and Carmina's son, Alberto."

"I also remember a park. One of the cousins fell from a tree and broke his ankle."

"That was Alberto. His ankle still bothers him every now and then." Celia seemed restless all of a sudden and rose to her feet.

Mariana was right—she did remember it. "I walked by that park on my way here yesterday. There were dead men hanging from the same tree Alberto had fallen from."

Celia closed her eyes and shook her head.

"And men were hanging from the telegraph poles along the railroad track."

"Not the best way to welcome people to Guadalajara," Celia said, "but an unequivocal warning about what will happen if you defy the government."

"Why is the government so brutal?"

"Because President Calles has no soul." Her eyes hardened and filled with tears. "He has outlawed our religion so all power will be in his hands."

"People are willing to die for it?"

"The government thought we would go scampering away like whipped dogs. They thought we would let them murder our priests and shoot up our churches. Calles is the beast in human form. He wants us to kneel before him rather than Christ the King."

"Can you win against the government?"

"Maybe we cannot, but it is an honor to die for God. You cannot take everything away from people and expect them to simply exist as complaisant burros that plod along their paths with flies in their eyes and no hope in their hearts. We need our religion, our festivals, our God. If they take all of it away, what do we have?"

"Your families and your lives?"

"This life is a small amount of time compared to eternity in heaven—and heaven is guaranteed for martyrs."

"Even if they murder innocent people?"

Celia had a hard but confused expression. "The federal soldiers are not innocent."

"What about that train robbery? The one where the priest they call *Pancho Villa in a Cassock* killed innocent passengers?"

Celia gave a single nod. "That was General Father José Reyes Vega and his troops. General Vega lost his temper when his own brother was killed by the *federales* on the train. He will have to answer to God for that. It set us back. Without public support, we have nothing. President Calles has used that incident to justify his anti-clerical laws and gain support from the United States."

Was her papá willing to give his life for Christ? That would explain his unwillingness to come home to his family.

"Are you all right?" Mariana felt a hand on her shoulder. Celia now stood next to her with a look of concern.

"Yes. It's been a long few days."

Celia reached out and cupped Mariana's cheek in her palm. "I need to get ready for the men coming home, and you should get a bath to wash all the train-filth from yourself."

"I am excited to see my papá...and it will be nice to meet my cousins again."

Celia dropped her hand and pulled her shawl tight around her shoulders. "Your cousins are in the hills fighting and will not be home today."

"I'm sorry. It must be hard to have your sons facing an army."

"It is, but Carmina and I sent them to fight. Men are cowards if they are not willing to fight for their Lord." Celia's eyes brimmed with tears. "The men were not interested in fighting at first, but after our boycotts failed, we women stood guard at our churches. We confronted the soldiers and caused our men to take up arms to defend us."

Mariana's words caught in her throat. "Until death?"

"It is better to die than to deny Christ the King." The wetness in her eyes finally spilled over and dripped onto her cheeks. She took a step away from Mariana. "Get a bath and stay in your room until one of us comes to get you."

AFTER HER BATH, Mariana found an old leather-bound copy of *Don Quixote* in her room. She opened it, surprised to see a book written in Spanish. In school, all the books were in

158

English, so it felt strange to open it to: *El Ingenioso Hidalgo Don Quixote de La Mancha Compuesto Por Miguel De Cervantes Saavedra.*

A bell rang from an upstairs room, then a commotion came from downstairs—and several deep male voices. Mariana lay the open book upside down on the bedside table. Please, let one of the voices be that of her papá. She stood, smoothed down her skirt, and pulled her shawl over her belly to hide it. Maybe she can see one last look of love on Papá's face before he discovered her disgrace.

The heavy thud of boots came up the stairs, louder and louder until the door burst open and there he stood, in the flesh and bones.

"Papá!" Her voice sounded high and pleading, like a child.

"What has happened? Is everyone all right?" Every nerve of Papá's face constricted and formed two deep furrows between his eyes.

"Everyone is well."

His shoulders relaxed and he came toward her. "Why are you here?"

"Mamá sent you a letter."

"I have been away."

His room. She did not even know where her own papá slept. His face and hands were ashen and coated with dust, just like in Santiago when he came home from a day of picking. He seemed so familiar, but at the same time foreign to her.

"Why are you here?"

Mariana parted her shawl and exposed the round shame of her belly.

"Were you attacked?" His nostrils flared and his eyes became fierce like a barbaric flame had been lit inside him.

If only she could tell him she was attacked. "No, Papá. I was in love."

He took a step back when all she wanted was to wrap her

arms around him and have him tell her that he loved her and all would be well. "Has he married you?"

Mariana shook her head. "He deceived me. I found out that he already had a wife and a child, but it was too late."

"Did Lázaro run him through?"

Mariana dropped her head, barely able to whisper out the words. "No. He is an Anglo and he was my boss."

There it was—the look of absolute disappointment and disgust. His expression pulled the breath from her and drained the blood from her head. She needed to sit down before she fainted. When she lowered herself into the chair, her baby fluttered like the little gray moth it was.

She pulled her shawl back over her belly and stared at his pant legs and shoes that were both worn soft and dusty like they had traveled down many roads unfamiliar to her. Papá stood there motionless for what seemed an eternity.

Finally, with words balled up like fists, he spoke, "We will talk later."

His feet turned away from her and left the room.

Mariana opened the book and stared at the infinite lines of blurry black type. They all bled together until they no longer made any sense. What had she expected? She surprised him with her presence, only to tell him that she was no longer his cherished little girl but a woman shamed and disgraced.

Mariana shut the book and climbed onto the bed. Maybe she could sleep through all of it. Maybe she could sleep until Papá no longer hated her.

More heavy footsteps resounded in the hallway, along with men's voices. She closed her eyes and partially drifted off to sleep when a knock came to the door and Carmina entered with a lace veil over her head.

She gave a slight smile to Mariana and noticed Don Quixote on the bedside table. "You enjoy reading?"

"Yes, I was a good student. Once I finished school, though, I no longer had time or books to read. I'm afraid this one will take me longer since I was taught to read in English."

Carmina shook her head. "I am sad for you. Please, help yourself to any of our books. All reading should be done in Spanish since it is a much more passionate language—and it is the language spoken in heaven."

Without another word, Carmina sat an intricately stitched chapel veil next to Mariana. "Put this on and come downstairs."

Mariana unfolded the beautiful floral lace. Could it be Sunday? Without work or church, she could not keep track of the days. She draped it over her head and stepped into the hall.

Papá was not in the living room, and neither were either of her uncles. At the bookcase, Carmina removed an old photograph of a man in a suit. Behind it, sat a golden chalice and ciborium, just like the priests used for Holy Communion.

A muted knock came from the front door and caused Carmina to hurry toward it. She opened both the double doors leading to the entry chamber with its dark orange tiles and white plaster walls. Celia opened the small window in the door, and a strange feminine voice whispered through the grate, "*Con paz y amistad*—With peace and friendship."

Carmina opened the door. Two women, dressed in embroidered cotton dresses over full lace petticoats, entered. Both of them had leather-sandaled feet. Once inside, they pulled church veils from beneath the sashes of their dresses, covered their hair, and knelt before the bookcase. They crossed themselves and prayed.

Soon, another knock came, and a raspy male voice whispered the same words, "With Peace and Friendship." Celia opened the door, and a man in a business suit came silently into the living room and knelt beside the women.

They kept coming. Carmina acted as a sentry at the door to let in person after person, of every aspect of life, from mixed blood Mestizos like her to dark-skinned Indios, and tall, blue-eyed Criollos of pure Spanish blood—all of them came in, pious and silent. They knew what was expected and knelt in prayer before the chalice and ciborium on the bookshelf.

Celia came from the kitchen, straight to Mariana. She extended her hand and Mariana took it.

"Are we having Mass?"

Celia led her to the other side of the stairs, away from the worshiping people. "We cannot have Mass without a priest. Our house is a Eucharistic Center for people to give themselves the Blessed Sacrament."

"How?"

"Since the churches are closed, the Pope has given us dispensation to give ourselves Holy Communion. This morning, Celia went to a priest in hiding. He gave Mass, consecrated the Host and the wine, and sent them out with the women and children appointed by the Eucharistic Centers."

"Do you do this every Sunday?"

"Yes, but not here. We have to move the centers around so we are not caught. If we are found out, we will be executed or tortured."

Celia pulled her forward toward the two dozen people with their heads bowed over their praying hands. Some of them worked their rosaries while others rocked back and forth with their bodies swaying as they mumbled barely audible prayers. Celia sunk to her knees and directed Mariana to kneel beside her. Mariana lifted the rosary from beneath her shirt, slipped it off, and made the Sign of the Cross with the crucifix. Papá came down the stairs and lowered himself beside her. He now smelled of soap and hair oil, just like she remembered.

One by one, the people rose, went to the bookshelf, and administered the Sacraments to themselves. After Socorro, Carmina, then Celia returned, her papá went. At her turn, Mariana started to rise when she felt a harsh hand grip her arm and Papá's words in her ear, "Have you been to confession?"

She shook her head. How could she go to confession with the churches closed? They were not even safe to enter.

Papá held Mariana down. "You have committed a mortal sin. It is a sacrilege to take Communion until you confess."

Mariana stayed upon her knees. She was the only person in the house who did not take Communion. She was the only person in the house unworthy before God.

CHAPTER TWENTY-THREE

EVERYONE SAT AROUND THE TABLE WITH THE MEN DEVOURING Socorro's deep red *machaca mole colorado* with fried plantain. Silence smothered the room, with only the dull clinking of silverware on the plates and the tapping of Socorro's shoes on the floor as she brought in the food and the wine. It seemed as if the men's heads were filled with stories they wanted to tell, but because of Mariana's presence, they would not let the words slip out of their mouths. Mariana was an intruder in their home and at their dinner table.

Her uncles, Victoriano and Tomás, had not spoken a word to her. Mariana forced herself to take the food and swallow it. Once Socorro finished serving the courses, and Mariana had eaten enough not to be insulting, she would excuse herself and go to her room. Then, they all could relax and enjoy their evening— and her Papá could forget the disgrace she had brought to him.

A hard knock at the door caused all the eyes to seek one another around the table. Celia's husband, Victoriano, laid his fork and knife beside his plate and hesitantly scooted his chair back. Beside her, Papá reached into his waistband, extracted a pistol, and held it beneath the surface of the table. Who was this Papá, who instead of wrapping his fingers around branches and fruit closed them around a gun?

They listened to the slow tap of Victoriano's shoes. The door from the kitchen silently slid open just wide enough for Socorro to slip into the dining room and fade against the wall. Victoriano's steps had ceased and nothing but silence and held breaths filled the house. A moment later, the knock turned to a sharp pound as if the door had been struck by an object.

"Open the door!" a harsh command flared into the house.

Papá and Tío Tomás jumped to their feet. Carmina and Socorro rushed toward the kitchen. Celia took hold of Mariana's wrist, but she pulled free.

"I'm staying with my papá."

Papá grabbed Mariana's arm so hard that it felt as if his fingers had embedded into her bone. "Go with your cousins." He conducted her toward the kitchen and pushed her through the door.

"What is happening, Papá?"

Victoriano rushed into the dining room with bulging eyes and pistol in hand. "*Federales!*"

The sound of splintering wood erupted from the front entry, like the entire front of the house had been smashed in.

The kitchen had no door to the outside, only one to the living room and one to the dining room. They were trapped. Socorro went to a pantry and placed her hands on the edge of the wood.

"There's no time," Celia said.

Dozens of boots stampeded into the house. How was there not an outside door?

Soldiers, in their khaki uniforms and high boots, burst into the kitchen. Dusky faces beneath military caps, both Indio and Mestizo, pressed in and yelled commands with rifles up. Some of the men had hard, blank expressions and others had eyes filled with barbarity.

"Drop your weapons," a harsh command came from the dining room. "Turn around."

Carmina reached beneath her skirt and withdrew a knife in the face of all the armed men. One of them let out a laugh and reached for Carmina's hand. She slashed at him and drew blood across his palm.

"*¿Qué chingados?*"

When the other *federales* laughed at him, he advanced toward Carmina. She backed away, wild and slashing at him with her knife. The men called out and encouraged Carmina as if they cheered the bull over their own matador. Her backside hit the sink just as the door from the dining room flew open, and Tío Tomás tripped in, pushed from behind by the butt of a rifle. Papá and Tío Victoriano came in behind him with anguish smeared on their faces and more *federales* behind them.

Tío Tomás gave a slight smile at the sight of his wife before yelling above the excited men, "Carmina!"

The man seemed to find sport in disarming Carmina. He mocked her and danced around her like a luchador.

"Carmina!" Tío Tomás snapped. "Drop your knife. You are going to get us all killed."

Carmina glanced over at her husband as if she had forgotten he was there. The soldier took his opportunity to seize her wrist and twist it until the knife clanked to the floor. Groans of disappointment escaped from the soldiers.

An officer, older and in charge, stepped forward. "Get them to the floor."

Mariana put her hand beneath her belly, felt her baby roll beneath her quivering fingers, and lowered herself to the floor.

"Turn around." A soldier kicked at the knees of Tío Tomás. "Backs together."

They all shifted and closed their group, body to body.

The officer stood before the men. "We hear you have been holding Holy Communion."

"I am afraid you are mistaken," Tomás said.

The chalice and ciborium still sat on the bookshelf in the living room, hidden by nothing but a framed photograph.

"Maybe you are also Cristeros."

A pudgy little soldier with a broad nose came in with the statuettes of the Virgin and *San Miguel* in his hands. "These were in the living room."

The officer took them, turned them around in his hands, and inspected the statuettes. He let out a derisive laugh.

"You are willing to die for useless chunks of clay?"

"The only useless chunks of clay in this house are you and your soldiers," Carmina spat out at him.

"Please, Carmina!" Tomás said.

Then, Tio Victoriano spoke low and steady, "Are you willing to live in eternal hell because you bowed down to Calles and his Government?"

"Search the house!" the officer yelled.

All but two of the soldiers and the top officer dispersed. They tramped up the stairs and scampered like rats through the rooms—probably with their rifles lifted while they peered under beds and in closets. Did these men not have their own families? How had the president torn them from their God and their religion? How did he get them to turn on their own people? How did he strip them of their consciences?

Mariana sat with her back against Papá's right shoulder. His body felt hot, like an intense fire burned inside him. Mariana's entire body began to tremble, and a terrible chatter came to her teeth. Celia placed her hand on Mariana's leg. If not for Celia and Papá next to her, she would not be able to keep herself upright.

Soldiers came back with arms filled with crucifixes, hand-made retablos, and large paintings of the Virgin and child, Jesus on the cross surrounded by angels, and the *Virgen de Guadalupe* surrounded by an aura of red and gold. Their fingers dripped with beaded rosaries and lace veils—everything against the law and punishable by death.

The officer's face flushed red as if the beautiful and serene artwork set a spark to the fire of his rage. His jaw clenched, and his nostrils flared. "Take that trash to the street and burn it."

"No…" a low groan came from Celia that sounded as if someone squeezed the last bit of air from her.

The officer took a deep and controlled breath. "Will you deny your god?"

"Never!" Carmina shouted.

The officer ignored her and walked around to face the men. "Deny your god, and you will live."

One of the soldiers raised his gun to Papá's head, but he did not speak. The officer pulled a revolver from his holster, held it to Tío Tomás's head, and clicked the hammer back.

"Deny your god."

"*¡Viva Cristo Rey!*" Tío Tomás said, strong and defiant.

A shot went off and shocked every nerve of Mariana's skin. Even the baby jumped within her stomach. Shards of broken glass and plaster rained down from the ceiling. Mariana gasped and tried to breathe, unable to get air.

"Deny your god."

"*¡Viva Cristo Rey! ¡Viva la Virgen de Guadalupe!*" All three men shouted in unison, followed by Celia and Carmina.

A scream caught in Mariana's throat. "Papá!"

"Silence!" the officer shouted.

"Please, Papá," Mariana said. "They are only words."

"No, they are not. I would rather die than deny my God."

"Silence!"

"Please! Papá!"

"Rise to your feet!" The officers poked them with the barrels of their guns. They were impatient and prodded them like animals. Celia and Socorro helped Mariana to her feet.

"Take them to the roof!"

"Please, Papá," Mariana clasped onto his arm. "Please, Papá."

"I love you," Papá whispered to Mariana. "May God forgive you and bless my grandchild."

Then, just as he always did, he placed his fingers on her head and made the sign of the cross on her forehead with his rough and calloused thumb.

On the way through the living room, the officer tossed the statuettes into the fireplace with a dull egg-cracking sound. How could men lose their humanity? They were turning on their brothers and their cousins—on their priests and on their God.

Not a single breeze stirred on the rooftop patio. The temperature had not dropped and the air still hung hot and humid, bringing pinpricks of sweat to Mariana's skin. The fountain water lay still and gray, and hundreds of birds sat on the electrical wires that looped from building to building.

A black snake of smoke spiraled up from the street. It reeked of kerosene and carried the ash of her cousins' religious treasures toward Heaven. All the doors to the patio stood open, clogged with soldiers.

"Against the wall."

Mariana touched the rosary beads beneath her blouse but could not remember a single word of her prayers.

Papá, Tío Tomás, and Tío Victoriano all stood against the wall so handsome and tall—bigger men than any of the dogs demanding that they lower themselves. Mariana's knees gave way, and she crumpled, but she did not hit the ground. Like a rag doll, Celia and Carmina kept her upright.

"Close your eyes," Celia whispered to Mariana, but she could not take her eyes from Papá. She was finally with him and would not waste a single moment that she could look at him.

A straight line of men formed before her papá and uncles, and they lifted the barrels of their rifles at them. The officer stood with his pistol pointed at Tío Tomás and said one more time, "Deny your god, or you will die."

In unison, all three men stood defiant and declared, "Long live Christ the..."

In what sounded like the eruption of a hundred firecrackers, the soldiers fired and filled her beautiful papá and uncles with their bullets. The entire mass of birds fluttered up from the wires. The sin of her papá's and uncle's deaths rose in the throats of the birds as they screeched and beat their wings against the smoke and sky. Mariana slipped from the support of her cousins and crumpled to the ground

CHAPTER TWENTY-FOUR

Mariana woke to spirit voices in the house. She slid out of bed and padded barefoot down the dark hallway all the way to Papá's room to see if his spirit had come. Several times a day, Mariana ventured there to hold his shirts to her nose and remember him. Maybe by breathing him in, her baby would learn the scent of his own grandfather.

Mariana slid into the room and listened. The baby fluttered in her stomach and her eyes prickled with tears. Maybe losing Emilio and then knowing Mariana's shame made Papá not care to live. Maybe he did not want to lay eyes on his illegitimate grandchild.

She clicked on the bedroom lamp to nothing but an empty room. All Mariana had left of Papá in this world were his few belongings and his clothes that held his scent. She opened the wardrobe door to nothing but empty hangers. Someone took his clothes. She hurried to the bureau drawers and pulled them open one at a time. No clothes. Papa's letters and rosary now lay alone in the emptiness. *Oh, Papá*. Mariana looped his rosary around her neck and adjusted it until the cross lay in the center of her belly.

She used to watch the smooth dark beads move between Papá's fingers when he prayed—his fingers that smelled of orange blossoms in the spring and smudge pot oil on winter mornings when frost threatened the fruit. The same fingers that trembled when he prayed over the body of Emilio. Those fingers will never pray again—and he chose to die for the right to say them.

She scooped up Papá's letters and took them to her room before they too disappeared. She tossed them on the bed and watched all of Mamá's envelopes fan out, probably stuffed with frivolous words—whining about long work hours and Josefina's love for an ugly boy that must have weighed Papá down with nothingness before he died.

Mariana had not ventured downstairs since the day of Papá's burial when they closed all three coffin lids over the men and placed the palm branch of martyrs on top of each one. But now, she would not sleep worrying about where Papá's clothes had gone. Maybe Socorro, with her curious beliefs, had done something with them.

From the first day she arrived, Celia had told her to stay in her room at night and not to emerge for any reason, and she had not. It was a mysterious house and she preferred to stay in her room through the night anyway. Socorro burned sage and set idols and food offerings all around, footsteps creaked the floorboards all hours of the night, and strange voices interrupted her sleep—sometimes male voices even though their men were dead and their boys were off fighting in the hills. She had expected her cousins to return for the funerals of their fathers, but they did not.

Downstairs, the statuettes of the *Virgen De Guadalupe* and *San Miguel* had been recovered from the ashes and glued together once again—this time with chipped paint and cracks running through them. San Miguel's nose and the edge of his shield were now nothing but dull white plaster and one of his wings had broken off. The Virgin's face had a line running from the tip of her left ear, across her mouth, and to her right shoulder.

Several female voices murmured, faint and soft, from the kitchen. Against her orders to stay out, Mariana pushed open the door. Socorro and several unknown Indio women stood at the table wrapping some smoky-smelling meat in paraffin paper. They spoke to each other in their strange-sounding language, as if every word spoke of superstition and omen. The pantry doors stood wide open and the shelves had been shifted to the side to reveal a dark hole behind it.

Socorro turned and stared at Mariana with her emotionless black eyes. She set the bundle she had been wrapping on the tray, then went into the pantry and descended some hidden stairs. The other women kept on with their work as if Mariana did not exist in their realm.

Within a minute, Celia came up, her face flushed red. In a harsh and slow tone, she said, "I told you to stay in your bedroom."

"I'm sorry," Mariana said. "I heard voices. And my papá's clothes..."

Celia drew in several slow and deep breaths. She shook her head and looked over at Socorro, who stood there silent and firm.

"I guess the damage is done." Celia, dressed in her black mourning clothes, motioned for Mariana to follow her down some cement steps and into a musty-smelling cavern with plastered walls.

Women of different classes crowded the chamber, all intent and all with purpose, whether they wore peasant clothes or store-bought skirts and stockings. They packed baskets with food and clothing. Several wore pocket-covered vests that they filled with long silver bullets. One woman tucked an envelope into the waistband of her skirt.

Carmina, still beautiful but looking older and more harsh in her black clothes, made her way to a girl who looked the same age as Josefina. Carmina helped her pack the bottom of a basket with antiseptic, rolls of bandages, scissors, and bottles of medication. Carmina patted the girl on the head and turned in the direction of Celia and Mariana.

When Carmina caught sight of Mariana, her brows pinched together and she stood immobile with her hand still halfway in the air. She dropped her gaze, shook her head, and turned away to give instructions to one woman in Spanish, and another in an Indio language before heading toward Celia and Mariana.

"She should not be here," Carmina said, not even looking at Mariana.

Another woman, well dressed and looking like an office worker, stuffed a pocket waistband with money.

"What is all of this?" Mariana asked.

"Sit there." Carmina pointed to a chair at the end of the supply table.

Little by little, the women disappeared through the tunnels. Celia and Carmina finally lowered themselves onto two chairs next to the now-empty table.

"Is this why my papá didn't come home?"

Celia looked at Carmina and shrugged. "The harm is done."

Carmina did not answer. She closed her eyes and shook her head in resignation. "Your papá was very helpful to our division of the Women's Brigade."

"Women's Brigade?" Mariana asked.

"The Joan of Arc Women's Brigade."

"Women are risking their lives? Not only the men?"

"Yes." Carmina's voice sounded passionate and driven compared to Celia's loving and calm tone. "The family, the home, and the church are women's responsibilities. What sort of a life would we have without our Holy Communion? Without our sacraments? Without Catholic schools for our children? Calles only wants the people to bow down to him. He wants to teach the children to worship their government over their God."

"Can a small group of women make a difference?"

"We cannot, just like one small army of men cannot triumph —but many strategic and organized groups of men or women can." Carmina took the comb from her hair and let it cascade down her shoulders. She ran her fingers through it to work out the tangles. "We have divisions of women all the way from here to Mexico City, with thousands of mothers and daughters slipping between the cities, the villages, and the Cristero camps delivering supplies and information."

"Women can move more inconspicuously than men and stroll right past the *federales* in the streets and on the trains," Celia added as if Carmina had left something out.

Carmina twisted her long hair back up into a bun. "We are not content to sit around and do nothing but pray. We must take action and be instruments of the Lord. We pray for guidance—not deliverance."

"Will they kill the women if they are caught?"

"Yes, and much worse. Death is the easy part of it."

Images of the men hanging from the telegraph poles and from the tree in the park clouded Mariana's mind. Their ears had been sliced off, eyes cut out, and feet flayed and burnt. Thank God the soldiers had left Papá and her uncles on the rooftop patio intact, to be buried by their family. At least they had been spared that.

Papá and her uncles did not have a priest or a mass, but they were buried in an old cemetery by their family tomb. The tomb was surrounded by grave markers of aunts and uncles, cousins and grandparents, none of whom Mariana ever knew of, except for one—Tía Carlota, Lázaro's mamá. Hers was a simple headstone with her name and the words *Mother, Sister, and Aunt*, letting it forever be known that she was not a wife.

"I want to help," Mariana said. "This is what my papá died for."

"We will talk more later," Celia said. "You should go back to bed. This cold is dangerous for your baby."

"It is?"

Her cousins looked at her with pity, and Mariana knew it was because she was pregnant without her mamá's guidance.

"Pregnancy is a hot state," Celia said. "You need to avoid the cold."

Mariana nodded and turned to go back upstairs when she remembered what she had wanted to ask her cousins. "Where are my papá's clothes? I could not find them in his room."

"We sent them out to the men who are fighting." After a long silence, she added, "That is what your papá would have wanted. We also sent the clothes of our husbands."

Mariana's heart hung by a single string and ticked back and forth. It struck one side of her ribs, then the other.

"Did you write your mamá a letter telling her what happened?"

Mariana shook her head so slightly that she could not tell if it had moved at all. She wanted to write Mamá a letter but could not put the words together. How did a daughter tell her mamá of such terrible things? Especially a ghost daughter she had sent away?

"You need to do that," Celia said. "It is best to come from you and you need to tell her that you are coming home."

Every day that she did not write the letter was another day Mamá could live without grief.

For the rest of the night, Mariana tossed and turned and tangled herself up in the bedsheets. Her bad luck had followed her. Images of men fighting and dying in her papá's clothes slipped through her dreams. She saw his denim shirt, dirtied and bloody, buttoned all the way up to the neck of an Indio man. She dreamt of a Cristero in cotton trousers hanging motionless in a tree with Papá´s work boots laced up his skinny shins—until a barefooted man untied the boots and caused the dead man to swing and rotate on his rope.

CHAPTER TWENTY-FIVE

WHEN THEY HEARD THE KNOCK, MARIANA, CARMINA, AND CELIA all stood staring at the back of the heavy wooden door. They had expected it, but when it came, they stood like clay figures, unable to move. Carmina had changed from her black mourning clothes, but still wore dark lace and an olive-color skirt.

From all that her cousins had told her, this was a war where your enemy looked no different than your compatriot. Traitors lurked on both sides. In times like these, a person you had trusted one day could suddenly shift their loyalty because of threats to their family, fear, or seeking to fatten their wallets with a few pesos.

Carmina stepped forward and put her hand on the latch of the little window in the door. When she opened it, a dull glow from the street lamps and a deep and scratchy voice came through the grille, "Can I talk to Miguel?"

"You have the wrong house," Carmina said.

"I am sorry, I thought this was the house of my brother."

Carmina closed the window and put her hand on the door

latch. They had the password and now she needed to put her life into their hands.

Carmina opened the door to a dark figure in round eyeglasses. "Allesandra," he said, using her *nom de guerre*.

The half-shadow of a second man appeared to the left of the entryway.

"You are as beautiful as I have heard," his husky voice came into the room.

The sounds of an idling engine and the clopping of a lone horse came from the street. Carmina would be loaded into a motorcar, blindfolded, and taken across the city to meet with a contact she would never see in order to receive important information.

If one of the *federales* spotted Carmina, they could accuse her of treason, or of prostitution for being out in the night. She would be taken straight to one of their prisons—and what a woman faced in prison was too barbaric to even think about.

Carmina pulled her shawl tight around her shoulders.

Celia touched her sister's arm before she stepped out into the street. "Go with God," she said before kissing her on the cheek and latching the door between them. Celia crossed herself, and with her forehead to the back of the door, she stood for what seemed a terrible length of time.

The day after Mariana had come across the women in the kitchen, Celia and Carmina made her promise to never speak a word about their work if she wished to stay at their house. And after that, they no longer asked her to remain in her room through the night.

She helped roll bandages or sort through supplies as they arrived—work that needed to be done but required no risk or skill. Work simple enough to be done by a girl who showed up at their door like a stray cat, too pregnant and too pitiful to throw back into the street. Celia refused to let Mariana go down into the cold underground cavern with her belly growing so round and cumbersome, which made it extra work for people to bring them up to the kitchen table, then back down again when Mariana finished her meager tasks.

Celia and Carmina were colonels and in charge of an entire brigade. They organized over six hundred daughters, mothers, and even some grandmothers who reached all the way out to the villages and provided food, ammunition, intelligence, and medical supplies. Celia's *nom de guerre* was Colonel Arebela Rolón and Carmina was called Colonel Allesandra Ríos.

Divisions of women organized and ran field hospitals, provided housing, and distributed pamphlets—right under the noses of the federal officers. Sometimes, the wives of the government officials themselves used their positions to fight for their religion against the wills of their own husbands and brothers.

Carmina told her that a woman in President Calles's own family allowed the Cristeros to use her barn as an ammunition depot. Nobody knew exactly how many women fought for the cause all over Mexico, but Celia heard it was over twenty thousand. Guadalajara alone had five full brigades.

All the secrecy felt unreal, like a game she used to play with Emilio and Lázaro. They had built a secret hideaway by the river, and only the trusted children in the barrio were given a password to enter. The children who were not allowed into their fort did everything they could to be trusted and gain entry, or they tried to destroy the hideaway—but this was real, and Papá had died for it. Thousands and thousands of people were dying for it.

Mariana stared at the back of the door. She hoped Carmina would change her mind and come right back through it. After a while, Celia finally turned away.

"Come," Celia said. "You need to sleep for your baby."

"I will not be able to sleep until she returns."

"Even if you lie awake, the rest will do you good."

"But…"

"Socorro and I will wait. If you fall asleep, I will come to wake you when she returns." Celia kissed Mariana on the forehead. "Go for your baby."

When Mariana turned to leave, Socorro said something in her Indio language. A few of the words were familiar enough that she understood, *poor child* and *no mamá*.

CHAPTER TWENTY-SIX

CARMINA HAD COME HOME THE NIGHT THE MEN BLINDFOLDED her, and two more times since. It felt as if the entire house held its breath each time she stepped out, whether through the front door or down one of the tunnels. They always kept the house closed up and the curtains drawn. The only sounds came from the ticking clocks, the creak of the floorboards, or their own whispers—to one another or in prayer.

A sliver of morning light poked through the curtains and into her room. Celia had not come in to tell her that Carmina had returned the night before. Carmina had gone out to sneak one of the Cristero officers into town and pose as his wife. Maybe they had been delayed. Hopefully Celia had just forgotten to wake her.

Mariana sat up, dropped her legs over the side of the bed, and felt the top of the wooden step-stool with her toes. The baby moved and created a flutter in her belly. She put her hand on it. "*Buenos días bebé*. Did you dream of angels last night?"

Ever since the baby began to move strong inside her, Mariana became resigned to the fact that she would be a mamá

—and she wanted to be a good one. She would give the same love and care to her child that Mamá gave to Sofía and Catalina.

Mariana pulled the enameled chamber pot out from under the bed. She no longer had to stay in her room at night but found it quite convenient now that her baby pushed on her bladder and tormented her all the time. No sooner had she lifted her nightgown and squatted over the pot than her door opened.

"Señora Carmina is home." Socorro stepped into the room.

No *excuse me*, or *may I come in*. She just slid in and left the door open behind her. Mariana doubted Socorro even disturbed the air as she walked through it. If you did not watch for her, she could appear behind you and you had to wonder if she was a spirit or the flesh and bone Socorro. The only sound in the room was the sound of Mariana's water splashing into the pot.

"We can all rest now that she is home," Mariana said. "You can go."

Socorro did not budge. She stood in the same spot until Mariana finished, stood up, and smoothed her nightgown back down. Socorro took hold of the pot.

"I will dump it," Mariana said. She always made it a point to empty and rinse it first thing every morning.

Socorro ignored her and left the room with the chamber pot as quietly as she had entered.

Mariana pulled open the drawer of the bedside table and looked for her hair comb. Beneath the brown tortoiseshell comb was the letter she had started for Mamá but never finished. How could she bring so much pain to poor Mamá?

Above the table, a new painting of the Madonna and Child hung since the soldiers burned the other one. It seemed that the attic was full of rescued religious artwork. As soon as the front doorframe had been repaired and doubly enforced, Celia brought them down and placed them on the same nails the burnt paintings had hung.

The Madonna in this painting, with the naked baby Christ in her arms, had a look of sadness and compassion. Maybe she expressed sorrow that bringing forth life only to set their children in the hands of the world was the fate of all mothers.

A single carpenter ant crept out from behind the golden frame. It crawled down the wall, disappeared behind the bedside table, reappeared, and made its way to the floor. It hugged the baseboard and walked in the seam, barely visible, all the way to the door where it slipped beneath the frame.

One of these days, Carmina might not come home, and then what would they do? Mariana could not imagine Celia without her sister.

Mariana pictured all the women fanning out to the railway stations, calling taxis, or simply walking down the street with their baskets or with correspondence tucked into the waistbands of their skirts. Maybe some would go to maize lorries pulled by burros, where they would hide their contraband beneath the load, and clip-clop out of town. She imagined them moving through plazas, past public monuments, and out into the countryside—right under the noses of the *federales*.

The door opened again and Socorro entered with the empty chamber pot. She slid it beneath the bed before placing her small dark hand, no larger than Sofía's, onto Mariana's belly. "It's going to be a boy," she said.

"How do you know?" Mariana asked.

"Because it is pointy," Socorro said as if everyone knew that.

Celia skirted around Socorro to enter Mariana's room. "Did Socorro tell you that Carmina is home?"

"Yes," Mariana said.

"It is time for you to go home."

Mariana dropped her head. Another ant crawled along the seam of the floor and baseboard.

"You need to go before your baby comes. It is dangerous here and you need your mamá."

"She does not want me," Mariana said.

"She sent you to your papá, but he is no longer here. This is not a safe place for you or for your baby."

Nobody wanted her. She thought that her cousins had started to love her. She did not want to face her mamá and she did not want to take that long train ride again, especially with her belly so heavy now.

"I have asked Socorro to give you a vapor bath. We call it a *temazcal* bath and it is good for the baby. Come." Celia extended her hand to Mariana.

Mariana took it and followed her out to the patio. She averted her eyes when they passed by the bullet-scarred wall where Papá and her uncles were executed. They skirted a narrow walk between the wall and the house to a wrought iron gate that led to another open patio—much smaller than the main patio.

In the center, and taking up most of the courtyard, sat a round adobe oven, big enough to put an entire cow into, with a blue and white wool blanket covering the opening. The smell of burning mesquite filled the air.

Three fat brown chickens and two black ones fluttered down from nesting boxes and skittered toward them. Socorro pulled a handful of bread crumbs from her pocket and scattered them across the patio.

"This is a steam bath," Celia said and placed her hand on the adobe. "Take off all but your underclothes and step inside."

Socorro shed her dress and shoes until she stood there in nothing but her bloomers. Her small brown breasts and dark nipples were exposed and out for anyone to see. Mariana looked at Celia and hoped she would tell Socorro to cover herself.

"It's all right," Celia said. "Socorro is a curandera."

Mariana pulled off her nightgown and stood on the patio in nothing but her bloomers and chemise. "What about the soldiers? What if the soldiers come?"

"They know better than to interfere with a curandera, especially one helping a pregnant woman."

Socorro slipped beneath the wool blanket that covered the opening. Celia picked up the bottom corner and lifted it for Mariana. "Go on in," she said with a smile. "You will thank me later."

In a pit, a small fire burned beneath a pile of rocks right in the center of the hut. Socorro motioned Mariana toward a stone bench covered with folded wool blankets. Three baskets of herbs and a pail of water sat next to the hot rocks. As soon as Mariana sat down, Celia dropped the blanket and the room went black. All Mariana could see was the slight glow of fire around the rocks.

"If your head starts to spin, lay down," Socorro said with her heavy Indio accent.

Socorro began chanting something in her own language. In a loud hissing gush, steam saturated the air. The smell of rosemary and basil swirled around on the vapor and Mariana breathed it in. It reminded her of Mamá pouring broth onto a hot griddle. The smells made her homesick. She closed her eyes and imagined herself back in their kitchen with Mamá at the stove and Josefina chopping vegetables.

Socorro's chanting caused Mariana's muscles to relax, and sweat dripped down her spine and between her breasts.

Images came riding in on the rhythm of Socorro's song. Flashes of the church in Tijuana with its broken ceramic figures of saints and the altar filled with bullet holes. The squeak of the federale's boots. The click of his rifle cocking and Mamá telling her to take the girls outside. The train ride and the federales piled on the roof like vultures—and Indios who knelt at the train windows, as body after body drifted by, hanging by their necks from the telegraph poles.

Mariana drifted into a sleep-state and dreamt of sneaking in and out of an underground press to pick up newspapers and pamphlets. She passed through palm groves and haciendas with vaqueros sitting on their horses and the metal clink of their spurs. She dreamt of walking down a narrow path through rocks and the dry beds of the arroyos as she made her way to villages filled with houses made of sticks and mud. She walked in the night and passed baskets from hand to hand under the dusky moon while an owl called out its warning.

Mariana felt a gush of cool air and the room filled with light. Socorro knelt beside her with a tin cup in her hand. "Drink," she said.

She put it to her lips, sipped, and tasted a cool herbal tea.

"Go slow and come out when you are ready," Socorro said. "I will wait outside."

Mariana's head felt clear. She thought about her dreams and knew that she would not return to her mamá. In Tijuana, she was nothing but a ghost daughter and a shame to her family. Here, she could be part of something bigger. She could continue serving God by helping the Cristeros. She could finish her papá's work. Mariana did not know if she had it in her to be as brave as her cousins, but it would be penance for her sins. If she died doing it, she would be assured a place in heaven right beside Papá. It would be better to die a martyr than to live with shame.

Back in her room, she removed the letter she had started for Mamá, finally knowing how to tell her that she no longer had a husband and her children no longer had a Papá—and knowing it would probably be the last letter Mamá would ever open from her. After this, Mariana would be nothing to her own mamá. She would be the daughter who shamed the family. She would be the daughter who told her that she no longer had a husband and her children no longer had a papá. She would be the daughter who never returned and stayed to fight a war for their God.

CHAPTER TWENTY-SEVEN

PAPÁ'S PILE OF LETTERS STILL LAY ON THE BEDSIDE TABLE. IT FELT intrusive, but she needed to read them before finishing her own letter to her Mamá. One by one, Mariana opened the envelopes. She needed to know the things that Mamá had shared with Papá—and needed to know what thoughts and worries Papá had on his mind when he died.

She read about all of Mamá's uncertainty, how she felt abandoned, and the worry of what was happening to her family. Mamá wrote about how Lázaro worked very hard and how ill-suited he was to watch over the family. She cursed William and Salbatore and referred to them as *the Gringo with his eyes on Mariana* and *the dirty dog who follows Josefina around.*

Mamá complained that their children were turning into street children and how they begged and sold trinkets to tourists. She had written many angry words to Papá for fighting with the Cristeros rather than taking care of his own family. Poor Papá had died with all of Mamá's unhappiness on his heart.

Mariana ignored the tap on her bedroom door. Socorro

usually knocked, then entered without being invited, but the door did not open and the tapping came again.

Mariana refolded Mamá's letter and lay the envelope on top of it. "Come in."

Both Celia and Carmina entered. Dressed in all black, they looked like twin shadows slipping into her room.

"Is everything all right?"

Celia looked at all the letters strewn out before sitting on the edge of the bed, next to Mariana. Carmina lowered herself into the chair by the window. They had come for more than that.

"It is time for you to go home."

"I want to help you. I want to fight for God. I know that I cannot do much until I have the baby, but I can cook. I can also read and write in both Spanish and English if you need that." Mariana was rambling, but she wanted to get it all out before they said no. "I am a shame to my family. I can at least redeem myself in the eyes of God. Please let me do this."

Celia put her hand on Mariana's knee. She was about to deny her.

"I want to do it to honor my papá. He became a Cristero and I want to continue his work."

Celia stared down at the floor and Carmina looked through a gap in the curtain at a slice of the wall with the bullet holes and papery red flowers of the bougainvillea.

When Carmina finally spoke, she said, "What about the father of your baby? Will he come here causing trouble?"

"No." Mariana let out a laugh "He does not care about the baby or about me."

"And you still lay with him?" Carmina asked with a look of condemnation on her face.

"Carmina…" Celia said.

"Women need to stop being stupid when it comes to men."

"I thought he loved me. I thought we were engaged. He bought me a ring and we were looking for houses." Mariana's throat stung with tears, but she had to explain. She did not want her cousins to think so lowly of her. "After a while, his interest started to drift and I became more of a routine than a woman he wanted a future with."

"And you still wanted to be with him?"

"I thought once we were married, it would get better."

"Marriage will not turn a scoundrel into a good man," Celia said.

"Men act like they are doing you a favor by marrying you, and before you know it, you are doing nothing but cooking and cleaning their house and scrubbing their piss from the bathroom floor." Carmina's tone turned bitter and her face flushed red. "Once you have a baby or two, they stop coming home after work. Instead, they go to the cantina with their friends and expect you to spread your legs for them when they get home— and you know all they are thinking about is some puta they had been desiring all night."

"Carmina!"

She ignored her sister. "Soon, they get so tired of making the money, they put you to work somewhere. Then you have an outside job, housework, children, and a husband to take care of —while he works one job and acts like he is the king of all of Mexico."

"Carmina!" Celia said. "Do not listen to her. Not all men are like that."

"Your Victoriano was not, but most men are and you know it," Carmina said. "I say you should write to the father of your baby and ask him to send you money every month for his child."

"My baby will still be illegitimate and I will still be unmarried. What would that make me?"

"A little bit richer," Carmina said. "Then maybe you will only work one job and not have to answer to a man. You will be much better off."

"I will still be unmarried."

Celia put her hand to Mariana's cheek and turned her face so that their eyes met. "You do not need a scoundrel to make you a good woman. You are already a good woman. You are just a vulnerable woman who believed the wrong man."

"Celia is too nice. You are a stupid woman. You cannot believe what a man tells you when he is trying to get you into his bed. I say to demand money from him to help with the baby, and if he sends it, you don't have to be his peon wife. It will be half the work and half the heartache."

Carmina went to the window and parted the curtain with her hand. Mariana could see the entire section of wall where Papá, Tío Victoriano, and Tío Tomás had been shot. "You say that you can read and write in English. Can you do it well?"

"Yes, I got top marks in school in the United States."

"That could come in very handy for us."

"Us?"

"The Women's Brigade." Carmina let the curtain drop shut. "Could you translate and write letters for us?"

"Yes! I can do that!" Mariana's heart rose up inside her chest. "I need to be of value. I need to continue what my papá believed in."

"It is still dangerous," Celia said. "The soldiers can raid our house again—and next time it could be the three of us at that wall. Are you willing to die for it?"

"If I go back to Tijuana, I may still be breathing air, but I will be dead."

"What about your baby?" Carmina asked. "Your baby will also be in danger."

"My baby will be in God's hands."

"That is easy for you to say now. You may feel differently once you hold your baby in your arms." Celia scooted off the bed and smoothed her skirts down. "You may stay and help—and you can change your mind any time you want."

"I will write to my mamá and let her know."

"And tell her about your papá. Tell her he died a martyr. Tell her he died with dignity and honor."

The thought of what that news would do to her mamá was more than she could bear. It would ruin her, and then what sort of a mamá would she be to Sofía and Catalina? How much harder would Josefina have to work to care for the little ones? Josefina was barely more than a child herself.

CHAPTER TWENTY-EIGHT

Celia and Carmina had been somber for days, always together and speaking in private whispers. After all the months Mariana had spent in their house, and knowing their routines, Celia indulged Carmina more than normal. She spent extra time with her and asked Socorro to cook Carmina's favorite dishes. Something big was about to happen, but nobody would tell Mariana what it was.

Late in the afternoon, Carmina took a long bath and emerged smelling of exotic perfume. She had arranged her hair and wore a brass diadem around her crown with an opal resting on her forehead, just like some exotic goddess. Instead of her dark mourning clothes, she wore a white blouse, red skirt, bracelets, and big hoop earrings—but by her countenance, this was no fiesta. Such an exquisitely beautiful woman, out alone and dressed in those clothes, was asking for trouble.

"You look beautiful," Mariana said.

"Sometimes, I wish I were ordinary. Then men would leave me alone to live my life." Carmina glanced down at Mariana's belly. "It is the same for you isn't it?"

Mariana fidgeted with the fringe on her shawl. She had

thought she was lucky to get the job with William, but it had nothing to do with her skills or how hard she worked.

Carmina looked up at the clock for the twentieth time, then at Celia, Mariana, and Socorro. "Will you pray with me?"

Without waiting for anyone to answer, Socorro went to the credenza, pulled open a drawer, and lifted out four lace veils. She passed them out to each woman before lighting three candles and draping lace over her own head.

Carmina pinched some ashes from the fireplace and sprinkled them onto her hair before covering it with her veil. Mariana had never seen that done before, but she had never lived with a warrior woman either. Carmina knelt before the crucifix and the statuettes of the *Virgen de Guadalupe* and *San Miguel*—still with their cracks and glue from when Celia pulled them from the ashes.

Mariana and Celia covered their heads with the veils and knelt beside Carmina and Socorro. Carmina prayed aloud. "O God, my father in heaven, hear me, a widow whose husband is a martyr and was executed for his faith. The federal army is a vast force who has defiled your sanctuaries, murdered your holy servants, and blasphemed your name. You are a God of the people, helper of those without power, supporter of the weak, protector of those in despair, and the savior of those without hope..."

The knock they had been anticipating came to the door. They all turned toward it, still on their knees before the altar. Celia and Carmina looked at one another in concern.

"They are early," Carmina said and rose to her feet. She removed her veil and handed it to Socorro.

"I have a bad feeling about tonight," Celia said.

"I will have an escort and they will be armed." Carmina's voice sounded unsure but resigned. She picked up a white shawl embroidered with red roses and draped it around her shoulders.

The knock came again, and Carmina opened the small window in the door.

"*Hola,*" a young male voice came through. "Telegram."

Carmina looked back at Celia, her eyes wide and uncertain.

"This is not part of the plan," Celia whispered.

Carmina put her fingers through the small window in the door. "Hurry, give it to me."

Celia slipped open a drawer on the credenza and withdrew a pistol. "You need to hide," she said to Mariana.

Mariana looked around for a spot but could not move. Since her baby would come in a few weeks, her belly was big and cumbersome.

"For the love of God!" Carmina shut the peephole and latched it. "He needs to be compensated."

Celia turned to Socorro with wide eyes. "Get some money. Quickly, he might ruin the entire mission."

Socorro hurried into the kitchen while Celia stood there with the pistol in the folds of her skirt.

"What if this is a ruse? What if he was sent to fool us?" Celia asked.

Carmina opened the little window and spoke through it. "It will only be a moment. We are getting you a big tip."

She closed it again and turned to whisper. "It might be something important about the…about my celebration tonight."

Socorro breezed back in with a coin purse that clinked a dull sound as she plopped it into Carmina's outstretched palm. Carmina worked to open the drawstring with quivering fingers and extracted several silver coins. She passed them through the window and returned with a telegram in hand.

They all stood silent and still while Carmina unfolded the paper. Her eyes scanned it then she let out an exasperated sigh.

"It's for you," she said and thrust the paper at Mariana.

Mamá? No good news would come to her by telegram. Mariana's hands trembled and hung by her side.

"Just take it."

Mariana took the paper and held it against her skirt.

"Not looking at it will not change whatever it is telling you," Celia said.

Mariana unfolded the paper. Across the top, in big black letters, was "Western Union Telegram." She had never received a telegram. "I FINALLY FOUND YOUR FAMILY SAW JOSE-FINA IN TIJUANA SHE TOLD ME WHAT HAS HAPPENED WHAT CAN I DO TO HELP SEND REPLY TO HEWITT AIRFIELD IN SANTIAGO YOUR FRIEND JENNY STRATTON"

"Is your family well?"

She nodded. The shock of seeing Jenny's name muddled her thoughts. Her baby churned and rotated inside her belly. "They are fine."

Someone else knocked sharply at the door.

Celia took Carmina in her arms and held her longer than normal. "Stay home this time. I will tell them you are ill."

"I will be back. I promise." Carmina peeked out the tiny window, verified the identities, and opened the door to two men in fancy suits, bow ties, and top hats. Their entire posture and demeanor changed the moment they set their eyes on Carmina's beauty.

"Allesandra?" the man with the thick mustache asked with admiration.

Celia reached out and grabbed Carmina's arm to stop her, but Carmina moved away and whispered, "May God guide my hand tonight," before she slipped out onto the dark street lit only by the hazy light of the street lamps.

Celia stood in the open doorway and stared at the spot where her sister had disappeared until the sound of a motorcar coming from the opposite direction caused her to close it. Celia draped the black veil over her head. She sunk back down to her knees in front of the credenza where, in the dim light of the flickering candles, the cracks in the saints could not be seen and they appeared whole and new. Mariana picked up her veil and knelt beside Celia.

Like a spirit, Socorro slipped into the room with a handful of red roses. She placed them at the feet of the figurine of the *Virgen de Guadalupe* before she knelt beside them and folded her own hands in prayer.

CHAPTER TWENTY-NINE

THE TELEGRAM MADE MARIANA WANT TO FALL INTO JENNY'S arms, grasp hold of her, and let Jenny pull her back to the time when she still had a brother and a papá. Back to a time when life was simple and the only thing that exhausted her was hard work and her whining baby sisters. It also made her want to scream at her for whirling up all the memories.

Jenny had tried to tell her something at the cemetery, but she did not need to. Mariana knew that Emilio had snuck out to meet her and that Emilio had died because of her. All this time, Mariana had tried to forget about Jenny. She was from a different life. She was from a life when Emilio and Papá still breathed the air and before she was a ghost daughter to her mamá.

Every night, Mariana lay in bed just on the other side of the door from where her papá was murdered. She hoped that his spirit would come in, trace the sign of the cross on her forehead, and forgive her. Her baby would be born at any time now and Mariana needed her papá.

Mariana went to the door that led to the patio. She put her hand on the iron bolt and ran her fingers over the metal. She wanted to slide the latch and step out into the night to the spot where Papá's spirit had lifted from his body. Carmina and Celia's warnings about keeping the door bolted and not opening it at night felt like a lump in her chest. Images of the *federales* with their guns, their squeaky leather boots, and evil black eyes made the lump grow and expand in her chest until she felt she could not breathe.

Mariana slid the bolt slow. A cold shiver ran up her spine as she creaked it open just wide enough to let a wash of moonlight in and to slip her body and big belly out. She pulled it shut behind her, so it would not draw the eye of any *federale* on the rooftops.

Slipping like a ghost in the night, she padded barefoot on the cold tiles to the spot on the wall where Papá had been shot. She put her hand to the plaster wall and felt for the holes made by the very bullets that had pierced through Papá. Her fingers passed over a chink in the wall, just about the height of Papá's heart. Putting her cheek to the spot, Mariana took in a deep breath where Papá had taken his last.

The sound of footsteps came from somewhere in the dark. Her baby turned and flipped inside her. Mariana hunched down against the wall, still and listening while she tried to slow her heartbeat and breath. The sound of a motorcar came from below and a dog barked somewhere in the distance. She could not hear any footsteps, but the feeling of being watched overwhelmed her. A *federale* could be standing right over the patio, looking down upon her, hunting and watching for any movement in the dark. Celia and Carmina would be furious with her for not listening. How could she be so stupid?

She heard footsteps again. This time, they stepped hard and faded away. He must not have seen her. Mariana rose slow. She kept her body against the wall and her eyes on the door. She moved, quiet with bare feet, and held breath until she finally had her hand on the door. She slipped in and slid the bolt shut.

Pain spread across Mariana's lower back. She needed to lie down. Mariana lit her altar candle on her bedside table. She needed to burn it for Papá and for Emilio—whose spirit Jenny had agitated with her telegram.

The baby turned over inside her again, more active than usual, pressing on her heart and her ribs. After dozing off and on for half the night, Mariana finally slid out of bed and into the dark hall, lit only by the dim light coming from the candle in her room and the light rising up the stairwell.

Downstairs, Celia sat on the couch staring at the tiny flames in the fireplace.

"Can I join you?"

Celia looked up, dazed like she just realized Mariana stood before her. "You should be sleeping."

"The baby and I have been tossing all night."

Socorro padded barefoot into the room.

"I guess none of us can sleep. Can you make us some…"

Someone pounded on the door and caused Celia to jump from the couch. She looked out the viewer and unlatched the door in one fluid movement. Carmina rushed in, shaking with her shawl pulled over her face. As soon as Celia latched the door, Carmina dropped her shawl, now smeared with blood. She held a knife. Her hand shook and was covered in blood up to her wrist. Her white shirt had red splatters all over it and her diadem sat crooked on her head.

"I killed him," Carmina said.

Socorro slipped away.

"Who?" Celia asked. "Who did you kill?"

"The General."

Celia's eyes filled with fear.

"Which General? You killed a General? God protect us."

"General Almondos Espinal Ballestero," Carmina said. "I slit his throat."

"Is that what you were sent to do?"

"I need a priest," Carmina said. "I need absolution."

"You did what you had to do," Celia said. "Come, let's wash it away."

In the kitchen, Socorro hurried to prepare supplies and towels. She took a bottle of iodine and bandages from a shelf. Steam rose from a large pot of water on the stove.

The name, General Ballestero, had been spoken by her cousins many times. He had ordered the massacre of an entire village. His soldiers raped the women before killing them, then sat down at their tables to eat their food. He was also responsible for the execution of Father Oseas Escalante Carvajal and the attack on the Cathedral del Sagrado Corazón de Jesus where nine people were killed, including children.

"You did what you had to. The General would never have ceased his attacks. You took one life to save many others."

"Maybe that should be for God to decide."

"Maybe he did—by your hand." Celia stood close to her sister and unbuttoned her blouse "Let's get you out of these."

The knife dropped from Carmina's hand and clanked onto the tiles with blood still on the handle and blade.

"I killed him," Carmina said.

"Are you sure?"

"Yes."

Mariana remembered waiting outside the church in Tijuana, helpless, while the soldier had raped her mamá. Secretly, even though it was a sin, she felt happy that Carmina had killed him.

"May God forgive me," Carmina said.

"God forgive the General." Mariana's words sounded harsh, unlike herself.

Both of her cousins looked at her in surprise.

"He has committed countless mortal sins, not you."

Celia peeled her sister's shirt off, unbuttoned the waist of her skirt, and let it drop to her feet like an extra skin.

"Step over it." Celia guided her sister forward. Socorro took the shirt and skirt to the stove and was about to drop them into the steaming pot.

"No!" Carmina stood there in her chemise and slip. "Burn them."

"We should not waste," Celia said.

"They are bad luck." Carmina stood there with skinny arms and a delicate frame. She looked unable to harm anyone, and yet, there she stood, trembling and covered in blood.

A gush of warm water broke from Mariana and ran down her inner thighs. All the water she had been drowning in since she had arrived, spilled out onto the floor. It puddled around the knife and caused a pink halo to form around it. Mariana, Celia, and Carmina stared down at it, silent and not comprehending, until Socorro said, "The baby is coming."

"I'm sorry." Mariana's entire body began to shake.

"For what?" Celia guided her toward the stairs.

"Carmina needs you now, not me."

"A baby is a blessing," Carmina said from behind her, but Mariana knew different. A baby was not a blessing on a day blackened by death.

CHAPTER THIRTY

MARIANA KNEW NOTHING ABOUT CHILDBIRTH OTHER THAN THE closed-door dreadful screams of her mamá when Sofía and Catalina were born and the panting bloody birth of the neighbor's puppies. Celia held onto Mariana with one hand and unbuttoned her blouse with the other while Socorro placed an oilcloth on the bed. Celia took hold of the bottom of Mariana's chemise.

"No." Mariana held it down. She could not let them see her like that.

"This is not the time for modesty."

Tears slid down Mariana's face. How much more humiliation could she endure? She had allowed William to completely know her body. And in pregnancy, the world could see what she had done.

"It will be all right, *Mija*," Celia said. "We are all women and we have all experienced childbirth. Your clothes will only get in the way or be ruined."

Socorro stood beside the bed and stared back with her clay face and the body of a child. She had given birth? Where were her children?

"As soon as I take your clothes off, you will lie down on the bed, and I will cover you."

Celia's words caused her chest to constrict. She did not deserve her tenderness. Mariana doubled over with an agonizing pain. When it ended, Celia pulled off her chemise and left her bare and heavy breasts for everyone to see. Mariana covered them with her hands while Celia unbuttoned her skirt and let it fall down Mariana's legs into a ring of fabric around her feet. Her bloomers, wet and clinging to her legs, were shed by Socorro until Mariana stood in all her shame before them— naked and swollen with the end of her braided hair brushing the top of her stomach.

Celia led her to the bed and steadied her while she stepped onto the stool. "Lie down and try to relax."

How could she relax with such terrible pain, Carmina's agony, and all the spirits of the memories Jenny's telegram had brought with it? What would she do with a baby and how would she care for it? She could not free her mind from the images of her train ride, of the bullet-ridden villages with crumbling walls and poor unbathed and wide-eyed children—hungry and sad with their hands out, calling, *For the love of God.*

Celia stood by the side of the bed and ran her hand up and down Mariana's arm. Socorro returned with strips of cloth, herbs, and a stone mortar and pestle. Carmina entered. She had changed back into her black mourning clothes, looking stark— like a completely different woman than she had hours earlier on her way to carry out her murderous plan. A sharp pain pierced through Mariana and pushed out a horrible scream she could not believe came from her mouth.

Between pains, Celia soothed her while Carmina mumbled prayers and worked a rosary. Socorro tended to Mariana with a blank face and silent mouth.

Tears dripped down Carmina's cheeks and onto her hand that worked the rosary. When she finished, she put the beads to her lips. "I cannot stop thinking of his face when he realized what I had done."

Mariana had another pain, one so strong it burned and pierced her from spine to navel. Birth alone should be repentance for a woman's mortal sin.

Carmina sat with her nerves on edge. "That was when I saw his humanity. That was the moment he was nothing more than a man."

"Try not to think about it," Celia said. "You did what you were told."

Socorro wiped Mariana's forehead with a damp cloth. Her tiny hands, scarred and tough as a rabbit hide, never stopped tucking, wrapping, or wiping.

"I lay with him." Carmina confessed to Celia as if it would lift the burden from her soul. "They brought me to his fiesta as a concubine. I did not have an opportunity to fulfill my mission until afterward when he lay spent beside me."

A long silence swallowed the room. Finally, Celia broke it with her soothing voice. "We will need a priest for the baby's baptism. While he is here, you can ask to give your confession."

"How can I admit such a thing to a priest?" Carmina asked.

"How can you not?"

The waiting, the praying, and the pain went on for hours. Carmina sat in the corner with her head tipped against the wall, stiff and turning to salt. She would doze off, only to be jolted awake by Mariana's screams.

"You should go to bed," Celia said. "We will be here with Mariana."

"I'm afraid of what will come to my mind if I am alone. What if his seed takes root in me?"

Celia rose and went to her sister. She knelt beside her and took her hand.

Eventually, Mariana's pains came quick, one after another,

unceasing. She was going to die right there in the bed. Right there with William's child tearing her from the inside out.

"It is time." Socorro pushed Mariana's feet apart.

Celia signaled Carmina, who rose and came to Mariana. Her cousins stood on either side and each one took a hand. Celia assured Mariana that soon she would hold her baby, and the pain would be forgotten.

They gripped Mariana's hands to give her solid support when she pushed. The veins in her head throbbed and felt as if they would burst. Her insides ripped apart. She would never be the same. She would never be whole.

With a final spine-piercing pain, the baby slipped out, and just like Celia said, the pain went with it.

"A boy." Socorro lifted him up, wet and limp.

Mariana's chest wracked with deep and gulping sobs. Her baby came out with his fists clenched tight, ready to fight. Waxy patches of white velvet lay in the creases of his thighs and armpits. He let out a single wail as he began breathing in the air. Socorro set the baby on Mariana's belly and tied a string around the cord.

Socorro took hold of Carmina's wrist and placed a pair of scissors in her hand. "You will cut one more time tonight. This one will bring forth life."

Carmina shook her head and motioned to Celia. "You should do it."

Socorro held the cord up to Carmina. Carmina looked to Mariana then to Celia. "I am not pure."

"In the service of God," Celia said. "Your strength should set him into this world. God knows he will need it."

"Yes," Mariana said. "I would like that."

Socorro grabbed Carmina's hand and guided it toward the baby. "Above the string."

Carmina cut the cord and stood there sobbing. Socorro took

the baby to a basin, squeezed warm water over him, wiped him down, and wrapped him in a blanket.

"He is a beautiful boy," Celia said. "You should be proud."

Tears slid from the corners of Mariana's eyes when Socorro placed the baby on her chest.

"Do you have a name for him?" Celia asked.

"Yes," Mariana said, "I am naming him for my brother, Emilio."

CHAPTER THIRTY-ONE

MARIANA NEVER TIRED OF STARING AT LITTLE EMILIO AS HE SLEPT —at his perfectly formed face and his tiny fingers. He slept next to her in the wooden rocking cradle Celia had used for her sons. Emilio had become the sole focus of her days, and her lone purpose for living. She may be a ghost daughter and a ghost sister, but she had Emilio and his warm flesh was the only thing real that tied her to the earth.

Her poor baby boy was born on the same day Carmina had killed the general and the same day José de León Toral was executed for assassinating President-elect Obregón. Little Emilio had been born on the souls of an enemy general and a martyr, so hopefully, they would balance out the bad luck.

Mariana gave her son a blessing every night and set a glassful of water behind their bedroom door to absorb any negative energy. Socorro tied a piece of black amber to his wrist to ward off the evil eye and Celia and Carmina placed a statuette of *San Nicolás* above his cradle—for they all knew he needed protection.

When Emilio slept, Mariana translated letters for the Cristeros. Most of them were to the Knights of Columbus and world leaders in the United States, pleading for intervention or financial support—telling them of the atrocities committed by Calles who still controlled the government through President Portis Gil. And trying to get them to understand the Mexican government was massacring whole villages of its own people, men, women, and children simply for wanting their religion.

Translating was far more difficult than she had first imagined. There were terms she was not familiar with. Between Celia's explanations, a Spanish dictionary, and an English dictionary, she worked her way through the correspondence.

She also answered Jenny's telegram in care of the Hewitt Airfield in Santiago. Unless Jenny wanted to join a war she had nothing to do with, she could not be of any help to Mariana—but she could help Mamá and her sisters. In her letter, she asked Jenny if she could financially help her family in Tijuana. It was a lot to ask from her, but Jenny was the root from which all their troubles had grown. Emilio was killed because of her and Jenny's own father had deported Mariana's family.

It would have to be in secret, though. Mamá would not touch Jenny's money and Mariana did not trust Lázaro's greedy hands. Josefina was their only hope. Mariana explained that Jenny must approach Josefina without Mamá knowing. She also wrote out exactly what Jenny should tell Josefina and what she should do with the money.

Mariana unraveled her messy braid and ran the comb through the long strands. Her hair had always been so long, it brushed the top of her waist—except for once when she was nine years old and Jenny cut it off.

Jenny had told Mariana that they would be playing hairdresser, and she led her into the grove, away from all the people. Jenny had always coveted Mariana's hair and told her that when she grew up, she would have big girl hair like Mariana's instead of the fine straw-color hair she had.

While Mariana sat on the bank of the river, Jenny knelt

behind her. She brushed and braided Mariana's hair into a single long rope. While Mariana sat like an idiot, eating an orange and staring out over the river, she felt something strange, an odd tugging and sawing. She asked Jenny what she was doing and Jenny told her to sit still—and of course she did, Mariana always complied with the wishes of others.

With a final snipping sound, Mariana turned to see Jenny with a pair of scissors in one hand and the shiny foot-long cord of her hair hanging over Jenny's hand like a dead snake. Even seeing her hair in Jenny's hand, she did not believe that she would do that to her—until she touched the back of her head to feel nothing but her neck and the chopped ends.

Papá had grounded Mariana for a month and did not allow her out of Mamá's sight for letting Jenny cut off her hair. Jenny had come to the house to apologize, tell him it wasn't Mariana's fault, and confess that she had tricked Mariana.

Papá's face, tight and frog-like, reddened as Jenny spoke. He stood there at the mercy of a nine-year-old and unable to castigate her because she was the daughter of El Patrón—and the owner of the land where their house sat. The moment Jenny left their house, Papá turned to Mariana, and with a tight and sour face, he said, "The shrimp that falls asleep is carried by the current."

Emilio stirred on the bed next to her. His tiny lips moved and he nursed in his dream. He was so perfect that her heart ached. She did not deserve him and prayed that God would not take him from her.

Papá was right. She had always been a shrimp carried by the current. She had been swept up by both Jenny and William, people she loved. Right now, for the first time, she chose which stream to swim in. Joining the Cristeros to fight for religious freedom for Emilio's future and to honor her papá was what *she* wanted to do.

Two weeks later, when Emilio's umbilical cord fell off in his diaper, Socorro placed a silver coin on the area and wrapped it with a cloth to keep his navel from poking out.

When Mariana and her cousins discussed the burial of Emilio's umbilical stump, Mariana wanted to find the hacienda where her own umbilical stump had been buried, because where a person's umbilical stump is buried, is the place their heart belongs forever. She wanted Emilio to belong to the same place as her. Celia told her it was too dangerous and assured Mariana that they would find a place close by. Both would be buried in the state of Jalisco, which was close enough.

A few days later, Celia announced that she had found a garden that belonged to some friends—Manuel and Rosa. Rosa was a captain in the brigade, and Manuel ran the underground press, *El Cielo*. If the wall where Papá had been shot had soil beneath it, Mariana would have buried it there. Maybe it was for the best that it didn't. Maybe that would have brought even more bad luck on her poor baby.

The day of the burial was the first time Mariana left the sanctuary of her cousins' house since papá's funeral. All the women: Celia, Carmina, Socorro, and Mariana, slipped out the front door quietly. The first step into the street with Emilio clutched to her chest was the most difficult. Mariana cradled her child, completely wrapped and hidden in blankets, while she stared straight ahead, afraid to draw attention to their little procession.

Out of the corners of her eyes, she watched the potbellied town men in their little black hats, the dark-skinned Indios in huaraches, and the old women dressed in greasy black satin with white powdered faces. She tried to listen for the tap of soldier's boots through the clamor of streetcar bells, the clomp of burro hooves on the stone, and street vendors calling out for customers. Life kept moving forward, even in a city heavy with death.

Carmina took them down a narrow alley lined with foul-smelling garbage cans. The buildings in the city took up an entire block with individual homes and businesses recognizable only by the number of doors and barred windows. Carmina stopped at an archway with a thick wooden door.

"This is it." Carmina slipped a key into the latch. When she opened the door, they stepped into a large hidden garden teeming with the thick green leaves of banana plants, mango, and orange trees—like a tiny Eden abundant with life in a city tainted with corruption, death, and hate. They dug a hole in a shady spot beneath a group of orange trees that felt perfect to honor the spirit of her brother Emilio, as well as an enchanted place with rich soil. It was a good omen for her baby.

CHAPTER THIRTY-TWO

ON THE MORNING OF EMILIO'S BAPTISM, MARIANA ROSE EARLY. After nursing him and putting him back to sleep in the cradle, she wandered downstairs to find Celia arranging the living room with a baptismal font, dozens of candles, and white crepe paper flowers to make the room look as sanctified as possible. She used a large enamel basin for the font and set it on top of the credenza that she had draped with a white cloth.

Even with all the festive decorations, fear tickled Mariana's spine. This was the first sacrament held at their house since the raid. The ghosts of the memories of the people coming to the door with their passwords and dropping to their knees, her Papá not letting her take communion, and of the soldiers skittering through the house like rats, appeared in the corners of her eyes, but when she turned to look, they were no longer there.

And worse of all, the spirits of her papá and uncles marching to the roof at gunpoint. Emilio would have softened Papá's heart. She knew that he would have bounced him on his knee and sung, *Little pony, little pony, do not throw me, galloping, galloping, watch us go—Long live Emilio!*, and he would have tucked him into bed at night and traced the sign of the cross on Emilio's forehead to bless him while he slept.

Carmina came downstairs holding a small gift wrapped in white tissue. She looked to Celia for approval before extending the package to Mariana. "This is not new, but it is treasured. Celia and I would like to give it to Emilio for his baptism."

The present was the size of Mariana's palm and tied with a white ribbon. Beneath the tissue, she uncovered a silver scallop shell dipper with intricate ribbing and a cross on the hilt.

"It is for the priest to scoop the holy water for Emilio's baptism," Celia said.

Mariana nodded. She knew what it was but could not speak for all the kindness her cousins had shown to her. "It is beautiful and more than Emilio or I deserve."

Mariana had asked Celia to be Emilio's godmother. Before she had a chance to ask either of them, Carmina suggested that Emilio deserved a godmother with a purer heart than she had, and she had cut his umbilical cord anyway. It was perfect for Emilio to be cut free by Carmina's strength and to be brought to the Lord with Celia's heart.

She had a problem finding a godfather. Since her cousins were off fighting, and Mariana did not know any men in Guadalajara, Celia provided him with a godfather—Manuel Valentín Acosta, the owner of the garden where they had buried Emilio's umbilical stump. The connection with the garden made him an appropriate choice and gave him a tie with Emilio. She would meet him just before the baptism when he arrived with the priest.

MARIANA FINISHED BUTTONING the white satin jacket of Emilio's baptismal suit that Celia lent to her. It had been the one Celia's own sons wore for their christenings. The embroidered silver satin with intricate designs made Emilio look like a tiny torero in white, ready for his first bullfight.

At seven weeks old, Emilio was an easy baby, and nothing like Catalina had been. He slept, ate, and spent his time smiling, laughing, or making tiny baby noises. Catalina had wailed and wailed, which caused the family to take turns walking the room with her.

Emilio was the most beautiful baby in the world with his dark hair and long eyelashes. He had her nose and big almond-shaped eyes, except they were blue like Williams's. He also had her brother Emilio's big smile that made all of their hearts sweet on him. Mariana even caught Socorro's stone face cracking smiles at him.

Mariana wrapped Emilio in the white blanket that Carmina had made for him and lifted him from the bed. On the other side of the hallway, Celia sat writing at the desk in her office with neat piles of envelopes, letters, and ledgers all around her.

"He's ready," Mariana said from the doorway.

"Oh, look at him," Celia said. "He is such a handsome baby."

Celia kissed the top of his head. Go on downstairs. I need to put these away and I will be right behind you. As they waited for the priest and Manuel, Celia, Carmina, and Mariana sat in the front room taking turns holding Emilio and listening for the bells from the underground passage. Their sound was not like the deep gong of the church bells but more like the *ding, ding* of a priest's bell just before he placed his hands over the bread and wine to consecrate them. Her own Papá had come up with the idea of the bells. He had attached a small rope underground that branched off to the kitchen, Celia's bedroom, and her office that alerted them when someone arrived in the secret passage below.

The dim lights and flickering candles transformed the living room into something holy that caused the women to speak in whispers. The sounds of Socorro preparing the food in the kitchen and the ticking of the grandfather clock made the wait seem eternal. Mariana's entire time in Guadalajara lay on the edge of waiting for something to happen.

Finally, the bells rang—mysterious and emanating from below the earth. They all went to the kitchen where Socorro had just finished preparing enchiladas in white sauce and bread pudding for the celebration.

When Celia opened the pantry door and pulled open the shelves, a short round man with black whiskers, a black suit, and a little black hat peered up from the bottom of the steps.

"Manuel!" Carmina said. "Thank you and welcome."

He climbed up and into the kitchen, followed by a woman in a canary-yellow chiffon dress. She wore so much light face powder over her dark skin that she looked dusty and parched, like an apparition rising up from the dry earth.

"It is nice to see you, Rosa," Celia said. "You look beautiful."

Below them stood a priest, surrounded by men with straps of bullets across their chests and guns clutched in their hands. All the Catholic priests of Mexico were either fugitives or bandits and therefore had to travel underground or in disguise.

The priest climbed and slowly ascended through the pantry in white lace vestments embroidered with gold thread. His sleeve was dirty at the cuffs and swayed back and forth like a hammock when he reached a hand up for Manuel to steady him.

Some priests had turned half-priest, half-soldier, and fought for the right to hold mass and give the sacraments. Based on the age of this priest, he could not be a soldier or a bandit. She imagined they kept him hidden and escorted him around to deliver the sacraments for select occasions. She did not know how the christening of her son merited his presence but figured it had to do with the rank of Celia and Carmina in the Women's Brigade.

Once the priest reached the top, both Celia and Carmina stepped forward, bent down, and kissed his ring. Celia motioned for Mariana to do the same. Father Hugo Ruiz de la Cruz looked to be ninety years old, almost skeletal except for the thin layer of papery skin. His eyes floated in fleshy sockets, red-rimmed and watery, and he had an air of peace and love. Mariana felt honored to have this ancient and holy man give her baby the sacrament.

Two of the armed men, both dark skinned and stoic, followed the priest up into the kitchen. The rest stayed down in the cavern, armed and waiting like a pack of armadillos in a burrow. Since there was such a demand for Father de la Cruz's time and it was dangerous for him to be there, they moved straight to the front room to commence with the baptism. Usually, both parents and the godparents stood up with the baby, but Emilio had no Papá.

Mariana held Emilio with Celia and Manuel on either side of her. Carmina, Socorro, and Rosa sat on the couch as witnesses. The priest welcomed everyone and reminded them that children are gifts from God and the sources of new life.

"What name do you give your child?" he asked in a milky voice.

"Emilio Hector Castillo," Mariana said.

"What do you ask of the church for this child?"

"Baptism," Mariana, Celia, and Manuel all answered in unison.

After consecrating the baptismal water, Father de la Cruz offered prayers in Latin and traced the sign of the cross on Emilio's forehead. He chanted, *Ego te baptizo in nomine Patris et Filii et Spiritus Sancti*, baptizing him in the name of the Father, and of the Son, and of the Holy Spirit while he scooped the Holy Water over his head three times. After more prayers, and just as he was about to anoint him with oil, excited voices came from the kitchen.

The priest only hesitated a second, then continued dabbing the oil on Emilio's chest and chanting more prayers. Mariana,

Celia, and Manuel kept glancing toward the kitchen. Socorro sat perched on the edge of the couch, ready to dart away.

The voices became louder, a mix of male and female. Father de la Cruz prayed in a soft and unwavering tone. Manuel seemed barely able to stay put and kept turning his head toward the kitchen and back.

The priest picked up the baptismal candle and handed it to Manuel, who lit the wick from an Easter candle flickering next to the font. Manuel stood there with his rapid breaths blowing the flame in a frantic dance and threatening to extinguish it. The voices turned to scuffles in the kitchen and the only thing holding them all in the living room was the priest's unwavering prayers. He placed his fingers on Emilio's ears and mouth saying, *Alabanza y gloria de Dios Padre.*

In the middle of the Lord's prayer, a woman burst into the living room. She froze when she noticed the priest and what she had interrupted. One of the armed Cristeros grabbed her from behind. He pulled her backward and she called out, "Excuse me, Father. Sorry for…"

The Cristero was so rough that the woman would have hit the ground if he did not have such a hold on her arm. Father de la Cruz finished the Lord's prayer, blessed Emilio, Mariana, the godparents, and everyone in the room before finally turning toward the kitchen.

The Cristero guards stood over the woman, who was now seated in a chair. Tendrils of dark hair stuck out of her braid, and she had rings of sweat under her arms.

"What has happened?" Celia asked, then addressed the men. "You can let her be. She is one of my Captains."

"They have found us out," she panted. "They have discovered us women. Many are being arrested and the soldiers are now searching all women for ammunition."

"Right now?"

"At this moment."

Without a word of protest, the ancient priest allowed the men to whisk him back down and into the tunnel. Emilio had received his baptism, but Carmina did not get the chance to have her confession. She needed absolution, and now she would not have it.

CHAPTER THIRTY-THREE

MARIANA TRIED TO SWALLOW, BUT HER TONGUE STUCK TO THE roof of her mouth while she followed the dark shape of Carmina through the tunnel. With the discovery of the brigades, the women had to be especially cautious. Carmina refused to let it delay their supplies to the Cristeros, so she took on extra tasks and needed Mariana to do more than translate.

Their path was lit only by one kerosene lantern and they headed to God knows where. Only dead people and rodents walked beneath the earth. She belonged in the open air, not in a narrow passage in the throat of the city—beneath its cathedral, its heavy buildings, and all the burros and motorcars.

"Are there earthquakes in Guadalajara?"

Carmina stopped and turned around to face Mariana. With her lantern between them, it cast strange shadows and ghostly distortions on her features. "What?"

"There were earthquakes in California where I lived. Do you have them here?"

"We have terrible earthquakes that shake down our buildings." With a teasing smile, she added, "And collapse our tunnels.

It is such a nuisance to remove all the debris, especially the dead bodies."

Her lantern swung and threw light and shadow across her face. Carmina put emphasis on the word *bodies* and let out a laugh. "Are you afraid of a tunnel? *Dios mío.* I assure you, it is safer to travel in the tunnels than on the streets with the *federales* searching all the women. Even if we are crushed by the rocks, it would be an easier death than the soldiers would give us."

"But…" Mariana was not looking for any sort of death, whether by torture or suffocation. If the soldiers found the tunnels, they could easily gas them out and eradicate them like pests—just like Walt used to do on Stratton Ranch with his truck exhaust.

"The faster we go, and the sooner you stop asking questions, the more rapidly we will be out," Carmina said.

Mariana followed her across uneven planks of wood for what seemed an eternity, sometimes passing by alcoves with crude wooden ladders that led up from the damp and airless passage. She had not been so far away from Emilio since the day he was born. Her arms felt empty—and what if she never returned to him?

Carmina finally stopped at the end of the passage, but once they got to it, it turned out to be an intersection of sorts that branched off three ways. She turned to the right, and within steps, she stopped again at an alcove and withdrew a clanking ring of keys from her pocket.

"Hold this." Carmina extended the lantern to Mariana.

She flipped through the keys, each with a different color paint on the top. She chose one with a red stripe. "Hold the light up so I can see."

"What's up there?"

"Why do you ask questions when you are about to find out?"

"I want to know what to expect."

"You sound like an Anglo."

"What do you mean?"

"Needing to know everything ahead of you. You will enjoy life more if you stop talking and take time to wonder at what unfolds before you."

"Maybe I want to prepare myself."

"What will you do to prepare yourself? You are in a tunnel with nothing. Be quiet now." Carmina shook her head, turned, and placed her foot on the first rung of the ladder.

She climbed to the top and stopped at a trap door above her. Carmina cocked her head and listened before placing both palms on the door and pushing it open. She climbed through, disappeared, and left Mariana alone in nothing but a ring of light.

Suddenly, Carmina's head popped back over the hole and she stared down at Mariana. "I thought you wanted out of the tunnel. Come on."

Mariana climbed up and passed the lantern to Carmina. At the top of the ladder, she scrambled out of the hole and into a room as small as their outhouse in Santiago. Carmina placed her ear to a closed door before sliding the key she had selected into the lock.

They stepped into the light of a long hallway lined with windows that looked out onto an arched breezeway and a courtyard where two red-tasseled burros stood facing a wall with their heads down. A breath of bad odor drifted on the air and grew thicker and thicker as they walked.

The hallway spilled out into a large room crammed with beds and pallets—all of them filled with women and children and old men. The smell of unwashed bodies, urine, and something rancid constricted Mariana's throat and made her feel as if she would get sick. Every face looked tense with pain or slack in despair. Children sat, unnaturally still, at the side of their mamá, grandfather, sister, or tiny brother.

One woman, whose head was wrapped in cloth with a large spot of blood seeping through, had three small children huddling at the foot of her bed. Everyone had some sort of an injury, from scrapes to gashes, to splinted arms and legs. All the injuries were external and evident, not due to sickness but to attack.

Every eye followed Mariana and Carmina while they wove through and looked for bare spots on the ground to place their feet. People shifted and leaned to let them pass. Big-eyed children with dirty feet and wounds wrapped in cotton fabric held their hands out. Carmina reached into her satchel and dropped small chunks of bread and boiled eggs into their palms. Mariana smiled in apology that she had nothing to give.

A tall and slender red-cheeked nurse, who looked to be in her late twenties, approached Carmina with her hands out and a big smile on her face. Her dark-brown hair was twisted-up, neat but not severe, beneath her cap.

"Señora Allesandra," she said to Carmina. "It gives my heart joy to see you."

"Antonia!" Carmina gave a slight, almost imperceptible bow. "Let me introduce you to my cousin, Isabella."

It took a moment for Mariana to realize she was referring to her. It was a good name.

"Delighted to meet you," she said with a smile. "I see that beauty runs in your family."

"It is more of a curse than a blessing," Carmina said and removed her satchel. "We have some medical supplies."

"You are an angel." Antonia motioned for them to follow. She led them to a storage closet with brooms and cleaning supplies, and also half-empty shelves scattered with bandages, iodine, scissors, and medicines.

After Carmina and Mariana emptied their satchels, Carmina turned to Antonia in the cramped space. "Will you give us a prayer, Sister?" she whispered.

Sister? She was a nun?

Antonia closed the door to the closet and the three of them dropped their heads. She prayed so quietly that only God and the angels could hear every one of her words. When she finished, Carmina kissed her hand.

Back out in the hospital, swarms of fat lazy flies droned in the open windows and landed on the people, some of whom were too tired to shoo them away. They let them buzz around their heads, poke about their wounds, and probe for a place to lay their eggs.

A woman with untidy dark hair and a milk-soaked blouse leaned up against one wall with no baby in her arms. Her hands hung limp at her sides but her body still rocked as if she had a baby to soothe.

Thankfully, Carmina kept walking. She led Mariana to the other side of the building where a woman sat behind a desk. Mariana expected Carmina to stop and speak to the woman, but she only greeted her and placed some money on the counter before stepping out into a courtyard that smelled of manure. An old bewhiskered man crouched on the ground and stared off ignoring them. Up close, the festive-looking burros had dusty coats and flies buzzing around their eyes.

When they stepped outside the courtyard, Mariana realized they were no longer in the city, but on the outskirts with low-slung adobe huts lining the street.

"Is Antonia a nun?"

"Shhh," Carmina said and glanced around. "Most nurses in Mexico are of religious orders. They must serve clandestinely or they will be deported or killed."

"What happened to all those people in the hospital?" Mariana asked.

"Their village was attacked by federal soldiers."

"How can the government win the favor of their people if they massacre them?"

"They don't need their favor," Carmina said. "They only need fear and subservience."

Carmina took Mariana down the lane and past a spring cluttered with women doing their wash. The further they walked, the more rural the landscape became until they reached a hacienda with fallow fields and a squat cluster of adobe huts in the distance. A wrought-iron gate squeaked when she swung it open and stepped into a neglected courtyard with weeds growing up through the cobbles. Carmina lifted the giant ring of the knocker and pounded it on the heavy wooden door with three strikes. The peephole in the door slid open, and a set of small black eyes stared out. Carmina nodded her head and the door swung open.

"*Hola*, Yatzil," Carmina said to the small Indio woman who let them inside. "Is Esmerelda waiting for us?"

With the nod of her head, she led Mariana and Carmina into the house. The elaborate hacienda was filled with heavy leather-studded furniture and several generations of family portraits. Based on the clothing and style, they looked as if they could have come right off the walls of a Spanish palace.

Yatzil led them into a study where an elegant woman, dressed in a high-collared emerald green gown and looking as Victorian as Jenny's mother back in Santiago, sat waiting on a sofa. She stood when Carmina approached, and the two women kissed one another on each cheek as if they were old and dear friends.

Carmina introduced her as Esmeralda.

Esmeralda looked Mariana over from head to foot with bewilderment on her face. "There is something not Mexican about her."

Carmina looked as if she could barely contain her laughter. "She was raised in the United States."

"That is it," Esmeralda said with a smile thrown in Mariana's direction. "I'm sure Carmina will cure you of it."

"There is a lot Carmina needs to cure me of," Mariana said.

She gave a short laugh. I hear the women in the United States cut their hair short and wear pants. Is that correct?"

"The younger women do."

"The men of the United States must be in mourning for the loss of their women," Esmeralda said.

"The women of the United States have the freedom to dress as they please and the men have adapted to it," Mariana said. Afraid that she had insulted her, she added, "Men's libidos are sometimes louder than their reason."

"That is a universal trait of all men." Esmeralda smiled, then looked over to Carmina. "I think I like your cousin."

Mariana took a deep breath. She had not realized how tightly her fists had been clinched under the scrutiny of this woman.

"We need to speak for a moment," Esmeralda said to Yatzil.

Mariana figured she was dismissing the servant until Yatzil placed her hand on Mariana's arm and guided her toward the door.

Mariana followed Yatzil into a kitchen where giant black cooking pots and skillets hung from a wrought-iron ring attached to the ceiling of the enormous room. A fire flickered beneath a black pot that hung on an iron hook in the fireplace. The smell of onions and garlic rose with the steam. A woman who looked very much like Jenny's housekeeper, Señora Hernández, stood before a giant metal table slicing chunks of red meat into strips with a cleaver.

The sight of the woman gave Mariana a pang of homesickness, She remembered Señora's stories of hummingbirds, armadillos, coyotes, and Pepita, the girl who had no gift to offer the Christ child. Señora used to tell her and Jenny the stories as they sat on the back kitchen step while Señora tended her garden.

Yatzil led her all the way through the kitchen and to a small leather stool outside. Mariana took in the beautiful, but neglected hacienda. Past a well-tended vegetable garden and chicken coop, there were empty corrals with weeds growing inside them and a barn with smaller pens on the far side of it.

When Carmina finally appeared, she was with Yatzil but not Esmeralda. The servant girl took them to the barn, opened a padlock, and unraveled a chain that held the doors shut. When she swung them open, light swept across the wings and propellers of airplanes—so many planes that two of them hung from the rafters.

"The Cristeros have an air fleet?"

"No."

"Is Esmeralda's husband a Cristero?"

"You ask too many questions," Carmina said. "Esmeralda's husband is a federal general and she is Calles's cousin."

"Ex-President Calles? The former President of Mexico, Calles?"

"Yes, the very one who pulls President Portes Gil's strings."

"Are we stealing the airplanes of a federal general? What if we get caught? Will we be executed?"

"How would you and I steal an airplane? We are here for the ammunition." Carmina grabbed a crowbar and headed toward a wooden barrel. "But, yes, if we are caught, we will be executed—whether it's airplanes or ammunition, it does not matter."

CHAPTER THIRTY-FOUR

MARIANA LAY IN BED WITH EMILIO BESIDE HER. SHE FINISHED nursing him, and now he rested on his stomach gnawing on the edge of the pillowcase. For all his unfortunate circumstances, he was a blessing that she did not deserve. He depended on her for everything, but she had nothing other than the charity of her cousins.

Soon, she might not have a house for Emilio either. Women all over Guadalajara, Mexico City, and the outlying villages were being arrested, kidnapped, or killed. The tinkle of bells ringing from the tunnels became a regular sound in the household as people brought news, and with every ringing bell, the odds of them being discovered increased.

What would happen to Emilio if the soldiers came to arrest them? Or kill them? Would the soldiers line them up against the wall of the patio and lay their blood and bullet holes over the top of her papá's and uncles? Would the soldiers shoot little Emilio? Would he end up in an orphanage? Or would they leave him in the empty house to slowly die alone?

The bells rang again in Celia's office across the hall. Emilio rolled over onto his back, which seemed to surprise and delight him. He gave Mariana a big smile and cooed.

"Do you think you are a big boy now?" Mariana tickled him under his chin. "Next thing you know, you will be leaving me for…"

She almost said *school*, but that was another thing her poor baby would not have. She would not allow the government to turn her son against his religion—against God and the saints who could protect him.

Jenny had sent a letter and it sat on her bedside table. She wrote to tell her that she was giving money to Josefina and she offered to come to Guadalajara to bring Mariana home with her to Santiago. But Mariana did not want to go. She and Emilio did not belong in the United States where the schools would not let him speak his own language and where the teachers would make him feel dirty and incapable of learning anything more than basic arithmetic and writing—Americanizing him and robbing him of his culture.

She wanted to stay in Guadalajara, where her son belonged, and where she had been born. She wanted to stay in Mexico to fight for her people and her religion so maybe one day, Emilio could attend a Catholic school with his own people, his own culture, and his own God.

The bells rang again.

"It is time for us to get dressed," Mariana said to Emilio. "You may have had your breakfast, but I have not had mine."

Mariana pinned a new diaper onto Emilio and put a clean sleeping gown on him before she dressed. Just as she finished buttoning her blouse, the bells rang again and a wailing cry rose up from the kitchen. Mariana scooped Emilio up and hurried toward it.

In the kitchen, Celia and six other women had expressions of shock and grief smeared across their faces. Celia paced the floor, while the other women stood and wrapped their hands in the loose folds of their skirts or bit their fingernails. One of the women, taller and with a look of authority, had a black ribbon around her neck.

"What's wrong?" Mariana asked. "Is it Carmina?"

"No. Carmina is out and warning others. The *federales* have captured Tesia Richaud, our General," Celia said.

One of the women let out a moan.

A thick woman in a store-bought dress and lace petticoat said, "If she is still alive, we can help her escape."

"Not all the *federales* believe in the government. Some will secretly help their people." The woman wearing the black ribbon said. "We need to pray for that."

Celia turned to Mariana. "You and Emilio need to escape. It is time for you to go home to your own mamá."

"I want to stay and help," Mariana said. "My mamá does not want me."

"Your mamá will not turn you away with her grandson in your arms."

"Please…I cannot go."

Celia closed her eyes.

"Emilio and I are safer here than on the streets or at the train station."

Celia did not say a word. She only stared down at the tile floor. None of the other women spoke, as if they had intruded on a family matter and felt ashamed for it.

"I want to stay and fight for God."

"God does not need you," Celia said in such a low voice that Mariana wasn't sure that she had said it.

"You do not mean that."

"Yes, I do." She did not take her gaze from the floor. "We cannot keep worrying about you and Emilio and about what the soldiers might do to you."

Celia sat in silence for what felt an eternity, while nothing but the ticking of the clock and the restlessness of the women shuffling with pent-up energy disturbed the silence. Finally, Celia looked up at Mariana and held her eyes. "You are a burden to us."

Mariana did not know what to do or say in front of these people. She opened her mouth to object, but had no air left in her lungs.

Something heavy pounded on the front door. All the women turned toward the banging, staying rooted and unmoving like sheep in a pasture.

"Into the tunnel, quickly." Celia put her hand on Mariana's shoulder and turned her toward the open pantry. "Everyone."

With Celia's hand at her back, Mariana moved to the stairs. She held Emilio tight to her chest and stepped down into the tunnel. The coolness of the cavern seeped through the fabric of her shirt.

Once at the bottom, she turned to see the women descending right behind her—huaraches, patent leather shoes, and swishing skirts came down the steps. They all gathered together, lit only by the glow from the kitchen light where only Celia and Socorro stood looking down.

"Go," Celia said.

Socorro would not move. "You go down."

"Both of you," one of the women called up. "Hurry."

"The pantry cannot be shut from below. It will give us all away," Celia called down to the women.

Socorro did not budge. Celia put her hands on Socorro's shoulders and pushed her forward. "I need to get the door. Maybe it is Carmina coming home by the front."

Socorro took Celia's hand and kissed it. "Let me get it."

"No," Celia said. "If it is the *federales*, I may be able to turn them away."

Celia pushed Socorro until she stepped down onto the first step, shut the door, and left them all in darkness. A key clicked in the lock, then the pantry slid into place and left nothing but the sound of the women's breaths, the rustling of their skirts, and water dripping somewhere in the cavern.

Emilio's wet hand touched her face and she kissed it. He stuck his fingers into Mariana's mouth and she closed her lips over them. She did not hear Socorro come down the stairs and knew that she would be waiting on the top step while she listened and lamented that she had left Celia on the wrong side of the door. Emilio began to fuss.

"Shhhh," Mariana whispered and unbuttoned her blouse. The cold air brushed across her breast and her milk came in with tiny stinging pinpricks. Emilio took her nipple and warmed it while a chill ran through the rest of her body. *Oh, blessed Virgin, protect us. Protect Celia. Protect my child.*

A man's muffled voice barked an order from above, followed by the pounding of boots—maybe an entire squad in their belted uniforms spread through the house again to search. Celia's voice came from above. Her words were incoherent, but they sounded calm and pleading.

Someone draped a rebozo over Mariana's shoulders and in a soft voice, said, "God's will be done."

The smell of mesquite rose up from the fibers of the rebozo and filled her lungs with a mystical scent—like the incense of a church or of the distant campfires in the desert villages along the railroad tracks.

"Nooooo…" A shrill cry came from above. Mariana flinched and it popped her breast from Emilio. Emilio nuzzled, unaware of anything other than his need for milk while the women shifted around her and tried to swallow their gasps and cries.

Celia…..oh, no God…please….

A long and piercing scream came from above then trailed off like the shriek of a hawk. The men above began to howl like feral animals, full of malevolence—men without a God, answerable only to their own feral natures. All around her, the women's cries bubbled up to low whines. This was not God's will be done. God does not will terror or brutality.

Every thump, scream, and crash of things banging and scraping above reverberated in Mariana's core.

"We need to help," a voice whispered in the dark.

"The door is locked," another of the women said.

Something slammed to the floor above, sounding as if the table had been overturned.

"We have to do something," Mariana said and shifted Emilio to her other breast.

"I will go for help," one of the women said.

"So will I," another said.

There was a stirring in the air as the women moved. Mariana wanted to reach out, touch them, count how many were still with her.

From the top of the steps, in a faint whisper, Socorro muttered incoherent prayers while Emilio sucked at Mariana's breast, contented.

A voice came from beside her. "Maybe they are only ransacking the house," but the voice held no conviction. Women knew what Godless men wanted.

A shot. One, single shot. Oh, blessed Virgin, let it be Celia's gun in her own hand. More boots stomped over their heads, but they were the sound boots retreating, fading away, then silence.

A whiff of cold air blew in from the tunnel, then drew back out as if the earth itself took a single deep breath. Emilio slept. His tiny body lay warm against Mariana's stomach. The sounds from above had ceased, leaving only the dripping of underground water. After what seemed like an hour, the sound of the pantry sliding and a key in the door came. Socorro scampered down the steps and the women moved, bumped into one another, and scattered like bugs.

Light came in from the door. Mariana peeked out from behind a shelf. The ashen face of a man in a suit and tie stared down into the cavern. Behind him, the woman with the black ribbon around her neck peered down.

"Hello. Are you all still there?"

The women emerged from their hiding spots and stepped into the wash of light. The man and woman did not have the looks of relief that they should have had to find the women safe. Socorro darted between them and scurried up the steps.

Someone grabbed Mariana's arm and held her back.

"Stay and wait with your baby." She stepped in front of Mariana and placed her foot on the first step. "I will let you know if it is safe."

All the women climbed up and disappeared into the kitchen without a sound. They rose, one by one, and were swallowed into nothingness. Emilio stirred. Nobody called for her.

Mariana could not wait any longer. Celia was her cousin, and she needed to be there for her. She climbed into the upturned kitchen, strewn with chairs and an overturned table. All the women stood, gathered around someone on the floor. Mariana stepped forward, afraid to look. *Please God, let her be alive*. When she got to the line of women, one of them shifted to let her in. Celia lay with her head in Socorro's lap with her face beaten and a bloody hole through her temple.

The woman with the black ribbon pulled Celia's skirt down to cover her thin and bloody legs. She pulled both sides of the torn blouse over Celia's breasts to cover the bite marks and bruises, then lifted Celia's arm and placed her hand on her chest. Her fingernails had been ripped down to the quick.

Someone pounded on the front door. The women glanced around at one another, then back at the tunnel, but did not move. Socorro slid out from beneath Celia and lowered her head to the floor. With Celia's blood smeared over her white blouse and skirt, Socorro walked to the door. Her bloody footprints faded with each step she took.

Celia lay there, alone. Mariana hugged Emilio to her chest

and stepped forward into the blood. She lowered herself to the floor and knelt beside her cousin. Mariana dipped her finger in the blood and traced the sign of the cross on Celia's forehead.

The scrape of the iron door latch came from the living room followed by the sound of someone running. Carmina rushed into the kitchen and let out a wail so horrific that Mariana would never be able to stop hearing it. Mariana's curse had followed her to Guadalajara. Being born on the tail of a comet did not simply bring misfortune or disgrace—it was an omen of complete disaster.

CHAPTER THIRTY-FIVE

MARIANA WOULD NOT BE ABLE TO HOLD VIGIL FOR HER COUSIN OR attend her burial. Celia wanted her to leave and Mariana could not deny her dying wish. She would have to throw herself and Emilio at her mamá's feet and beg for forgiveness.

Mariana would no longer be able to step onto the patio where Papá's spirit had left his body—or sleep in the room where her son had been born. They would leave Emilio's umbilical stump buried in the garden of his godfather who he would never know. She would not have the opportunity to fight for God or guarantee herself a place in heaven next to Papá.

Mariana took out the flimsy cardboard suitcase that Mamá had sent her off with and placed it on the bed. She had not laid eyes on it since the day she had arrived. She opened it and exposed the brown stain in the shape of a rabbit on the lid.

Mariana placed a stack of Emilio's diapers, washed and bleached by Socorro, into the suitcase along with two of his sleeping gowns and baptismal suit. The white satin suit stood stark against the pulpy color of the suitcase fabric. It was not his. None of this was his. Her son did not own anything. He had come into this world with nothing but skin and breath—and that was all he still had. She removed the suit and laid it on the rose-color bedspread. She took out the sleeping gowns and the diapers. Mariana stared into the empty suitcase.

She pulled off the beautiful skirt and blouse that Celia had lent her—and the chemise and bloomers. She stood there naked and staring into the empty suitcase. None of it belonged to them. Emilio slept sound and tranquil next to the suitcase. His long dark lashes rested against his pink cheeks and his hair curled in soft black curlicues. His tiny lips puckered and sucked in his sleep.

Mariana opened the drawer of her bedside table and pulled out Papá's letters and his rosary—and Emilio's baptismal shell. He did own something and it was beautiful. She placed the shell and letters inside her suitcase and looped Papá's rosary around her neck. The dark beads that had moved between Papá's dirt-stained fingers lay strung against her bare breasts and the cross that he had brought to his lips touched the top of her belly.

The door creaked. Mariana turned to see Socorro standing in the threshold. She stared, not even asking why Mariana stood in nakedness.

"Do you know where I can find my clothes? The ones I was wearing when I arrived?"

Socorro went to the bureau and slid open the bottom drawer. Buried beneath a blanket, she pulled out several folded blouses, skirts, and the white wool blanket with blue and black bars that she had bought in the market with Palma. She placed them on the bed, next to Emilio.

Socorro lifted Celia's skirt. "You can wear this."

"It is not mine."

In her usual silent way, Socorro shrugged before picking up the stack of diapers and the two dressing gowns. She placed them in the suitcase. "These were gifts for Emilio. Carmina bought them."

Socorro picked up the baptismal suit and Celia's clothes and placed them in a drawer before leaving and shutting the door behind her. Mariana wished she had a photograph of Emilio in his baptismal suit so he would have something to look at and know where he had been born.

Mariana had forgotten that she still stood there wearing nothing but Papá's rosary. Carmina would be waiting for her, ready to whisk her to the train depot and throw her back on the train—ready to be rid of her burden. Mariana pulled on her own undergarments, skirt, and blouse. The fabric felt cheap and thin. She had never realized that there could be a difference until she had worn Celia's clothing and gotten used to the feel.

She closed the lid of her suitcase over her old clothes and Papá's letters and latched it. Mariana lifted Emilio and left the room with one last look at the bed and the painting of the Virgin and Child. A cold wave of nausea swept over her.

In the kitchen, Carmina and the woman with the black ribbon around her throat bent over an unfolded map. Celia's body still lay on the metal chopping table. Candles burned all over the kitchen. Carmina looked rumpled and still wore the clothes she had on the night before.

The woman, dressed in a skirt and blouse with a blue rebozo draped over her shoulders, ran her finger along the map. "Is this the way I should go?"

"I'm ready," Mariana said.

Both of them looked up at Mariana standing there with Emilio and her suitcase. Carmina's eyebrows pinched together. "Where are you going?"

"You said to get ready to go."

"Go to the market with Socorro. She will need your help."

"But Celia said..."

Carmina pushed the wild tendrils of her unkempt hair from her face. Her eyes held a weariness and uncertainty that Mariana had never seen in her.

"Celia said that Emilio and I needed to go..." Her chest tightened and she tried to hold in her tears. "She said that we are a burden to both of you."

Carmina looked fragile. Her shoulders trembled and she shook her head. "No...we did not...she did not mean it."

"She said it, didn't she?" Mariana asked the woman with the black ribbon. "You were there."

Carmina looked to her and the woman nodded.

"She was probably just worried and wanted you safe." Carmina stepped toward her with her arms out. All the tension in Mariana's body dissolved when Carmina's arms wrapped around her and Emilio. "I need you here to help me. This is your home."

CHAPTER THIRTY-SIX

THE TINKLE OF BELLS CAME ALL DAY AS PEOPLE ROSE UP FROM below the earth for Celia's vigil or came knocking on the front door with new passwords. They all entered with flowers and rosaries and somber faces. Her body lay in a pure white casket on top of the credenza with the palm branch of martyrs beneath her crossed arms. The people buried her person by person with the flowers they carried in. Every chair in the house had been brought into the living room and remained filled, others stood or knelt. The mumbling of prayers and feet shuffling on the hardwood went on for days.

Toward the end of the last day of the vigil, just as the sun set and the candles cast their flickering lights across the room, the bells rang. Socorro rose from her knees to open the pantry. Minutes later, the door from the kitchen flew open and caused all the people to flinch and turn their heads.

Three dusty and road-worn young men, with straps of bullets across their chests and red armbands, rushed into the room. The woman with the black ribbon around her neck came in behind them, nodded at Carmina, then joined the women at the back of the room.

Mariana let out a gasp at the face of her brother Emilio on one of the men. He came in hard and solid, and very unlike a spirit. They all fell to their knees before the casket and let out deep groans of grief. Mariana could not take her eyes from the back of his neck, the shape of his shoulders, and the intake of his breath. Carmina's entire body seemed to go lax and she set her head against the shoulder of the man beside her.

Mariana shivered with cold and sweat and little Emilio began to cry. The big flesh-and-blood ghost of Emilio turned and caught her eyes. The room began to sway and pinpricks of cold washed up her face. She felt her baby being lifted from her arms and the room went black.

CHAPTER THIRTY-SEVEN

THE NEXT MORNING, ON CELIA'S BURIAL DAY, MARIANA WOKE TO the morning light coming in through the gap in the curtain. It cut a slice across her bed and shined on an empty cradle beside her. Emilio! Where was Emilio? The ghost of her brother had come in her dream. Was it a dream? Had he stolen away his namesake?

Mariana slid off the side of the bed, dropped to the floor in her bare feet, and rushed out into the hall. "Socorro, Socorro," she called.

The house was quiet with all the doors closed. Her heart quickened. Where could he be? Our dear Virgin, take her to Emilio. She hurried down the stairs. "Socorro."

Celia still lay in her casket in the living room with Carmina and two other women still on their knees. Flowers covered Celia's entire body, with only her beautiful, but swollen, face uncovered. The living room smelled sickly sweet of flowers and death.

Mariana walked into the kitchen to find three men sitting at the table with Emilio between them and Socorro at the stove.

Everyone turned to look at her standing there like a crazy woman in her nightgown and bare feet. Emilio! And big Emilio.

"Is that you little butterfly, all grown up?" Big Emilio smiled at her with his broad and handsome smile. His nose and jawline were just a bit off and made him a different person.

"We have been entertaining our new little cousin," another of the men said. He was a bit shorter and round-faced.

With their rough-cut hair and scraggly beards, they did not resemble the boy cousins she remembered.

"I think you have struck her dumb, Lorenzo," the oldest looking of the three responded.

"He does that to all women," the round-faced one said.

Emilio started to whine and reached out for Mariana.

"You look like the same little butterfly, only more beautiful. It is too bad that you are our cousin."

"I...I'm sorry, none of you look as I remember. I cannot tell who is who." She went to the table, took Emilio, and placed him on her hip.

"I am Alberto," the round-faced one said. "The scruffy mean-looking one there is Leon, and the heartbreaker with the smile is Lorenzo."

"You look like my brother, Emilio."

Lorenzo's smile faded. "That is what your papá told me also. I'm sorry to hear about Emilio."

"And your papá," Alberto said.

Mariana tried to hold back her tears before remembering that they too had lost their papás—and Leon and Lorenzo just lost their mamá.

Socorro sat plates of eggs, chile, and tortillas on the table just as Carmina entered the kitchen. She stopped when she saw Mariana, then looked from young man to young man accusingly.

All of them shot their hands into the air in surrender. "We did nothing."

Carmina looked to Socorro for confirmation. "I brought Emilio down to let the poor girl sleep. Mariana woke up in a panic. It was my fault."

"We have a very long and sad day ahead of us. I expect all of you to behave and keep watch for the *federales*. At the first sight of them, you are to flee without us."

"We are not cowards, Tía," Leon said.

"It is not for you. I do not want to bury another member of my family."

CHAPTER THIRTY-EIGHT

THE GROUND OVER PAPÁ'S AND HER UNCLE'S GRAVES HAD NOT even settled before they had to remove the earth over Tío Victoriano's to place his wife above him. Women in black, professional city women, and rural women with their children clinging to their skirts crowded the cemetery. Leon, Lorenzo, and Alberto had not been found in time for their father's burials, so it was an extra heavy mourning for them.

Her cousins did not stay long, for they needed to be back in the hills with their units. They left clean and shaven, with most of the dirt stains scrubbed from their clothes. They disappeared down the tunnels wearing their red armbands over white shirts —the colors of Christ. Without uniforms, it was the only outward thing that all the Cristeros wore to declare themselves an army.

The day after Celia was buried, Carmina went right back to the business of God. She took Mariana into Celia's office and opened a secret compartment in the wall filled with ledgers, correspondence, and maps. Mariana needed to familiarize herself with them.

Carmina was a woman of action, not a woman of paperwork. She needed Mariana to be in charge of the logistics of supplies, propaganda, money, and communications. She needed her to understand the depth and breadth of the brigade before she would be put under the wing of Leta De la Mora, the woman with the black ribbon, who would teach her the rest.

Mariana read through the ledgers whenever Emilio slept. She learned that their brigade alone consisted of six-hundred and thirty-eight women who came from various backgrounds as shop keepers, seamstresses, office workers, teachers, and typists. They were working-class girls, peasant girls, and girls from the closed Catholic girls' schools.

The women had originally been organized by a trade union, the Catholic Employees' Union of Guadalajara, which was affiliated with the Unión Popular. It was originally founded to promote morality for working-class women. At the beginning of the anti-clerical laws, the women took action by supporting a boycott, and at one time, they helped release six hundred balloons tied with leaflets for the defense of religion.

The women were spies, organizers, money collectors, and suppliers of ammunition and intelligence. They provided channels of communication for the Cristeros—and the rural women organized dances in the villages and softened up the officers to gain their trust and obtain information. The women used violence, published propaganda, and even resorted to kidnapping. They made bombs and they provided nursing and field hospitals.

Women in the villages traded food to starving federal soldiers for magazines full of ammunition. The Cristero army, in addition to needing arms and ammunition, much of which was confiscated from federal soldiers after a battle, needed sandals since many of their men arrived with bare feet. They needed coats and blankets, horseshoes, salt, tobacco, aspirin tablets, salve, and soap.

Mariana set all the letters and ledgers aside in complete

bewilderment. She had thought this was a battle of good and evil. She imagined the Cristeros fighting only to defend themselves and their God. Not kidnapping or theft. How did one justify killing and stealing for the Lord?

The ring of the bell from the tunnels startled Mariana. She scooped up the ledgers, letters, and maps, and placed them back in their hiding spot. If the government got ahold of them, all would be lost. Everyone would be discovered. She hurried back to her room and scooped Emilio from his cradle to hold him while he slept. The sound of footsteps came from the hall moments before Carmina appeared in her doorway.

"Have you had much time to work today?"

"Yes," Mariana said without meeting her gaze.

Carmina moved into the room and sat on the bed facing Mariana. "And you are concerned?"

Mariana nodded. "I thought we were on the side of good."

"We are on the side of God."

"But we are killing and stealing. Those things are sins."

Carmina stiffened. "You knew that I killed that General."

"But that was to save lives..." Mariana's mind clouded and she did not know how to express what she felt. "I know you. You are a good woman."

"What did you think our army was doing?"

Mariana shrugged. "Defending themselves?"

"It is a war. Only at the end will there be any glory—and only for the side that is victorious."

"And we need to steal?"

Carmina's face tensed up and turned red before she took a deep breath and slowly released it. "The government steals from us every day. They demand our money in taxes, confiscate our land, and take our religion. Now they want to indoctrinate our children in their secular schools to make them worship the government. Do you think it is right for the government to tell us what is best for us—over our own desires and the desires of our God?"

Mariana could not answer. Everything Carmina said sounded reasonable, but they were committing sins.

"Regrettable things happen in the name of war." Carmina slid off the bed and placed her hand beneath Mariana's chin and lifted Mariana's face until their eyes met. "We do not take things to fatten our wallets and live like kings. We use what we take in the defense of God—and our soldiers do not rape and kill women. The government cannot make those claims."

Mariana looked down at Emilio in all his innocence. She did not want him to grow up in a world where men chased nothing but money and power. She did not want him to grow up where he did not have their saints, their festivals, and their God. And she remembered Mamá on the floor of the church beneath the dirty *federal*. She looked up at Carmina. "Do we have a chance against the government?"

Carmina shrugged. "I do not know, but we are not losing. We are winning just as many battles because we fight for what is in our hearts and our men do not fear death. All we want is the right to worship and have our sacraments and festivals."

Mariana nodded and looked down at Emilio sleeping peacefully in her arms.

"*¡Viva Cristo Rey!*" Carmina said.

"*¡Viva la Virgen de Guadalupe!*" Mariana answered. "*¡Viva Cristo Rey!*"

As she spoke them, the words took root. She had a purpose. She was fighting for a future where her son, and her sisters, could live without having to bow down to the government.

CHAPTER THIRTY-NINE

THE BELLS IN CELIA'S OFFICE RANG AND RANG IN A FRANTIC CALL. Mariana hurried to the hall and down the stairs. She opened the kitchen door just as Socorro pushed open the pantry with a wash of fear across her face. Carmina had gone out that morning and whenever she was gone, the tension always hung in the house like cotton until she returned.

Socorro fumbled with the key and the bell kept ringing and ringing. Socorro's nervousness sent Mariana's blood pulsating and throbbing in her temples. Socorro was always the smooth and soothing water for them, but her hands quivered. She finally turned the key and the door opened.

Carmina, half-unconscious and bleeding down the side of her leg, was carried in by a man and a woman who struggled to get through the pantry doors. Socorro ran to the table where they had prepared Celia's body and spread a table cloth over it. Carmina groaned. Most of the blood came from her leg, but tiny flowers of red splotched her face and her body.

"What happened?" Mariana asked and helped them get Carmina to the table.

"There was an explosion."

"Where?"

They got Carmina to the table, and as they lifted her onto it, she let out a scream. Mariana rolled up a towel to put beneath her head.

"Where did this happen? How many were hurt?"

Socorro put a pot of water to boil on the stove then brought antiseptic, aspirin, bandages, tweezers, and scissors. The man, dressed in a suit, looked like an office worker with thick bottle-brush hair and a mustache that he greased down. Other than the blood, the woman also looked like she had just stepped from an office building in a fancy dress and heels.

"Two women were killed," the man said. "They were making bombs and one detonated."

When Carmina left that morning with batteries and wire, Mariana had no idea they were for bombs. Carmina lay on the table. She was barely conscious and groaning. Socorro slipped off her shoes, poked the end of a scissor through her stocking, and started cutting it off.

"I'll go for a doctor," the man said.

"Yes, hurry." The woman took Carmina's hand and kissed it. "We are getting you a doctor."

The man hurried down the stairs, back into the cavern.

"Should I close it back up?" Mariana asked.

Socorro did not seem to hear as she focused on the scissors chewing through the fabric of Carmina's stocking.

"Should I lock the door and close the pantry?" It seemed wrong to leave it open for any spirit that lurked beneath the city to rise up into their house.

"Yes, please close it," the woman finally said. She held Carmina's hand and whispered comforting words into her ear.

With the door to the cavern in her hand, a shiver ran up Mariana's spine—like a spirit had passed through her. She crossed herself before she shut the door and locked it tight.

When Socorro peeled the stocking off, it pulled away the

thick and clotted blood. Fresh red blood oozed from numerous places where bits of material were embedded.

"What can I do?" Mariana asked. She needed to get busy. She needed to stop watching before she became sick.

"Give her some aspirin, then clean the blood from her face," the woman said. "Use the tweezers on anything protruding first."

Carmina swallowed the aspirin with the water Mariana poured into her mouth. With the tweezers, Mariana pinched a sliver stuck in Carmina's face. As she pulled, Carmina flinched and caused Mariana to drop the tweezers with a dull metallic clang.

"It's all right," Carmina said.

"Want me to wait until the aspirin takes effect?"

"No." Carmina sounded tired and weary with pain.

The kitchen felt thick and humid with prayers, blood, and the steaming water on the stove. Socorro worked to stop the blood flowing from her leg, Mariana plucked slivers of wood and glass from her face, and the woman comforted Carmina. The ring of the bells startled them all.

"That was fast. Thank God," the woman said.

Mariana opened the pantry, then unlocked the door. Instead of the man and a doctor, a woman in an embroidered blouse rose up with urgency on her face.

"I have a message for Allesandra..." her eyes landed on Carmina and the blood. "Oh dear Lord, what has happened to her?"

"I'm not dead," Carmina said. The weakness of her voice betrayed her humor.

"There was an explosion," the first woman said. "We lost María and Petra."

The newly arrived woman, who looked to be in her thirties, put her hand over her mouth and let out a gasp. Her hair was pulled back from a slanting forehead and beautiful almond eyes. "I have an urgent message."

"There is nothing she can do," the woman who brought Carmina home said.

"She is the only one. I do not know who else to take it to."

"What is it?" Carmina's voice sounded weak and thick.

The woman stepped beside her. "We received a message that Esmeralda has been discovered. The *federales* will raid her house tomorrow."

Carmina closed her eyes. The tears that had not been there from the pain came spilling over. "We must get her out." She tried to sit up but groaned in pain and dropped back onto the table.

"There is nothing she can do," the woman said again.

"Nobody knows who Esmeralda is but her."

"Isabella knows," Carmina said.

The women looked at one another with confused expressions. Mariana stood beside Carmina with the tweezers hovering in her hands while she waited for the women to be done with her.

"Who?" the woman with the message asked.

Mariana tried to swallow but it felt as if she had a mouthful of ash. She was Isabella. She knows who Esmeralda is. "Me."

Everyone looked over to Mariana. She felt small and helpless. "I am Isabella."

Nobody looked confident or relieved by the information.

"I know where to find Esmeralda."

The distant cry of a baby drifted into the kitchen.

"Emilio!" She had forgotten about her own son. "He is awake."

"You need to go," Carmina said. "Socorro can care for Emilio."

Without a moment to consider, the messenger led Mariana

to the top of the passageway. She handed Mariana her lantern and she said, "*¡Viva Cristo Rey¡* Bless you and go with God."

Mariana turned to plead for another solution, but Socorro had already disappeared to take care of Emilio and Carmina lay on the table covered in blood.

"Quickly, so you can return before dark," the woman at Carmina's side said.

Carmina turned to look at her.

"You can do it." Carmina's voice came out thin. "I have faith in you."

The tunnel was lit only by the lantern that Mariana held out in front of her. She kept turning around to look over her shoulder. It felt as if someone followed behind her, but every time she turned, she saw nothing but darkness.

Mariana had never been brave. Emilio and Lázaro had always looked out for her. They always walked her home and made sure no harm came to her. She never rolled down hills in a tire or neared the river when it ran swift. Carmina was a fool for trusting her to carry this out.

She emerged from the tunnel and climbed up into the hospital that smelled of stale sickness and blood. Three children sat huddled around a girl of about twelve who had her arms around them. All of them looked tired and dirty. Several other women and children, wrapped with bandages, lay on blankets spread next to the walls. The children rose and walked toward her with hands out. Again, she had come unprepared. "I am sorry. I have nothing."

Sister Antonia rose from beside one of the patients and stared at Mariana with a knowing sadness in her eyes. "I heard about the accident. How is Allesandra?"

"She is injured, but alive," Mariana said.

"Thank the Lord," Sister Antonia said. "I have been praying."

Mariana nodded. "She needs your prayers."

"Shall we pray together?"

"Can we on my return? I must go, it is urgent."

"Of course," Sister Antonia said. "Go with God."

Mariana hurried to the door and stepped out into the street of small adobe homes. Half-naked children ran after a scraggly dog and tormented it. An old man sat next to a mesquite tree and whittled a chunk of wood—just like her Papá had been doing in her dream. Without a word, he looked up and beckoned to Mariana with a withered hand.

Mariana shook her head. She had nothing to give and she needed to find Esmeralda. He motioned to her again. She looked at the mesquite tree with its gnarled limbs in the same branching formation as the tree her papá had been sitting beneath in that dream she had just after he left Tijuana. He motioned again, intent on calling her over.

When she approached, the old man struggled to get to his feet, half-bent, with skinny legs and elbows sticking out like a plucked chicken. He hobbled toward her, all fabric and bones. His head bobbled like a withered pumpkin in a straw hat as he walked toward Mariana. His toes, with yellow and thickly ridged nails, curled over the lip of his huaraches.

"I do not have anything to give you," she said to him.

"No, but I have something to give you." He smiled a toothless smile.

"I cannot pay you..."

He only nodded as if he knew the course of their encounter. "There are *federales* in the cantina around the corner. You can get around them if you go this way." He pointed east.

"*Federales?*" Mariana gasped in tiny breaths that did not quench her lungs. She could not do it. She was not brave enough. A cold hand touched her shoulder. She turned to see the old man staring at her with milky eyes. He took Mariana's hand and placed something in it.

She looked down to see a carving of Christ with

outstretched arms, just like her Papá had been whittling in that dream.

Mariana's body wanted to stay planted right there, right on that spot of earth instead of walking into the hands of the *federales*—or getting caught with Esmeralda, where she could be raped and shot.

"It is time to swim on your own, Señorita," the old man said to her.

Swim? Papá's words of her being a shrimp came to her… She looked into the man's eyes and searched for some spark of Papá. Could he be Papá's ghost? She glanced down, again, at the figure in her hand. In her dream, it did not bring a bad omen. Her papá himself had been whittling it.

"Go with God," the old man said. He turned back toward the tree and left her alone on the road.

Mariana forced herself forward. After several wrong turns down lanes crowded with chickens, children, and women sitting in front of their adobes frying tortillas, she finally found the hacienda. A young boy of about twelve years skittered out from the back kitchen door. He wore white cotton clothes and had a mass of black hair, too big for his skinny body. He ran toward the pigpen with a heavy cloth sack.

The wrought-iron gate squeaked when she swung it open and stepped into a courtyard that was still overgrown with weeds creeping up through the cobbles. Mariana lifted the giant ring of the knocker and pounded it on the heavy wooden door with three strikes, just like Carmina had done. The peephole in the door slid open and Yatzil's black eyes stared out at her.

"Allesandra is injured and I have an urgent message for Esmeralda."

The peephole closed, but the door did not open. Mariana stood there in the dusty breezeway hearing nothing but the distant squeal of pigs and the buzz of a fly circling her head.

Mariana knocked again and waited. Finally, the peephole

opened again, but this time, two heavily lashed dark eyes peered out. "Allesandra is injured and I have an urgent message."

The door unlatched and swung open with barely enough room for her to squeeze in. Esmeralda stood behind the door with a rifle at her side.

"Thank you, Yatzil." Esmeralda said. "You can go have your lunch."

Yatzil left them alone in the entryway and as soon as she disappeared through a door, Esmeralda turned to Mariana. "What happened to Allesandra?"

"Her leg was injured from an explosive."

"Will she be all right?"

"I think so. They are getting a doctor." Mariana's stomach fluttered. She needed to give her the message and hurry away, back to Emilio and Carmina. "You have been discovered. *Federales* are planning a raid on your hacienda tomorrow morning."

Esmeralda's face drained of color and she swayed on her feet. "Tomorrow?"

"Yes," Mariana said. "Some are already in the village cantina."

Esmeralda stood like stone for a moment, then shook her head in resignation. "You need to leave."

Mariana did not want to go back through the hospital with nothing for the children. "Do you have some bread or fruit for the children in the hospital?"

Esmeralda stared at her with a blank expression, then blinked her eyes. "Oh…yes, yes. Follow me."

As they moved toward the kitchen, Esmeralda's pace quickened.

Yatzil, and the same woman who reminded her of Señora Hernández from Santiago, sat at a table with two plates of beans and tortillas before them.

"The *federales* will be here in the morning. We have much to do."

Dire looks washed over the faces of both women.

"Get a bag of Oranges for Isabella to take to the children in the hospital." Esmeralda turned to Mariana. "I will be right back."

Yatzil disappeared into a pantry and returned with a burlap sack. The bottom hung heavy and looked just like the bag where Señora Hernández had placed the dead peacock on that terrible day—the day when she had woken up safe and in the love of her family and went to sleep with a dead brother and her house filled with black crepe and burning candles.

"Are you all right?"

Mariana blinked and noticed the woman standing before her.

"Yes, it's been a hard day."

Yatzil placed the burlap sack on the table between the two plates.

"Hurry and eat," Yatzil said to the woman. "We have much to do."

Esmeralda returned with a small leather handbag. "Unbutton your blouse."

With only a second of thought, Mariana complied and slipped the buttons from their holes. The double crosses of her's and Papá's rosaries lay on the white fabric of her chemise.

Esmeralda looked at them, then up at Mariana with a tight and determined smile. "*¡Viva Cristo Rey¡*"

"*¡Viva la Virgen de Guadalupe!*" Mariana answered.

Esmeralda slipped the strap over her head. "This is most of the money we have. I will not let the federal pigs get their hands on it. Give half to Sister Antonia at the hospital and the rest to Carmina for the Cristeros." She dropped the purse inside Mariana's chemise and began buttoning her blouse over it.

"Won't you need it?"

"Whether I end up in prison, with God, or with my husband, it will be of no use to me anymore." She kissed Mariana on the forehead, then led her to the back door of the kitchen. "God bless you, Isabella, and thank you."

Yatzil handed her the burlap sack and Mariana stepped from the kitchen. The barn, filled with airplanes and stolen ammunition, sat beyond the empty weed-filled animal corrals. The hacienda must have once been beautiful with gardens, horses, goats, and cows. Families must have lived in the houses and vaqueros in the bunkhouse. But now, with the war, it all went to waste.

She took one look back at Esmeralda and Yatzil who stood in the doorway waiting for her to leave. She lifted a hand to wave goodbye. Esmeralda gave one nod, then shut the door. In the morning, all three of those women could suffer the same fate as Celia. Tomorrow may be their last sunrise and the last time they ever wake to the crowing of a cock or the sounds of birds chittering outside their windows.

When Mariana passed by the mesquite tree, the old man was no longer there. Mariana put her hand into her pocket to feel the carved figure and to make sure it truly existed. It was there. She ran her fingertip over the face and the furrows in the robe of Jesus Christ. May God bless Esmeralda, Yatzil, and the other women whose names she did not know. God bless all the women and all the men she could not name—who all fought for their right to worship and have more than their meager earthly labors.

Mariana entered the hospital and found Sister Antonia wiping the forehead of a woman whose face was flushed with infection. The children, all with bare feet and skinny legs, stood and began to step toward Mariana, so she opened the sack. Their eyes widened at the sight of the bright oranges.

Mariana scraped her fingernail into one of the orange skins and brought it to her nose. It brought back the familiar scent of sunshine and the warm green trees of the grove. It brought back the memories of Emilio and Lázaro as children playing hide and seek in the branches—and of the pickers filling their bags with fruit while their little boys clipped the oranges below them.

These children, with their hands out begging for a bit of fruit, deserved a life without war. They deserved a life with a mamá and a papá, surrounded by their cousins and aunts and uncles. They did not deserve their lives to be filled with violence from their own government. They did not deserve to have their lives ruined for the glory of a few powerful men.

The children gave her smiles or tiny kisses on her hand before walking away in their dirty white cotton clothes, grateful for their gifts. They took the oranges back to their little family groups and distributed them to their loved ones surrounding the bed of a mamá, or a sister, or a brother wrapped in bloody bandages.

Once the oranges were distributed, Mariana looked up to see Sister Antonia watching her with a smile on her face. Mariana went to her. "I have something for you also."

As soon as they stepped into an empty hallway, Mariana unbuttoned her blouse and pulled the soft leather purse from beneath her chemise. She opened it to more money than she had ever put her eyes on. It was a thick stack of pink, green, and coral-color banknotes. She took half of the bills and held them out. "This is from Esmeralda...for the hospital."

Sister Antonia's eyes shot open. "Why so much?"

"She said she will not need it."

Tears rose in the sister's eyes and when she closed them, they slid down her cheeks. She crossed herself and muttered a prayer too silent for Mariana to comprehend.

Sister Antonia slipped the money into her pocket and Mariana buttoned her blouse. When Mariana finished, the sister reached both hands out to her. Her hands felt strong, calloused, and warm. After the prayer, Mariana kissed the top of her hand, just as Carmina had done.

"I will continue to pray for Allesandra and also for you."

"Your prayers must take you hours," Mariana said.

"Taking care of our people, both on my feet and on my knees, is all I have to give. Go with God, Isabella."

Mariana hurried down the breezeway to the closet that led to the tunnel. She unlocked it, stepped in, and closed the door behind her. She did it on her own. Of her own free will. Of her own choice to be a part of something bigger than her fears. She was swimming against the current. If she could do this, she could do many things. She could be a good mamá for Emilio. She could help her people. She could help her own family.

CHAPTER FORTY

MARIANA WOKE TO THE CALL OF A PEACOCK. IN THE HAZE OF waking, the *may-AWW, may-AWW, may-AWW* made her feel as if she was back in Santiago, safe in her childhood home. The big four-poster bed and the dark beams in the ceiling confused her like her two worlds had somehow converged.

May-AWW, may-AWW, may-AWW. She peeked through the curtain at the terra-cotta patio. A beautiful peacock stood atop the bullet-scarred wall. Mariana slid open the bolt and crept out onto the patio, not wanting to startle the bird. The grout beneath the wall was dark, still stained by Papá's and her uncles' precious blood. The peacock turned his head toward her. A warm wash of water seemed to rise in her chest and she felt the spirit of her brother, Emilio.

She let out a tiny laugh. "You always were a peacock."

Her voice did not scare it away. Instead, it raised its beak into the air and let out a resounding *may-AWW, may-AWW, may-AWW* that echoed over all the rooftops.

"Your breakfast is ready."

Mariana jumped at Socorro's voice behind her.

"You should not sneak up on people like that. You about

made my heart leap from my chest. Can you bring my breakfast out here? I have a guest," Mariana motioned to the peacock. When it shifted, the sun turned its feathers into iridescent gold, emerald green, sapphire, and amethyst.

"Carmina is in the dining room waiting to eat with you."

"Should she be out of bed?"

"Not if she listened to the doctor."

The deep gong of a church bell rang. Mariana looked to Socorro, who stared back at her and tipped her head to the side. Then, another bell rang in the opposite direction, and another, and another—until all the bells in every church in Guadalajara rang out.

The peacock dipped its head, took wing, and soared over the rooftops in all his magnificence. Mariana watched until it disappeared and all that remained was the ringing of the church bells and people wandering out onto their rooftops. Mariana kissed her fingers and ran them over the bullet holes in the wall before going in and lifting baby Emilio from his cradle.

Downstairs, Carmina sat at the dining room table beside the woman with the black ribbon around her throat. Carmina looked pale but appeared much better than she had been the day before.

"What is happening?" Mariana asked. "Why are the bells ringing?"

"It is done."

"What?"

"The war, it is over."

Mariana took a seat at the table and adjusted Emilio so as not to wake him. "How can that be? We just sent out ammunition and medical supplies yesterday."

"The bishops negotiated a reconciliation. I just received word."

"That is wonderful!" Mariana said.

Carmina's expression did not match the occasion. "The anti-clerical articles will remain in our constitution, President Portes Gil and Calles remain, but the government will allow us to have our churches, our Mass, and our sacraments."

"Why is that not a good thing?"

"The people have been appeased, but I do not trust Calles. Without removing the articles, what is to prevent him from doing it again?"

"Can we push to have them removed?"

"No, it is done. The bishops, who did not fight with us, have spoken for the church. Calles knew he could not defeat us, so he called the bishops and mollified them. They gave the people what they wanted—for now."

If only it had been twelve days earlier, Celia would have escaped her fate and Esmeralda's hacienda would not have been burned to the ground. So many people lost their lives for an appeasement rather than a victory.

CHAPTER FORTY-ONE

THE FIRST-CLASS TRAIN CAR HAD BEDS WITH CURTAINS AND padded seats—nothing like her trip down to Guadalajara on the hard bench with her head bumping against the window while she tried to sleep. She and Emilio had made this trip together last time, but that was before he was good company.

One week earlier, right after the reconciliation, Mariana asked Carmina if she could bring her family to live in Guadalajara. She told Carmina that she did not want an answer immediately. She wanted her to think about it and be certain, but Carmina quickly agreed to welcome her family into her home and give them a place to live.

Mariana lay on the berth with her arm around Emilio so he did not roll off, but she was unable to sleep. She felt the comfort of knowing that someone needed her. She could face anything for him. She took the carved figure of Jesus from her pocket and lay it next to Emilio, finally able to expose a religious icon without fear of being shot. She ran her finger over the figure. She could not help but believe that her papá's own hands had whittled it—if not his, then his ghost in the body of the old man.

This time, when the women and children came to the train

windows with their wares, she no longer looked on them with pity. She saw their strength. She saw women fighting to care for their children. They may even have been women who uttered ¡*Viva Cristo Rey*¡ to one another—even though they could be shot for saying it. Maybe they were women who handled and passed on the supplies she had sent out. Or women who sacrificed themselves for information that was then passed to Carmina. Women were stronger than anyone ever gave them credit for. Women can fight. Women can stand up for what they believe in—and women always find a way to care for those they love.

As word had trickled through the women's brigade, Mariana found out that the *federales* did not burn Esmeralda's hacienda. She and her servants loaded her most valuable possessions into a truck and set fire to the house and barn themselves. Word had it that Esmeralda did not even turn around to watch it burn. She drove off, still the wife of federal General Enrique Nevarez and still cousin to Plutarco Elías Calles—doing what she believed in, right beneath their noses and returning to them without any proof of her betrayal.

The train finally pulled into the Tijuana station. Tourists, excited to gamble and drink themselves to oblivion, had boarded at the Nogales stop. A high-heeled woman, followed by a peacock on a jeweled leash with the dusty tips of its train dragging across the floor, sat in the same car with Mariana.

Her family did not belong in Tijuana, always in the shadow of the United States. Always catering to Anglos and working for Anglos—always on their leash and being robbed of their own dignity. They belonged in Guadalajara where they began. They belonged with their family.

No matter what, Mariana promised Carmina that she would return to Guadalajara—with or without her family. Her help was needed and there was a lot of work to be done rebuilding the churches and raising money for the people who had lost everything. There was also a lot of uncertainty with the Catholic schools and if they would be able to open.

Mariana waited while the train car emptied before she stood with her suitcase in her hand and Emilio on her hip. "Are you ready to meet your grandmother, aunties, and Tío Lázaro?"

With each step toward their half-a-house beneath the Padilla's feet, Mariana's belly filled with the dread of facing her mamá. It became more real with every step and a hard lump formed in her stomach.

Tijuana had not changed. It was still a dirty version of an American town. Tourists acted like mischievous children, there to get drunk behind their parents' backs and running around like caged animals finally set free.

The establishments were owned by Anglos for Anglos while the Mexican people worked for them for a pittance—and the Anglos thought they had done a great thing for Mexico. *Look at the improvements to the town. The business they brought in. The jobs.* Had they ever seen Guadalajara? The grand city with its Cathedral of the Assumption of Our Lady, its parks, and elaborate buildings? A city much older and ornate than any city in the United States.

The sight of the crooked and dilapidated half-a-house, with the Padilla's caged canaries on the balcony above, brought Mariana's feet to a stop. It felt like her belly was filled with stones, weighing her down, cementing her feet to the ground. She was a cursed daughter returning with her illegitimate baby and asking them to follow her. Who was she to tell Mamá what was best for their family?

"I cannot do it," Mariana said to Emilio.

He gave her his irresistible and innocent smile and reached up to touch her face.

"What if she tells me to go away?"

Emilio stroked her cheek with his tiny baby hand. She had brought Emilio this far and risked both their lives alone on the train. She was no longer the shrimp in the current. If she could go alone through a tunnel and elude soldiers, she could face her mamá. Maybe.

A drunken American man staggered down the street, probably lost, with a liquor bottle swaying back and forth from his limp wrist. He stumbled toward Mariana and forced her to move.

One step at a time, she walked toward their gate, opened it, and stepped into the dirt courtyard. Behind the iron grilles, the windows were still unwashed and covered in flyspecks. Mariana smoothed Emilio's hair down. "Do you want to meet your grandmother?"

With Emilio in her arms, she knocked. Feo let out a string of ferocious barks, followed by Josefina's normal, "Shut up you stupid mutt."

The door opened and Josefina stood there blinking as if she thought her eyes might be playing tricks on her. She reached out and touched Mariana. When her hands felt flesh and bone, she squealed and wrapped her arms around them.

"Come in, come in. Oh my God, come in."

"Is Mamá home?"

"Yes, she is in the kitchen."

Sofía and Catalina came bounding into the room. They had grown. Sofía was missing her two front teeth and Catalina's hair reached all the way to the middle of her back. As soon as they spotted Mariana, they stopped and hid behind Josefina.

"It is all right, it is your sister, Mariana."

Her sisters stayed behind Josefina and peeked out at her and Emilio with shy smiles.

Mamá stood in the kitchen chopping scallions.

"*Hola* Mamá," Mariana said.

Mamá looked up from her cutting board with a slight smile that quickly disappeared. She glanced at Emilio, then forced her gaze away and turned her back to Mariana.

"This is your grandson."

Without turning around, Mamá asked, "Are you married?"

"No," Mariana said.

"Then I have no grandson." Mamá's strong and persevering shoulders drooped. This was hard for her. "I do not need another two mouths to feed. I do not need a daughter who cannot be a good example for her sisters."

Please turn around, Mamá.

Her entire body shook with silent sobs. "Leave before your sisters see you."

'No," Mariana said. "This is my family."

Mamá turned around and stared at Mariana like she had no idea who this insolent woman was. She refused to look at Emilio. Her strong mamá who had survived a rape without telling anyone, even pretending that Mariana did not know, and not allowing her to give comfort. Mamá, who found a way to support her family, even without a husband, could not bear to look at her grandson.

Emilio gazed up at Mariana with his fingers in his mouth. She opened her mouth and pretended to gobble up his entire hand, which made him giggle.

Mamá began to shake and Mariana feared she would collapse to the ground.

"I am not leaving. I am your daughter and this is your grandson. Family is not a burden. Family is a blessing."

Mamá stared and tried to remain hard, but her whole body quaked. Mariana stepped closer. She wanted to take Mamá into her arms and hug her with Emilio between them before she uttered another word. Mamá took a step back.

Mamá groaned, a deep and defeated sound that wracked Mariana to the core.

"I'm sorry for letting you down, but there is nothing I can do about it now. It is time to move forward. Papa would want us to stay together."

At the mention of Papá, Mamá sank to the floor and gasped for air. Her pain sunk so deep, that instead of tears, she could not breathe.

Josefina rushed into the kitchen. "What's wrong?" She put an arm around Mamá.

Sofía and Catalina peeked in with worried eyes. "Mamá?"

Mariana held her arm out to them, but they ran to Josefina.

"It will be all right," Mariana said to her little sisters. "Mamá is just sad."

Mariana knew that was true. They would all be fine as long as they had one another. She sat down on the floor of the kitchen with Emilio in her lap and waited for Mamá to calm herself—and to show Mamá that she would not leave.

"Who is that?" Sofía asked. She took Catalina's hand and came toward Mariana.

"This is your nephew. He is my baby."

Mamá looked up, almost as if she wanted to grab hold of Sofía and Catalina to keep them away from Mariana.

"What is his name?" Catalina asked.

"His name is Emilio."

Mamá took a deep and quivering breath. "You named him Emilio?"

Mariana nodded. "Would you like to hold your grandson?"

Mamá's whole body relaxed and she wept, this time with thick tears.

"Please, Mamá," Josefina said.

Mamá reached out. Mariana leaned forward and placed Emilio into the arms of his grandmother.

CHAPTER FORTY-TWO

"Why did you agree on Nero's?"

"Does it matter? It is Mamá's day off."

"It's pushing our luck. If Mamá finds out, she will feel a double betrayal."

Mariana would not have chosen to meet Jenny at the restaurant where Mamá worked—or bring Emilio into town on a weekend when the streets were crowded with drunken tourists, but she had no choice. She had written to Jenny and told her she was back in Tijuana. Their friendship was from a different time when she was a different girl, but she owed it to Jenny to at least meet with her.

Josefina walked beside her with a shoebox full of her bracelets under one arm and Catalina's hand in the other. Sofía walked beside them, used to their routine, so Josefina did not fear her running off.

"*Hola, chicas*," one of the shop owners called to them. He stood outside his store filled with puppets, pottery, bins of shells, and blankets. "Who do you have with you today?"

"*Hola*, Señor Garcia. This is our sister, Mariana, and our nephew, Emilio," Josefina said.

"Will she be selling with you from now on?"

"No, she is too glorious to be on the street."

"Josefina!"

"It is true and you know it."

Before she got her job at the Hotel De Obregón, Mariana had applied for work in his shop. How much different her life would have been if she had worked there instead. She would never have met William, or been sent off to Guadalajara. She would not have seen Papá one last time or met Celia and Carmina. Mariana kissed Emilio on the head, glad that things turned out the way they did—she could not imagine her life without him. He brought her more joy than she ever thought she would have in life.

"Are you and Emilio selling bracelets with us today?" Sofía asked.

"Emilio and I are having lunch with a friend."

"I want to have lunch."

"Well, you cannot," Josefina said. "That is not a restaurant for us."

"Do not tell her that." Josefina talked to the little ones as if she were teaching them to believe that they were lower than others.

"I am only speaking the truth."

"Maybe another time," Mariana said.

"And your lies are better than my truths?"

It hurt Mariana's heart to hear it. Her little sisters should not be told they were lower than the drunk and wild Anglos. It was sad to know that Josefina believed that to be the truth.

When they approached Nero's, Mariana's heart beat in her throat. Seeing Jenny would bring back the memories of all they had lost, but she needed to thank her for getting money to Josefina—and to tell her that they did not need it anymore.

Josefina told her that Jenny was a pilot and she flies an

airplane into Tijuana. Of course she had an airplane. There was no end to her father's money. And no end to what he would purchase for Jenny.

Mariana stopped before she reached the window of Nero's. "Peek in and see if she is there," she said to Josefina.

She did not want to walk into a restaurant full of tourists like some confused local girl. Josefina cupped her hands around her face, leaned forward, and plastered them to the window.

"Josefina!" Mariana said. "That is rude."

"It is the only way I can see in."

Poor Josefina. Salbatore's manners had rubbed off on her and made her a street girl, just like Lázaro had warned.

Josefina straightened up. "She's in there."

Mariana's heart beat like a rabbit's. She smoothed down Emilio's hair and shifted him onto her other hip. She had not put her eyes on Jenny since the day of Emilio's funeral and she kept picturing her the night he was murdered, dressed in that bloody white dress and the people calling her *Sante Muerte*.

She recognized Jenny instantly. Jenny jumped from the table as soon as their eyes met, very excited to see her. She still had short and messy hair and wore pants and high laced boots, just like Esmeralda had remarked about women from the United States.

Jenny hurried to Mariana and embraced her. "I have finally found you. I cannot believe you are actually here."

Emilio squirmed between them.

"I did not think I would ever see you again," Mariana said. Every eye in the restaurant was on them. If only she had worn a shawl or a rebozo so she could pull it over Emilio to protect him. She had felt so invincible just weeks earlier, but facing her past and being in an Anglo establishment made her feel inept. That was ridiculous. She was a mamá and she was a member of the Joan of Arc Women's Brigade.

"Josefina said you had a baby. He is beautiful."

"Thank you. You are looking well."

"Come and sit. I cannot believe it is you. You are even more beautiful than I remember."

Jenny led them to a table where paper menus sat before each chair. Mariana put Emilio on her lap and pushed the silverware out of his reach.

When the waiter came, he tried to exchange a Spanish menu for Mariana's. "Thank you, the English one is fine."

"I cannot believe that you are a mother. It seems like not too long ago we were running through the groves pretending to be pirates."

"A lot has happened since then," Mariana said. She did not need to tell Jenny about Papá because she had already told her in their letters, and she could not tell her about the brigade. She had been sworn to secrecy, and even if she had not, that was a part of her life that she wanted to keep and not give pieces of it out to anyone. "Josefina told me that you fly an airplane."

"Yes. That is what my father bought me for my birthday just after everything happened. I'm trying to figure out how to turn it into a career."

Jenny did not need a career. Her father had money and she would probably marry a rich man. Mariana felt as if the Jenny she knew was no longer the person in Jenny's body. She still looked like the girl who ran after adventures, but she did not seem as reckless as she used to be. Maybe losing Emilio had been hard on her too.

Mariana tried to focus on the menu, but her stomach felt weak ever since Josefina told her Jenny was in town.

"Order anything you like," Jenny said. "I'm treating."

When the waiter appeared, Mariana ordered the first thing her finger came to. "Potted Long Island Duckling, please."

"I'll take the Creamed Chicken," Jenny said and held the menu out for the waiter. "And two lemonades."

Every table was occupied with loud people drinking beer, wine, and mixed cocktails while slowly nibbling on food.

"It is good to see you," Jenny said. "So much has happened...I..."

"Why did it take you so long to come looking for my family?" Maybe if Jenny had found her sooner...

"I didn't know where you were. My father said you moved to Texas."

"Texas?"

"Yes, I could not understand why you would go to Texas and not say goodbye to me. You have no idea how long I have searched for you."

"Your father had us deported."

"I know." Jenny's smile faded. "I just found out. I'm not speaking to him and I will never forgive him."

Emilio leaned forward and reached for the knife. Mariana pushed it further away and handed him a spoon. There was nothing she would like better than to have Warren Stratton pay for what he did to their family. He may not have killed Emilio himself, but he protected whoever did—and if not for that, Papá would have never gone to Guadalajara. Jenny's father deserved to have his only child hate him. He deserved worse than that.

Emilio started to bang the spoon on the table.

"What's your baby's name?"

Mariana hesitated and put her hand beneath the spoon so it did not make any noise. "His name is Emilio."

Jenny stared at Emilio for what seemed an extreme amount of time. The waiter came with their pale yellow lemonades and placed them on the table.

Tears came to Jenny's eyes and she began to nod. "He is as handsome as his namesake. I am sorry. I am sorry for everything. If I could go back and change it, I would. I would never have met Emilio that night. I would have never let myself fall in love with him."

Mariana swallowed the words she wanted to scream. Yes, it was Jenny's fault. She had warned Jenny just that morning when she had put the baby bird back in its nest and when that man from the grower's association had seen them. The back of Mariana's throat clenched as if it did not want any kind words to pass through. "It was hard not to fall in love with Emilio."

Jenny clamped her lips together and tears dripped down her cheeks. That reminds me, I have something for you." She pulled a long piece of rolled-up paper from beside her and handed it to Jenny.

Emilio reached for it.

"This is not for you." Mariana held it out of his grasp. "What is it?"

"Open it up." Jenny's eyebrows pinched together. "I hope it is okay."

Mariana unrolled the paper and came to the edge of a field of bumpy and smeared grease pencil, then ghost letters and numbers began to appear. *Emilio Castillo de la Vega* and *February 2, 1908 – August 17, 1927.* A pair of wings fanned out over the epitaph. They looked morbid in black grease pencil, like the wings of a crow rather than an angel.

"It's a rubbing of his headstone. I thought you would like to know what it looks like…and that he has one."

Cold fingers walked up Mariana's spine. "The wings are black?"

"That's just the relief," Jenny said. "The stone is marble."

"Thank you." Her voice came out as thin as tissue. She appreciated the rubbing but preferred to think of Emilio's spirit as the essence of a peacock, not his solid body beneath the soil. She ran her hand over the waxy texture that captured every bump of his headstone. She could not breathe and felt the weight of the earth on her chest.

Mariana rolled the paper back up and leaned it against the side of her chair. "Have they found who killed him?"

Jenny's eyes went down to the table and she shook her head. "Not yet."

"They will not try," Mariana said. "The sheriff and your father are protecting someone."

"I know." Jenny brought her eyes up to Mariana. "I am trying. I keep asking and I promise you, I will not stop until we find out who did it—and that person is arrested."

The waiter brought their food. On her plate, fancy strips of meat fanned out beneath a small mound of mashed potatoes sprinkled with herbs and tiny cooked onions. She did not have the stomach for it. This was how she used to eat with William. She had no idea if he still worked at the Hotel de Obregón, or if he had returned to California with his family. She did not care. She only cared that he would never discover he had a son. She would not take the chance of William taking Emilio away from her.

Mariana put a bite of mashed potatoes into Emilio's mouth. "Thank you for helping my family while I was in Guadalajara. It is very much appreciated, but we do not need it anymore."

"I want to keep helping," Jenny said. "Maybe I can find a way to get you all back to Santiago. Or another city if you want to avoid my father."

"Thank you, but we can take care of ourselves now."

"Here? Don't you want a better life for your sisters? And for Emilio? This town is full of drunks and…"

"Thank you," Mariana said, "but we want to stay in Mexico."

"Just think of the life…"

"No," Mariana said. Her voice came out more bitter than she wanted.

Jenny sat up straight and her face flushed as if Mariana had slapped it.

"I do want a better life for my sisters and Emilio. There are opportunities in Mexico, we just need to get further away from

277

the border. Guadalajara is a beautiful city. Have you ever been there?"

Jenny shook her head and took a sip of her lemonade. Beads of sweat dripped from the bottom of her glass and made tiny water-filled craters in her cream sauce.

Mariana wanted to tell Jenny that Guadalajara was grander and more beautiful than any city she had ever seen in California. She wanted to tell her that Guadalajara held more promise for Lázaro and her sisters than Santiago. In California, their opportunities were limited and they would always be second class. She wanted to tell her that she did not want her son and little sisters to go to a school that would not let them speak Spanish, checked their heads for lice, and made them feel dirty. She wanted to tell her about Carmina and Celia and what she had done for the brigade, but all of that was her story.

"We have family in Guadalajara." Mariana put one of the tiny onions in her mouth. It tasted good but felt slimy and slippery as she bit into it. "After all that has happened, and losing both Emilio and Papá, we need our family."

"Maybe one day, I can fly down there and visit you."

"That would be nice," Mariana said. She knew and accepted that would probably never happen.

They spent the rest of lunch chatting, eating, or interacting with Emilio. Jenny talked about the miracle of flying and how free she felt in the air—which sounded like a nightmare to Mariana. The planes in Esmeralda's barn looked like giant deathtraps of metal and wood. Toward the end, Jenny told her that her mother was ill. It sounded dire, but she did not give any details. Poor Jenny did not have family. She had no brothers, sisters, cousins, aunts, or uncles—at least none that Mariana had ever heard about.

At the end of lunch, Jenny promised to fly down to Guadalajara and visit them.

As much as Mariana resented Warren Stratton and wanted him to suffer, she put her hand on Jenny's arm. "Give your father some grace. He is the only father you will ever have."

Jenny's eyebrows pinched together and she looked about to object, but instead, she nodded and forced a smile.

CHAPTER FORTY-THREE

As they approach Guadalajara, the towers of the cathedral still rise over the city with their crosses pointing straight up toward heaven. The telegraph poles pass by the windows with nothing but the ghosts of the men who hung from them. Next to Mariana, Emilio sits on Lázaro's lap with his forehead pressed against the glass and being hypnotized by the passing poles. Maybe Emilio senses that he is headed home, where Aunt Carmina, Socorro, Leon, Lorenzo, and Alberto are waiting for them.

Four months have already passed since Mariana and Emilio left Guadalajara. It took her that long to convince Mamá that the fighting was over. Mamá waited and tested the peace before she agreed to go where Papá had wanted his family. Carmina helped by writing several letters to Mamá, inviting them to come and fill their big house with family—and for the love of God, more women.

Now Priests can wear vestments and step into their churches without the fear of being hung or shot. Hopefully, her and Papá's sacrifices had made a difference. Maybe something they had done changed the course of the war, no matter how small. She had stayed in Guadalajara to honor her Papá's memory and fight for her God, and now, by bringing her family, she was finishing what he had set out to do.

Only Josefina feels sad to move away from Tijuana because she had to leave Salbatore behind. Lázaro told Salbatore he can come to Guadalajara, once he is a man, and claim Josefina. Mamá would not speak to Lázaro for two days after that, because, knowing Salbatore, he will do it. But next time, he will have four male cousins to deal with instead of one—and surely, one of them can deal with unwanted suitors better than Lázaro.

Soon, the spirits of the Guadalajara house will have all their living family. Celia, Tío Victoriano, and Tío Tomás will have Carmina, Leon, Lorenzo, and Alberto—and Papá will have his wife, his children, and his grandson.

Guadalajara has more opportunities with better schools for Sofía, Catalina, and one day, Emilio. Lázaro can make his own way, finally working for his own people, instead of Anglos. He will finally have a chance to feel proud of who he is. He will also have his three male cousins to help him support the family. Josefina and Mamá will love helping the brigade rebuild the churches and restore the Catholic faith. And maybe Mamá can open her own restaurant there.

Mamá sits in the seat before Mariana with Catalina beside her. Across the aisle, Josefina leans against the window with Sofía lying across her lap, asleep. She did it. Her family is here with her on the way to their new life.

Outside the window, an airplane flies along the same line as the train, almost as if it is escorting them into the city. It cannot be Jenny, but Mariana would not put it past her.

Poor Jenny still suffers from what happened to Emilio, but life is easier for her. Jenny's father is alive and he has more money than any one person should have. He is also an important man in Santiago with the power and influence to get an entire innocent family deported just to cover up his own evil.

Emilio looks up and points at the plane.

"Airplane," Lázaro says. "Maybe one day you can fly one."

He opens his mouth to say more, but Mariana slaps him on the arm. "Do not put dangerous ideas into his head."

Lázaro laughs. "Then maybe you should not bring him to Guadalajara where he will have three extra uncles to teach him how to be a man."

It seems unimaginable how something so cataclysmic as a war can be stopped by the signing of a single paper. Over 200,000 people died, offering their lives for God or for the government. They only wanted their faith, their traditions, and their festivals so their lives would have more meaning than simply working until death with no hope of Heaven.

Hopefully, Mexico is done killing its people and the people will have no more reason to rise up. Mariana cannot imagine having Emilio grow up to be another man sacrificed for freedom—or for the right to step into a church and worship his God.

AUTHOR'S NOTES

It is estimated that 25,000 women were part of the Joan of Arc Women's Brigade between 1926 and 1929, without a single recorded defection. The network of women stretched from Guadalajara to Mexico City, including fifty-four villages and surrounding hamlets, who all provided monthly reports. They were professional women and rural women who fought for their religion and encouraged their husbands and sons to fight. A majority of the women were between the ages of fifteen and twenty-five.

The women and girls were recruited from all social classes but were mostly working girls and peasant girls from the country. The brigades were organized in a military hierarchy with generals, colonels, majors, lieutenants, captains, sergeants, and soldiers. The women smuggled food, supplies, and ammunition to the *Cristeros*. They not only transmitted information but they obtained it by setting up dances in the villages for the federal officers. The women were spies and resorted to violence, kidnapping, and executions in order to protect the combatants. They also set up field hospitals and an underground hospital in

Guadalajara where many of the Catholic nuns were in hiding as nurses. They worked with the Unión Popular, publishing propaganda and running an underground press.

The bands of *Cristeros* rose up independently of one another, fighting in small bands until they were organized by generals who fought in the Revolutionary War. In three years, around 90,000 combatants died. The deaths between the *Cristeros* and the federal soldiers were about equal. When civilian casualties are included, the number is estimated at 200,000 deaths.

The peace treaty only appeased the masses and got them to lay down their arms. The day after the peace, the government began to hunt down and kill all the *Cristero* leaders and they placed detachments in the villages. Between 1929 and 1935, they killed approximately 5,000 additional *Cristero* leaders and combatants.

After a respite, the government, still under the control of Plutarco Elías Calles, reinstated the anti-clerical laws of the constitution, persecuting priests and Christians again. They also instituted a 'socialist education' for the schools. The bands of *Cristeros* that remained became bitter at the church bishops for mollifying the masses, so they fled to the hills and fought against the government, schoolteachers, and agaristas—but it never became the mass uprising as the first *Cristiada*. The final step of removing the anti-clerical laws from the Mexican constitution was not achieved until 1992.

Below is a list of the priests and laymen beautified or canonized by various Popes for their martyrdom during the *Cristero* War:

Beatified 1988 by Pope John Paul II
• Bl. Miguel Pro (1891-1927)
Beatified 1997 by Pope John Paul II
• Mateo Elías Nieves Castillo (1882-1928)
Canonized 2000 by Pope John Paul II
• Cristóbal Magallanes Jara (1869–1927)

- Román Adame Rosales (1859–1928)
- Rodrigo Aguilar Alemán (1875–1927)
- Julio Álvarez Mendoza (1866–1927)
- Luis Batis Sáinz (1870–1926)
- Agustín Caloca Cortés (1898–1927)
- Mateo Correa Magallanes (1866–1927)
- Atilano Cruz Alvarado (1901–1928)
- Miguel De La Mora (1874–1927)
- Pedro Esqueda Ramirez (1897–1927)
- Margarito Flores Garcia (1899–1927)
- José Isabel Flores Varela (1866–1927)
- David Galván Bermudes (1882–1915)
- Salvador Lara Puente (1905–1926)
- Pedro de Jesús Maldonado (1892–1937)
- Jesús Méndez Montoya (1880–1928)
- Manuel Moralez (1898–1926)
- Justino Orona Madrigal (1877–1928)
- Sabas Reyes Salazar (1879–1927)
- José María Robles Hurtado (1888–1927)
- David Roldán Lara (1907–1926)
- Toribio Romo González (1900–1928)
- Jenaro Sánchez Delgadillo (1886–1927)
- Tranquilino Ubiarco Robles (1899–1928)
- David Uribe Velasco (1888–1927)

Beatified 2005 by Pope Benedict XVI
- Anacleto González Flores (1888-1927)
- José Dionisio Luis Padilla Gómez (1899-1927)
- Jorge Ramon Vargas González (1899-1927)
- Ramón Vicente Vargas González (1905-1927)
- José Luciano Ezequiel Huerta Gutiérrez (1880-1927)
- Salvador Huerta Gutiérrez (1880-1927)
- Miguel Gómez Loza (1888-1928)
- Luis Magaña Servín (1902-1928)
- Jose Trinidad Rangel Montano (1887-1927)

- Andreas Sola y Molist C.F.M. (1895-1927)
- Leonardo Pérez Larios (1883-1927)
- Darío Acosta Zurita (1908-1931)

Canonized 2016 by Pope Frances

- José Sánchez del Río (1913-1928)

ACKNOWLEDGMENTS

Nothing in life is done in isolation, and this novel would not be possible without all the love, support, instruction, and feedback from the people in my life.

Thanks to my biggest supporters: My children, Brittany Romo, Brennan Romo, and Ryan Romo. Brittany has spent countless hours sitting with me in coffee shops from the time she was in elementary school until now, as a professional graphic designer, helping me with my marketing and creating my beautiful cover design. Brennan and Ryan are always willing to let me bounce ideas off them and help me work through things when I feel stuck.

Thanks to my mother, Sandy Folk, not only for being a kind and loving mother but also for making audio recordings for me so I can hear how my work reads.

To my father, John J. Folk II who left this earth far too early but always encouraged me to do what I love in life.

To my siblings, John J. Folk III and Kristy Oliver, thank you for all your love and excitement about my writing.

To my newest family members: Chris Jungenberg, Cathy

Cogliano, Serina Savage, and Rylend Monroe Savage—thank you for all the love and encouragement, with an extra thanks to Cathy for helping me around my house so I have more time to write.

To Mark Overholtzer for taking me into the clouds when I started this novel and for helping ground me as I finish it.

I am also blessed by the rest of my big and loving family and my friends.

To Randy Hopp for all the love and support.

A very special thanks to my agent, Larry Kirshbaum, for all the patience, caring, expertise, and encouragement—and for sharing the depth of his vast knowledge, both personally and professionally, to help me grow.

To my readers, Bobby Plummer and Wendy Halstead, for their encouragement and feedback. To Martha Santamaria for all her insight and guidance. To Diane Peters, my beta reader, who isn't afraid to tell me like it is in a very constructive and encouraging way. And to my copy editor, Mike Magnuson, the guru of grammar.

I am grateful for all the instruction from Pacific University's MFA program, especially my advisors: Craig Lesley, Pete Fromm, Ann Hood, and Mary Helen Stafaniak. I especially appreciate the continued friendship with Craig Lesley. A special thanks to Deborah Reed for giving me the jump-start on my career—there are just not enough words.

Thank you to "Farmer Tony" Marquez from Pearson Ranch in California for sharing his expertise in orange grove management and for the delicious shipment of oranges at Christmas.

I am also grateful to all the people who so meticulously strive to preserve history and make it available to the public, specifically (for this novel): the Santa Ana Public Library, Orange Public Library, Orange County Archives, and historian Jean Meyer who has extensively researched and published works on the *Cristero* War.

And last, but certainly not least, to my "dictator"—you know who you are.

ABOUT THE AUTHOR

Kelly Romo grew up in Southern California and currently lives in Oregon, where she teaches language arts and social studies. She is the mother of three grown children: Brittany, Brennan, and Ryan. She is an avid outdoorswoman and is always up for a new adventure. *When Sorrow Takes Wing* is her second novel. Her debut novel, *Whistling Women*, was published in November 2015.

For more information or discussion questions for your book club, please visit www.kellyromo.com

Thank you for reading my novel. I hope you enjoyed it.

Reviews make a huge difference for authors! If you enjoyed

When Sorrow Takes Wing, please consider leaving a review on Amazon—I would greatly appreciate it, even if it is only a sentence or two.

Amazon U.S.

Amazon U.K.

I would love to have you join my **Fan List**!

My fans get exclusive updates on my writing, free downloads, and free drawings for books or other items. I also use my fan list for Advanced Readers before I release a new book.

If you are interested, visit my website www.kellyromo.com and sign up on my *Contact* page or my *Work in Progress* page.

facebook.com/kellyromoauthorpage
twitter.com/KellyAnneRomo
instagram.com/kellyromo.author

ALSO BY KELLY ROMO

Whistling Women

Coming Soon:
Silver Wings and Sinful Things
(Jenny's Story)

Drown Me Like A River
(A Thriller)

Made in the USA
Monee, IL
04 July 2023

38468500R00176